Uncharted Avenues

Lisa Keifer

To all the kind, loving, fierce, determined, protective single moms I've had the luck and the honor of knowing. Life isn't always easy or fair, but you have persevered and carried on. You all rock!

Note to the Reader

This book references bullying, anxiety, death of a loved one, and divorce.

Chapter 1

Kenzie

"THAT GORGEOUS SPECIMEN OF male over there can't keep his dark, smoldering eyes off you, and if you don't want him, I might have to brave twisting my ankle in these damn heels just to see if he'll look up at me the way he looks at you."

I don't even have to glance over to know this woman is talking about Trevor. He's chatted with me the whole time he's been here. It's what happens every time he comes to the diner, only this beautiful, obviously drunk woman doesn't know Trevor's my best friend.

I laugh internally, but also hate what this woman's suggesting. I don't care how single he is or that he might like a night with her. I just can't stomach the idea of Trevor getting naked with . . . anyone, really, though I know it happens.

"Sorry, he's taken." I give the woman and her friends a smile. Only one of them is sober enough to perhaps figure out how sorry I'm not.

The first woman looks a little disappointed, I admit, but still, I don't care.

I walk away from them, having already supplied the extra barbecue sauce they asked for. Then Trevor calls me over.

"Why do those women keep staring at me?" he asks in a whisper. I wish he could whisper it in my ear instead of just in my general direction. Then I remind myself that best friends are not supposed to do things like that—the same thing I've been telling myself all the time lately, it seems.

"The blonde one in the pink top wants to have you for dinner instead of her chicken strips."

Trevor laughs. "Wow, that's abrupt." His face tells me he's not sure what to think of my bold words.

"Maybe I should send her over," I tease. "I know you like the tourist types. The temporary women."

His eyebrows shoot up. "Please don't."

"Relax. I told her you're taken."

Now he grins. "By you?"

"I wasn't specific." But the way he looks at me has me wishing it were true.

From my vantage point, I can see the woman—Jacey, I think I heard a friend call her—watch us the entire time Trevor and I talk at his table. He gives a soft annoyed groan. I move my eyes back to his handsome face.

"Maybe I can make this believable."

I have no idea what he's talking about until he stands up. His rough hands cradle my face, his touch gentle on my cheeks. Before I have a chance to react to this or the sexy wink he gives me, he plants a kiss on my lips.

There are sparks immediately. It's an electric jolt, in the best freaking way. Trevor wastes no time parting my lips with his tongue, giving me tingles everywhere. The heat from him roasts my body as we passionately explore each other's mouths, both of us now tasting like the root beer he was drinking moments before I walked over here. His short, neatly trimmed beard rubs against my skin, and I have a flash of it rubbing on other parts of me.

But this is crazy.

He's my best friend.

I'm his.

This is our first kiss.

Kiss.

I'm at work in a town, in a diner, where nearly everyone knows both of us. Only the women in that booth don't know that Trevor and I are only friends.

Not a single person has said or done anything to stop us.

One of us moans. Then we both do. My hands are on his face. His arms are wrapped around me now, his body pressed into mine, hands gently caressing my back through my stretchy T-shirt. Then, slowly, Trevor moves his mouth in a way to let me know we should end the kiss.

By the time we've separated and I glance over, the women are gone. Dottie, my coworker and Trevor's aunt, walks by with a tray of food for a table of regulars. Trevor and I are still in each other's embrace.

"Are you not even going to ask what your nephew's doing to me?" I ask Dottie.

She smirks. "Nope."

Not a single coworker or regular customer, especially all my fellow Syracuse Falls citizens, seem at all concerned that Trevor and I just made out. No one's even batted an eye in shock.

"They've known both of us for years," I whisper to Trev. Neither of us has pulled away yet. I don't know why.

"I'm sure they know there's nothing to it," he replies as he steps back. My arms feel empty now. "They know we're just friends." His smile drops a bit. His deep brown eyes watch me, but I can't tell what he's thinking just by looking in them.

"Yeah," I say.

He's right.

I know he is.

But it doesn't sit well with me. Not in a bad way, I don't think. It just feels like there's something I'm missing, especially since there's something to Trevor's expression that I can't quite read.

"Yeah, I'm sure that's it," I add.

Something has changed with him now. I know he kissed me to save himself from the *thirsty* woman, but I feel like there's more to it.

This has happened a lot recently. This feeling of a change in Trevor, or perhaps a change in how I see him. It feels like he wants more, from me or with me. But it could also just be in my head. I've been single ever since my stupid-ass husband walked out on me and our baby daughter and suddenly became my stupid-ass ex-husband.

Whatever this is, I need to let it go. At least for now. I'm still at work in a diner full of people, for crying out loud. No time to dissect emotions.

Trevor gives me a nod and a smile, as well as a promise to call me in the morning, like we do every day. Then he's out the door.

I'm gripped with the fear that he might go find Jacey after all. She's definitely his type—most importantly because she isn't local. And if she's his type, as fancy and brash as she is, that means I'm not. She and I have a totally different style and a totally different vibe. I'm a local, which is number one on Trevor's list of *hell no*. Not to mention the fact that we really are just friends.

I give my head a quick shake and snap out of it, moving my feet and eventually grabbing the plates I need from the kitchen. Thankfully, Dottie covered the couple tables that needed me while I was lost in my stupor.

This won't happen again.

I will never try to convince myself that Trevor wants me as more than a friend.

And I'll make myself okay with that.

Chapter 2

Trevor

I visit Kenzie at the diner every day she's scheduled, even if we have plans later that day or night. It's too good and too gratifying to be around her no matter where we are. Running my family farm isn't easy, and it's sometimes difficult to get away from my responsibilities to go visit with Kenz, but I'd do just about anything to see her.

As I leave the diner now after the best damn kiss of my life, I see those women just down the street, at the corner. Hopefully, they'll cross the street, moving themselves away from me, but I don't want to take the risk of being spotted. I duck behind a car parked along the curb, hating the fact that I didn't leave my truck closer to the diner. I have to walk toward the women to get to it, placing me in an unfortunate dilemma.

My sister Polly texted me right before I walked out the door—my lips still on fire from Kenzie—asking me to return to the farm because there's something not adding up in the apple yield and the sales spreadsheets covering the past five years that she's been scouring through. It's late, but the work is often never over, especially the paperwork. Well, especially with Polly in charge of it.

Heading to my pickup truck could cause me to be spotted by the blonde. Even with that kiss I just planted on Kenzie, there's a chance that woman might still want me for dinner, the thought of which has me thinking maybe I'll hide out here behind Tysen's car for an extra five minutes, just in case.

·♥·♥·♥·♥·♥·

The next morning, as Kenzie pours me a cup of coffee and everyone who was here last night pretends nothing out of the ordinary happened, I watch my best friend with hopeful eyes, wanting her to intuitively know that kiss meant everything to me.

"Lemon meringue today, right?" she asks.

As an excuse that my staff won't get mad about, I buy pie for them every day at the diner. Mostly, they eat it at lunch or take it home for later. Some of them might never eat it. Some might throw it away. I don't know. I don't really care. Of course, I do give them the choice of opting out any day they want because the pie isn't really the point of the diner trips. It gives me a good enough reason in everyone else's eyes. I already have the best reason for me: my best friend.

I nod, watching the sparkle in her eyes as the sunlight from the window hits them just right.

"Coming right up." She starts to walk away, but stops short and turns to me again. "By the way, I saw that stack of books you bought Hayzel."

I feel myself grinning sheepishly. "She's been wanting to read that series for ages, and the library is always out of its copies. Same with online."

Now Kenzie grins, too. "You spoil her too much."

"We both do, but it's okay. She's a healthy, happy, well-adjusted child. You're doing things right with her."

Kenzie leans closer to kiss my cheek. When she leaves and comes back a few minutes later, she has the bags full of pie to-go, as well as a slice of carrot cake just for me.

It's literally just for me, too. Knox, one of the cooks here at the diner, lets Kenzie use his family recipe, but he's such a perfectionist that he'll only allow her to make it here. He also altered it so it would make a small cake, not a full- size one. Kenzie bakes the carrot cake—my favorite—once a week, and I get to order it any day. There's always some fresh in the fridge or freshly thawing from the freezer. I don't care either way.

Sometimes I take it to-go, but this time I'm glad Kenzie made the choice for me.

As I take my first heavenly bite—complete with the sweet, tangy cream-cheese frosting Kenzie spent hours practicing before she got it just right, when she first started offering me the cake—my best friend studies me with her eyes.

"Change your mind yet?" she asks.

I shake my head, hoping she'll let it go. Instead, she squeezes herself into the booth with me, though I'm in the middle of the bench and there isn't much room for her. "Kenz, no. Not gonna happen."

"Oh, come on. Jade said you'd be perfect for it. All you have to do is hold a banner and recite—"

"Recite a few lines," I say at the same time she does. I've heard this speech too many times. This makes me laugh to myself. "Already told my sister this. I am not an actor. That's what the performers are for."

"Yeah, but they lost one when he got that part in New York. Jade told us you're the same size and height as him. She wouldn't have to alter the costume like she would for a different actor."

I've already devoured my slice of cake. It never seems to last long. Kenzie just makes it too damn good, even though I wish I could slow down and savor it like she does when she eats a piece. It may be only for me, but I always share with her and Hayzel. The heady look Kenz gets when she eats it is worth a million times more than keeping the cake to myself.

Since my amazing dessert is gone too soon and I really need to return to the farm, I put my hands on Kenzie's hips and slide her out of the booth, allowing her to stand before following. Then I kiss the side of her head as usual and say, "Love you, Sweet Cake." Also as usual.

That's our thing. We tell each other *love you* every day. Have for nearly our entire decade-long friendship. Odd for best friends? Perhaps. I don't think so, though. I just wish she knew it isn't platonic on my side. I mean, I thought the kiss last night would have shown her that, but she hasn't given any indication this ever occurred to her.

"Love you, too, Trev." She gives me a soft kiss on the cheek. I wish I could turn and catch her by surprise on the mouth again, but it's not a good idea.

"Think about it," she calls as I walk toward the door.

"Not happening." I leave with these as my last words, though I do throw her one last grin that she laughs at, then blows a friendly kiss to.

With the pie safe on the back seat of my truck, hopefully without the risk of sliding to the floorboard, I drive back to Bernhardt Farms and Orchard.

I love my job. I really do. And I know it was necessary for one of my siblings or me to take over once Dad died. But damn. I miss my journalism job sometimes. Well, I miss having less decisions to make and less people who depend on me. Running a family farm is high risk and extremely stressful in a lot of ways.

The sound of a new text emanates from my phone. I'm sure it's Polly again. She and I already met up twice today so we could try to figure out this apple-yield mess since it was too late for phone calls and emails to our buyers last night. But I've also been busy with all our other crops and harvests—what with this June weather being wholly uncooperative—plus everything that's going on with our shops and whatnot. It's never-ending, it seems.

I don't check my phone until I make it back to the farm. The drive only takes a few minutes, anyway. Less than ten, most days. Only I see it wasn't my sister. It was actually my mom, with news that one of the doors just broke on the barn we use for the combine, and also that the track loader apparently now has a bad transmission, according to Rob, our worker who was using the machine at the time.

Like I said. It's always something.

·♥·♥·♥·♥·♥·

Hours later, I've distributed the pie, helped board up the open barn doorway with some scrap wood we had lying around, checked in with Rob again about what the track loader actually did or didn't do in addition to how it sounded, and called in a reliable mechanic we've used several times on short notice. I also helped Polly finish sorting the yield numbers and—with the assistance of a few of my workers—checked on the status of everything else on the farm, just in case something decided to play along with Murphy's Law today.

As far as I could tell, it all looked okay. My staff agreed with me, as did Polly, Mom, and my brother Dawson, who stopped by to lend a hand.

Kenzie's just about off work now, or she should be. She and Hayzel will be home soon enough, after Kenz picks Hayzel up from her parents' house. I could sit at home by myself, with my cats, missing my best friend, or I could invite myself to her house like I normally would before that make-out session last night.

Today is Friday. Kenz has often wondered why I don't have Friday night dates. Well, I do, just not in a way I can fully explain to her. Or rather, not in a way I ever thought she'd want to hear, at least until yesterday. Even now, I'm still not sure she's ready for it. The best I can do is go over there as a way to show her that she is and always will be more important to me than a date with any other woman ever could be.

Chapter 3

Kenzie

"IF YOU DON'T TAKE those plates to their tables, they'll be so cold, I'll have to make them again, and it'll come out of your paycheck," Knox whisper-shouts at me.

I've been stuck in the same spot, watching my best friend—the man I've loved in a strictly platonic way for years, until recently—leave the diner, oddly finding myself wanting him to come back again. Wanting him to cradle me in his arms like he did last night. Wanting his weirdly soft lips on mine again, aching for that little squeeze he gave me before our kiss ended.

Trevor *kissed* me.

More than just our friendly kisses. More than just my joking air kisses.

He kissed me with a hungry tongue and exploring hands.

Like, what the hell? What was that?

I don't have these thoughts in a mean or mad way. Just . . .

It was weird. It's weird, right?

I mean, I've thought about kissing him many times these last few months. I never thought it would ever actually happen. Why would it? We're friends.

But the wink. The kiss. The squeeze. The moan. The hard body against mine. Those things all meant something.

Didn't they?

It wasn't my imagination, or because of that woman. It can't be. Trevor isn't that good of an actor. He just said so. There's no way it was all fake.

Except now I'm thinking about my best friend Charisma. She's told me many stories where the passionate nights she has with men are simply perfect, then she doesn't even remember what they look like by the next day. They gave her what she needed in the moment, then she moved on.

Is that what Trevor did?

Did he need a really good kiss—an explosive, all-consuming kiss—without needing anything else after?

Then why would he have picked me? Or why would he not pick me for anything else?

Yet again my brain is screaming, *Because you're a townie!*

My ever-present reminder.

The reason Trev and I will never actually be more that what we already are. He is Charisma and I am a faceless date, perfect for a little bit of fun, but otherwise unremarkable. I told myself I'd accept this truth and move on from it. Time to kick that plan into high gear, because clearly, I'm faltering. No sense in bogging Trevor down with my mess, so I also promise myself to never talk about it with him.

I deliver the dishes to my tables, and thankfully, no one complains about cold food except for one customer who's new-ish in town and complains about every meal yet returns every day. I can't say I blame him this time, though, because I wouldn't want to eat cold scrambled eggs either.

Eventually, work becomes enough of a distraction, and Trevor is out of my thoughts.

At least until he stops over at my apartment after dinner. Hayzel's in her room reading one of those new books Trev bought her. I eye him carefully as he sits on the sofa with me, his attention caught by the video of cats in Santa hats that I'm halfway through. Trevor watches more of it than I do. I just can't stop looking at him. He's still giving no indication that anything odd happened last night.

Guess I'll continue to follow his lead.

No matter how much I want things to be different.

Tonight is different in other ways. Every Friday, Hayzel stays with my parents or my sister, and I go over to Trevor's. While I appreciate time to myself, I don't actually care for being alone at night.

I mean, I was okay at first. Then Trevor suggested I watch a movie at his house with him. I ended up falling asleep on the sofa, my head resting against his shoulder. He never woke me up to send me home. In the morning, we were still in the same positions we were when we drifted off to dreamland. It was the first good night's sleep I'd had on a Friday since Hayzel's overnights with my parents began the month before.

It's now been four months. That's sixteen weeks of sleeping next to Trevor every single Friday. At some point, we shifted from sitting next to each other and falling asleep to lying cuddled on the sofa and sleeping that way. It's been about fourteen weeks of me wishing he'd carry me to his bed and sleep with me or *sleep with me* there.

Except we don't have any of those options tonight. My parents had other plans with old friends who unexpectedly came into town and my sister is busy with her boyfriend, so Hayzel's home. Friend date is at my place. No falling asleep in a cuddle this time.

"Since yesterday was your last double shift and you're vegging out tonight, how would you like to go to Billie's Bar-B-Que tomorrow?" Trev asks when the short video is over.

I smile. "Love to."

"I'm sure Hayzel would like to go, too, right?"

Days and nights out with Trevor often feel like family time, like Hayzel is our kid and not just mine. Sometimes, he's confused for my husband or boyfriend, and he's never once corrected anyone who made the mistake. I used to think it was funny. For the past few months, it's given me hope. Now I'm not sure. What does Trevor think of me most? Friend? Great kisser? Wife potential?

I clear my throat, annoyed that I let my imagination start to run wild. "Usually, yeah, but she's going to the movies with friends tomorrow."

"So it'll be just us?"

"Yep. Friend date."

"Awesome." He has a wide grin, but was that a brief glimmer of sadness I saw? The teeny-tiniest flicker of him hating being friend-zoned? Or is that my stupid imagination again?

With our faces turned toward each other, sitting as close as we are, I would only have to lean about six inches to kiss him. Six inches between me and the thing I want most. Six little inches.

Could I do it?

Should I?

Damn it. Now I feel my cheeks pinking up at the palpable physicality of that first kiss in my memory. Why am I aching for my best friend to hold me and squeeze me again? Why am I longing to feel his muscles tight around me and against me? Why is he the only man I've dreamed and daydreamed of for months?

"You all right, Sweet Cake?" he asks with a bit of a laugh to his voice, dark eyes on mine.

Oops.

I've moved closer now.

It's no longer six inches. It's maybe three.

Is he breathing faster, too?

I swear he just looked at my mouth.

Unintentionally, I lick my lips. Just the idea of him looking at them caused the reaction.

Then I feel a warm, heavy lump land in my lap. An enormous, furry lump, forcing me to turn away from Trevor. Cinnamon, our giant one-year-old Maine Coon, has apparently decided I'm the best thing to sleep on.

This is what I always wanted when we got him. Hayzel just wanted a cat, but when Trevor was gifted a small litter of Maine Coons, I knew that would be the perfect kind of kitten. Sweet, warm, fuzzy, and the best to cuddle with. Now is not the time for that, however.

"Hi, sweet kitty," I say before attempting to shift him down to the floor, only he's not having it. He's relaxed his body to the point that it's like trying to lift fifteen pounds of fluffy goo. Not going to happen.

Only Trevor swoops in, easily lifting Cinnamon off me, carefully cradling the cat and setting him down on the other side of the sofa. "His siblings get me all the time."

We both laugh because it's so true. Though they're large, Trevor's cats are still young enough that they don't seem to notice or care about their size. Cinnamon is the same way.

My orange tabby isn't happy with this arrangement, though, and stands back up to climb on Trev this time.

Trevor gives him a hug and a good scratch behind his ears, which makes Cinnamon purr so loudly, it nearly vibrates into me. I mean, I love my cat, but this is not the kind of vibration I want to feel. I'd rather feel a humming or tingling from Trevor. I want to be the one in his lap.

That's an idea, though. If I straddle Trevor, there won't be any room for Cinnamon. He'll be bored or annoyed, but either way, he'll most likely walk away and let us get back to what we were doing. Well, what I was about to do.

But just randomly straddling the thighs of my only male bestie—something I've never done before—isn't nearly as easy and carefree as it sounds.

Trev's still snuggling with my sleepy feline, which doesn't help the situation. I can't exactly snatch Cinnamon up. They both look so happy and cute, cuddling together. Then Cinnamon yawns with a stretch and jumps down. I should not be this giddy, but I don't care. Now's my chance. Then again, with Cinnamon gone, I have no excuse to climb on top of Trevor except for the glaringly obvious one: I want him.

A kiss is one thing. I could come up with a dozen reasons to kiss him, then back away from it if it turns out he's not happy about it. But sitting on him like that? I'm not helping him cut his hair or shave his beard. He doesn't have anything in his eye I need to look at.

You know what?

I am not a timid woman.

Not usually.

I can do this.

If his reactions to our kiss last night were real—even if fleeting—then this will allow him to enjoy them again, at least temporarily.

Shifting my body, I pull my legs up onto the sofa, intending to get on my knees. I have to adjust my foot since I'm doing this very awkwardly and it's jammed against the armrest. This doesn't take long, though. I'm on my knees, watching Trevor watch me. I swear his pupils dilate as I place my nearest hand on his arm.

"Mom! Do you have my charger?"

Startled, I let go of Trevor. "What?" I turn and see my daughter standing in the hall.

"Charger? The battery died, and I was in the middle of the chorus. I have to finish that song."

I don't need her to tell me what song it is. It's Taylor Swift's "Today Was a Fairytale (Taylor's Version)," the one Hayzel's had on repeat for the last twenty-three days. "I haven't seen it, honey. Have you checked your desk?"

"Will you help me look for it?"

"Where was the last place you remember seeing it?"

"Why do people ask that question? If I knew where I saw it last, I would have found it," my ten-year-old going on sixteen replies snappishly.

Before I have a chance to respond, she sighs and turns her gaze to Trevor. "Trev, will you help me since Mom won't?"

"Watch the attitude, Hayze," he scolds gently. Then he looks at me.

I give him a slight nod, knowing he's asking what I want. Trevor always does this, and I love it. He wants to help and doesn't have any qualms about stepping in, but he also wants me to know he respects me and respects the fact that I obviously make the final decisions.

"Yeah, I can help you, Hayze." Trev smiles at me, then stands.

"Sorry," Hayzel adds quickly to me before heading back down the hall.

"I would say she's at a difficult age, but every age seems to have this effect on her." He gives a soft chuckle.

He comes back after maybe thirty seconds.

"Let me guess. She found it before you ever got there?"

"Yep."

We both laugh this time, then I reach for the remote control to find another video to watch. My fantasies almost got the best of me. Hayzel's still awake, and Trevor's not giving me any *go ahead* signs. Time to shove those feelings back down and spend the rest of the evening laughing at funny videos with my bestie.

After a while, it's time for Hayzel to go to bed. Trevor and I both give her hugs good night. He stays in the living room when she asks me to tuck her in. I know she's old enough to do this herself, but it's been a while since the last time she made this request, and I'm happy to do it for her. Then she wants to talk about one of the girls who's supposed to go with the group to the movies tomorrow, who hasn't been nice to her the past few weeks, and what she should do about that.

Once we've discussed her options, I kiss her cheek and leave her to fall asleep. In the living room, I see Hayzel isn't the only one who's ready for bed. Trevor's leaned back against the sofa, arms crossed, feet on the floor. He doesn't look very comfortable, but if I wake him, he might go home. I woke up this morning around the same time he did. For some reason, though, I'm both an early bird and a night owl and am not too tired.

Maybe I could snuggle up to him and fall asleep with my head on his shoulder.

Maybe that would be too weird. It's only normal when we both fall asleep like that, right? Just joining him when he's already out?

Yep. That's weird.

So I crouch in front of him and tap on his leg. Trevor doesn't react. I try again, to no avail. Then I get up on the sofa, next to him, and rub his arm.

"Trev, wake up."

He startles, and his eyes open. Then he blinks twice before his eyes seem to focus on me. "Hey." There's his beautiful smile that I love.

"You fell asleep," I whisper.

"Yeah." He gently scrubs a hand over his whole face. "Guess I should head home."

"Yeah." I pause. "Or you could stay."

Trevor turns his head more toward me but doesn't reply.

"Just that it's late. So you could sleep here if you want."

"Do you want me to?"

Yes. "If you want. I mean, I know it's more convenient for you to already be home in the mornings since your office is right there." If there were ever a queen of talking someone out of doing the thing she actually wants them to do, it'd be me. And now that I've begun, I can't seem to stop. "And you'd have to sleep on the sofa, whereas home has your bed. And your cats."

"You're sending me home so my cats won't be lonely?"

"I'm sure they miss you. Everyone misses you when you're gone."

"Including you?"

"Especially me," I whisper. Then the queen—who apparently can't help herself—adds, "But you'll come for lunch tomorrow, right? Knox is doing that bacon gravy and cheddar waffles special he's been talking about for weeks."

"Sounds delicious." Only his smile isn't very big and it doesn't last long.

After a stretch of both his arms and legs, Trevor kisses my forehead and rises to his feet. "Love you, Sweet Cake. See you tomorrow."

"Love you, too," I say, wishing so desperately I could tell him exactly how much. "Drive safe."

·♥·♥·♥·♥·♥·

A few days later, I stand with Edin in her tiny office at the back of her brand-new bakery in Syracuse Falls. Late last year, the bakery she had in Auburn suffered from an electrical fire. Most of it burned down or had to be ripped down to nothing. The fire was traumatic enough, but then the building's owner decided to just demolish instead of letting her help rebuild. With a loan from her parents—since the insurance money wasn't released yet—Edin set her sights on something new.

Some people in this town—especially my sister—think Edin chose the Falls because Edin's ex-fiance Rhett lives here with his wife Gwenn. Honestly, if that were her reason, I wouldn't blame her for it. Edin can be acerbic at times, salty at others. Not the warmest person one might meet. But she's also kind and loving and fiercely loyal when it comes to her friends. She just doesn't have many of those.

Aside from me and Charisma, Edin still has Rhett as a best friend. He's not in love with her, but he cares about her enough to stay her friend. After their rocky first meetings, Gwenn and Edin now respect each other enough to considers themselves friends as well. And Edin has Val and Phoebe, her two assistants who have been with her for years, since the very beginning of her bakery in Auburn.

The grand opening today is so important to Edin. Rhett and Gwenn won't be able to make it, but I hope the rest of the town shows up. I know everyone's been buzzing about it. Neither Capelli's nor the diner has a full bakery. Each only offers a few options. This town could use more choices for cakes and pastries. Edin also won last year's Butterscotch Pie Festival, which is a huge nod in her favor. I hope all that talk leads to customers.

I also hope maybe her family will come. Edin moved to town a few months ago, and in that time, not one of them has come to visit. Not even her brother Elliot, though they've supposedly always been close. In our nearly yearlong friendship, I've only seen him in person twice. He's a civil engineer and always has a huge workload, and he doesn't seem to make much time for her. I guess that's what close means when you're a Marchant. Totally different from being a Larkin.

We might annoy each other, but I know I can always count on my family, which is how I know all of them—my sister Lucy included—will show up and buy something today because I asked them to. I even offered to buy Lucy's treat for her since she initially balked at the idea, but she shot that down, too. She'll show. She'll buy her own cake or cookie. She'll smile a fake smile, then she'll be on her way. My brother Dom will probably be grumpy, but at least he'll enjoy his time here more than Lucy will.

I'm grateful to Jacqui for switching shifts with me, because there was no way I'd miss this. Despite her sometimes gruff exterior, Edin is a complete mess of nerves.

"The balloon bouquets are up but not blocking anything?" she asks.

"Yep. We checked them a few minutes ago."

"They're pink—the right shade of pink?"

"Yes."

"All the tables and chairs placed just right?"

"Already lined them up with both a tape measure and a ruler."

Edin nods, but I'm not sure how much she hears me or my joke. "And there is no glitter anywhere except for the edible glitter, right?"

"Yes, we triple checked that, too. Just breathe, Edes. It's going to be okay."

"Kenz, this is my whole world. I live for this bakery. If this bombs—"

"It won't. I promise. This town was not meant to survive on only a handful of fresh-baked choices and whatever's at the grocery store. We need you just as much as you need us."

She nods again, and I know she's heard me this time.

An alarm sounds on her watch. She turns it off, then checks her notifications, looking for texts from her parents, I'm sure. Her downturned expression tells me she doesn't have any. Looking up at me with a smile, she puts her arm down, the sounds on her watch now muted.

"There have been some really long days and really hard nights to get to this point, but you are going to kick ass, Edes. You hear me?

You already know how to run a super-successful bakery. The people of Syracuse Falls will support you. I know it. You're one of us now."

·♥·♥·♥·♥·♥·

I knew our town wouldn't let her down, but I'm still a little surprised at just how many familiar faces are here. Some of these people don't go anywhere except the grocery store and the gas station. Entire families, including those temporarily returning from out of town, showed up. Edin's glossy eyes tell me how relieved she is.

However, there is one person who could completely ruin the mood.

Lucy and Gwenn's bestie Lourdes talking to Edin is never good. Her showing up to the grand opening for the bakery to deliver flowers might seem innocuous to most others, but I know better. She isn't here by choice, and she is clearly in no mood for Edin's admittedly acerbic way of dealing with those she'd rather not have to face.

The situation takes a turn for the worse when Lourdes shoves the vase of pink and white blooms—ones that perfectly match Edin's Sprinkle Scene Bakery logo—at her with a look of annoyed disdain. It's really packed in here, and neither of them are actually making a scene, but I'm worried all the same. There isn't much I can do at the moment, though. When Edin's stressed like this, the best thing to give her is space.

Edin reads the card from the flowers, says something that looks like "thank you" to Lourdes, and heads to pick up an enormous tray of cupcakes that need handed out. I know she'd much rather be in her office, where she'd more easily fight off her tears and try her best to take deep breaths. Edin's suffering out here in public, and Lourdes can't be bothered to feel sorry about it. She's not even looking at Edin anymore. Based on the way she just rolled her eyes, I don't think she cares.

Now's my chance. I wave to Lourdes and rush over.

"Where is everyone?" she asks.

I can't help but laugh. She must be in a mood to not even notice the dozens of people filling the bakery. "What are you talking about? Almost the whole town is here."

Lourdes takes a look around, so I do as well. Every table and chair is full. Have been all day. So have all the stools at the counter. Those who can't find seats stand around, happily snacking on cakes and cookies.

"I mean, where are all the people I don't recognize? Where are her friends from Auburn?"

My smile falls immediately. "She has her staff."

"Two people. What about the rest?"

"She doesn't have a lot of friends. People are too hard on her."

"Maybe she should adjust her attitude."

I knew this was going to happen. When it comes to her loved ones—when it comes to most people—Lourdes is able to hold her tongue and keep the thing she shouldn't say to herself. There are only a few people Lourdes loses her cool about, mostly her ex-boyfriend Spence, a girl from our town named Pippa—though I'm not fully caught up on the story of that one—and Edin.

I give Lourdes a look I hope she understands as me asking her to chill out a little. "Maybe it's also been hard for her."

Lourdes doesn't reply. In fact, she almost looks like she's about to debate me on this.

Oh geez.

We should at least be sitting down for this. I lead her over to a newly opened stool at the counter, but before I have a chance to sit, Edin returns, holding a now-empty large tray. She spies Lourdes immediately.

"Oh no," she says, shaking her head in Lourdes's direction. "I don't need your pity. You are more than welcome to leave, so please do."

Lourdes turns to me. "Guess I'll have to buy a cupcake somewhere else." Then she walks out the door.

Edin passes the tray off to Val, then stalks toward the back. I slip past a group of customers near the counter and head toward Edin's office again. The moment I open the door, she turns toward me, eyes teary, voice shaky, tissues in her hands.

"Rhett and I are friends. Hell, Gwenn and I are friends. I've apologized a dozen times to both of them. Why won't Lourdes let it go already?" She lets out a sob, but tries to hold the rest back. This causes her to sputter a little.

"Lourdes has a hard time letting things go. Her anger, for one."

"You can say that again." Edes tilts her head up, looking at the ceiling. Though she's silent, I know what she's doing. Counting. Breathing. Calming down. There's no way she wants any of the customers to see her like this.

When her tears have abated a few minutes later and she's refreshed her makeup, Edin and I head back out to see what's left of the crowd. Honestly, there are more people in here now than there were ten minutes ago, which is saying something. More than three-quarters of them have nowhere to sit, but no one seems to mind. If I know my fellow townspeople, they genuinely don't. I always told Lucy that Edin opening a bakery here was a brilliant idea, long before Edin was sold on the plan.

By closing time, Edes has given away more cupcakes than I can count. She's also had the best turnout for a new business in the Falls in years, as far as I can tell. My entire family showed up as promised. Lucy smiled twice at Edin, though they looked seriously fake, as expected. She even bought two boxes of cookies for her boyfriend

Pete to share with his coworkers. Some of Val's and Phoebe's relatives came up from Auburn to help support them and Edin, too.

The only family that didn't show? Edin's.

We sit on the chairs in her office hours later, after everything is cleaned up to Edin's standards and she sent her assistants home. Well, to this new fancy restaurant they want to try in Syracuse. The four of us spent half an hour debating on Edin's attendance, which she was wholly against.

"But we have to celebrate," Val insisted to no avail.

"This weekend, I promise," Edin replied.

Phoebe and Val reluctantly took off. I stayed behind to see what I could do to help Edes.

She sighs now and slouches further into her plush chair.

"You wish we'd gone with them?"

Edin scoffs. "Not really. I'm far too exhausted for that. I just . . ." She heaves another deep breath out. "Where the hell was my family, Kenz?"

I don't reply. I know she doesn't need me to.

"Even my damn brother. Elliott promised he was going to get the day off, no matter what. Why didn't they come? I've been a success since I first opened the Auburn bakery when I was nineteen. What more do I have to do? Why can I never live up to their expectations?" Tears stream down her cheeks. She angrily swipes some away with her hands, then reaches for some tissues to get the rest.

While I don't know what it's like to not have a supportive family, I do know how it feels being disappointed by people I love. "Whatever their issues, whatever their hang-ups, it's not about you. Your family might not ever come around, and that sucks. But you know you're living your best life, kicking ass and being a total boss babe."

She gives a small smile with a tiny laugh.

"You are kind and loving, Edes. You—"

"No one ever says that about me," she interrupts with a deeper laugh. "They think the four of you are crazy for being my friends." Meaning Charisma, Val, Phoebe, and me. Then she sobers. "That's what my parents think. No one should be friends with me. No one should date me or marry me. No one should come to my stupid little bakery."

"Your parents are assholes, and you know it. They're also wrong, and you know that, too. Our entire town showed up for you. You're one of us now, Edes, and we will never let you down."

"Love you, bestie," she says with a soft grin.

"Love you, too." I check the time on my phone. "Guess I should go home and sleep. Early morning tomorrow. For both of us. You go home and sleep, too."

"Hayzel's going to miss all these sleepovers with your family when school starts." Edin laughs. "End of summer break is going to be a rude awakening for her."

I chuckle. "Don't I know it. Congrats on the most amazing launch."

"Thanks. If I ever expand to New York or Paris like my parents think I should, I'm bringing you with me, you know."

"Hayzel and I will go happily," I reply before giving my bestie a quick hug. Then I'm on my way home, wishing there was more time in the day because I doubt I'll get more than a few hours of sleep before waking for my daily hourlong workout. I also wish there was a way to invite Trevor over without it being obvious that I'd happily have sleepovers with him every day instead of only once a week.

Chapter 4

Trevor

Mom is, of course, outside when I pull up to her house. She's never been one to sit around and let things be done for her, even when Dad was still alive. So when she mentioned yesterday that the railing on her front deck was a little loose, I knew even though I'd go over there to fix it, she'd probably have it finished before I arrived. This seems to be the case.

"Need any help?" I ask anyway.

"I got it, thanks," she replies with a smile.

"Thought I'd still offer," I tell her.

Her smile grows even bigger. "And I appreciate that." I join her on the porch. She turns and gives me a hug. "So how are things?"

I shrug. "Things are good."

Mom makes a *hmm* sound. Then she says, "I heard about you kissing Kenzie."

"Aunt Dottie tell you?"

"My sister couldn't wait, that's true. But she wasn't the only one. Seems half the town was in there when you pulled Kenzie in for a lip-lock."

Now I laugh. "Mom, I didn't have any other choice. There was this tourist—this woman—I was trying to shield myself from, and—"

"Trevor, sweetheart, I've heard the whole story. I don't care one bit about this other woman. You and I both know it had nothing to do with her. Do not stand there and lie to me about what's going on with you and your beautiful best friend." She gestures with the hammer while she talks.

"Maybe you should put that thing down," I say.

"Don't deflect. I am perfectly safe, as are you. Now, tell me about Kenzie."

"She won't talk to me about it."

"Won't or hasn't? Because there is a difference. One means she's refused, the other means she just hasn't brought it up yet."

I amend my original answer. "Hasn't."

Mom's quiet for a few moments, the only sound the hammer and nail she's using on this next part of the spindle. Then she asks, "Is she still going to your house tonight while Hayzel is with her parents? You know, like you two do every weekend?"

This takes me by surprise. "How did you know she was coming to my house?"

"We share a lane, son." Mom laughs. "Your house is on the same farm as mine."

"Yeah, with a whole lot of land between them."

"Don't avoid the question."

"Yes, she is," I admit.

"Well then, that's the perfect opportunity, don't you think?"

"For what?"

"Talking to her about that kiss."

I almost want to laugh, to play this off, to pretend this is all no big deal, the way I normally do. But Mom's right. "I probably should. That kiss isn't something I'll ever forget. I don't like pretending it didn't happen." Even being best friends, there's only so much willpower I have to ignore it. I want it to happen a whole lot more.

Though I don't say the rest of this, Mom looks like she knows it anyway.

"Talk to her, sweetheart. What's the worst that could happen?"

Then she immediately puts a hand up. "And before you go to catastrophic, remember that Kenzie is your best friend. She kissed you as much as you kissed her. The worst is not that she hates you now or some such nonsense. That's not possible." Mom shakes her head. "The worst that could happen is Kenzie telling you she's not interested in dating. And now, look, I know that might feel like the end of the world or the end of your friendship, but you are grown adults. Friendships do not just end because one person has more feelings than the other. Not if you're mature about it. You still love each other no matter what."

"I want to be able to do that, Mom. I want to talk with her about it. We've both avoided it for so long now. Over a week. It feels like the window of opportunity has shut in that respect."

"Nonsense. It's only too late if you let it be or if you want it to be."

· ♥ · ♥ · ♥ · ♥ · ♥ ·

It's "date" night once again. Dinner, movie, and falling asleep with Kenzie in my arms, every Friday night since the beginning of March. She always seemed to be okay before when Hayzel stayed with her parents, Kerrick and Nadine, but I guess that was more sporadic. When the sleepovers with Hayze and her grandparents became a regular event, it began to affect Kenzie more and more. I could see it on her face and hear it in her voice every Friday when she mentioned having her apartment to herself. She tried to act like she was totally fine, but I knew better.

I mean, come on. We've been best friends for years. Why did she think she could hide that from me? So I suggested movie nights.

Another night per week that we got to hang out, and a way to keep either of us from being too lonely.

They've always been chaste, these overnights of ours. Only cuddles or snuggles, fully clothed. Well, I don't always wear a shirt, but that's how I sleep. Kenzie doesn't know I also do that as a way to feel her skin connect with mine. Of course, I have to position our bodies so she doesn't get too close to certain areas because there's no hiding physical reactions. I won't let her feel it if it might scare her off.

"Hey," she calls from what sounds like the mudroom.

I'm in the living room, making sure the blanket will be within reach when we need it and the throw pillows are already in place. I also moved the coffee table a little closer to the sofa in case she wants to sit with her feet propped up. She doesn't know I do this on purpose. What used to happen was Kenzie had to get up to bring the table closer, and inevitably, she didn't end up in the same spot, meaning she often returned to the sofa in a spot farther away from me.

Is it selfish of me to want to keep her as close to me as possible?

Maybe, but I don't care. If she's resting her head on my shoulder, the last thing I want is for her to move away for any reason. I want her next to me as long as possible.

I head her way, meeting her in the kitchen. She's holding two bags, one I recognize from the diner and one I don't know.

"Hey." I greet her with a smile that I couldn't hold in if I wanted to and watch as she unloads carrot cake and chili cheese fries from Button's Diner.

As she moves on to the other bag—which I see holds falafel wraps and some other items in closed containers from that new Mediterranean restaurant in Onondaga Hill—Kenzie smiles in return. "I promised a good dinner. We've got gyro fries, falafel wraps, lamb kabobs, and souvlaki since we've wanted to try Christo's for weeks.

And chili cheese fries because I couldn't help myself. The chili was so, so good today."

"And the carrot cake?" I ask with a smirk.

She grins wide and gives a sexy little laugh. "Only the best desserts for you, Trev."

I wish I could kiss her right now. Just grab her with a wink and crash my mouth into hers like last time. There was a moment last week when I thought she was about to make my dreams come true and kiss me first. She was really close to me, her eyes on my lips. Then she licked her own lips. Even with Cinnamon interrupting us, I swear it was about to happen.

Only Hazyel needed her mom to help her get ready for bed. I was exhausted that night and stupidly fell asleep before Kenz returned to the living room. My own damn fault, I know. But when Kenzie woke me up, she didn't give any indication she was still interested in doing whatever it was that had her mere inches from my face, on her knees in front of me. I couldn't force the issue by asking her about it. Then she let me go home.

Was I disappointed? More than, honestly.

Maybe now I know that she's not ready or perhaps not interested.

Then again, she keeps giving me flirty smiles as we eat. Different smiles than the ones she used to give me. I swear her cheeks have a pink to them they never had before. Something's changed with her.

Or maybe I'm reading her wrong. Maybe kissing her in front of everyone like that embarrassed her, and she's too nervous to tell me.

Damn it.

I didn't want that. I just wanted to show her how I feel.

"You all right?" she asks.

When I glance over at her, her head is tilted slightly. As her friend, I'm not supposed to think of how perfectly that exposes a little more of her neck, making it easier to kiss it on my way up or down somewhere else. Nope. Not supposed to do that.

"Yep." I nod quickly. Perhaps too quickly. I have zero chill right now, though.

Kenzie laughs. "Okay. Just seems like you're trying to rush through dinner."

Guess I am eating a lot faster than I normally would. We always eat first, then share junk food snacks during the movie as if we were at the theater, without having to share the time and space with others, allowing us to always be alone. I force a chuckle. "Must not have eaten a big enough lunch."

"What? The double bacon cheeseburger, mozzarella sticks, and large bowl of potato soup weren't enough? Not to mention a giant slice of carrot cake."

I hear her teasing, both of us knowing full well that's plenty of food for me. I just didn't know what else to say. Question is, do I now lean into the fib, or try to steer away from it?

"Think you'll ever tire of making that cake?" I ask, hoping I won't have to lie any more.

"Tire of doing something nice for you? Something you like?" She laughs again, then gives me a warm smile. "Never."

It's moments like this that have me questioning our friendship. Not that it shouldn't exist or that it hasn't been good. On the contrary. That we can have both friendship and a hell of a lot more, because I see it with her. I see how amazing we could be together. How the fact that being friends with Kenzie has led us to this place where we know everything about each other. We wouldn't have any awkward "getting to know you" stages. If we get together, it'll be forever.

But that's a pretty big "if."

That's what keeps me in my seat. What keeps me from grabbing her face. From telling her she's the only woman in this world I'll ever love.

"Good to hear. I don't know what I'd do without all that cake."

She gifts me with yet another beautiful chuckle. "Spoiled much?"

"Me? Nah. I only get cake. You haven't learned how to make my favorite chili yet," I say, motioning with the fry I hold. "Or the stew we had at that little Irish place in Ithaca. Or those mini chocolate lava cakes."

Kenzie puts a hand on my arm, leaning a little closer, and it suddenly feels like it did last week when I thought she was trying to seduce me. *Please let me be right this time,* I think.

Instead of kissing me or even trying to, she gives a small grin. "If that's the case, you might have to spoil yourself."

"Giving up already?"

She rolls her eyes with a laugh. "Already? Trev, I've tried to make Knox's chili for three years now and still can't get it right. Let's face it. I'm a server and not a cook for a very good reason."

I disagree and tell her so.

The blush that spreads her face with the compliment is so pretty, it takes me a little too long to look away.

Kenz glances down, eyeing what's left of her falafel wrap. Then she slowly—and slyly—looks back up. "Maybe I'll get it right for you one day."

There's a lot that could be read into that sentence. Too much for me to be able to think about right now. I finish the last of my helping of fries. My plate's mostly empty by this point. So is Kenzie's.

"Movie time?" I ask.

"Sure." Her tone is friendly and sweet, lightening what was quickly becoming a heady kind of mood.

We put all the dinner things away, then dig out the chocolate Kenzie likes most that I always have on hand and a bag of microwave popcorn. Kenz gets the popcorn started while I pull out the licorice candy from the cabinet and a bottle from the wine rack. She grabs two wineglasses without me needing to ask her to. When the popcorn's done, we gather it all and carry what we can into the living room.

I've already turned off the lights, giving it more of a movie theater feel. Also more of a romantic feel, but I ignore this fact as Kenzie and I settle into the sofa with our treats. Twenty minutes in, neither of us have touched the wine. She's only had a little chocolate, a piece of which she fed to me because it was almost gone and she didn't want me to not get any of it. I wanted to kiss her fingertips when they brushed against my lips. I ignored that urge, too.

Since we've both been yawning like crazy, I suggest we lie down, not waiting until the halfway point like we usually do. She agrees immediately.

As I hold her and breathe in the sweet scent that is so perfectly Kenzie, I can't help but wonder why she doesn't see that I should be more than just a cuddle buddy to her. I should be able wrap my arms around her for reasons that have nothing to do with her loneliness.

I've spent so many moments like this, curious why there's never been more between us. We're best friends. I know her, and I *see* her. I understand her better than anyone else does.

Was the interest she began to show last week and again tonight simply because she's lonely? Those moments when I thought she might have kissed me? As much as I love her, I don't think I could let her use me like that.

Kenzie's always maintained that she won't date so long as Hayzel is still living at home. She says she wants to wait to get into a serious relationship. Hayzel has to be off at school or out on her own first.

That's so far away, though. Eight more years. And if she meets the right guy before then? Or if she already knows him?

But I can't do that. I can't put myself into this. Kenz hasn't mentioned the kiss. It's been over a week. This has been driving me crazy. I think about her all the time. Hell, I'm fantasizing about her right now, with her in my arms, nuzzled together on the sofa. How is this situation not making her crazy, too? How is she not wanting to ask all these questions like I do?

With the way her hair has moved, her neck is exposed. I wish I could kiss it right now. I wonder what she'd do if I did?

It's probably a terrible idea.

I'm sure it is.

Only I lean toward her anyway. She shifts slightly at the same time, completely unaware what I'm trying to do. My lips hit her hair, not her skin.

Kenzie gives a small laugh. "What was that?"

"What?"

"Are you blowing my hair? I felt something in it."

I force a laugh in return, though it does sound a little ridiculous. "Nope, just moving it a little. It was tickling my nose."

"Oh, okay." She gives my hand a squeeze, then places her arm on top of mine, holding part of me while I hold her.

So . . . that didn't work. I should give up, yet I don't want to.

I wish I could call myself brave for trying again, but I can't, especially since I chicken out at the last moment and kiss her hair instead. Kenzie turns that beautiful head to face me and smiles. Of course, I give her a grin in return, one I hope conveys to her how much I want to cover her whole body in kisses.

Is that enough, though? I'm not sure. So I go for one last try, landing a soft kiss on her exposed shoulder. I want to pull down her tank top strap but can't. Well, *won't*. Not if we haven't discussed what happened in the diner. There's no way I'll make a move on her without knowing if she wants it, too.

But that kiss. I mean, how could she not? I know for a fact how much she enjoyed it. That is, unless it was all for show. Is it possible Kenz is that good of an actress? Or was she just really jealous of that woman and liked the kiss only as much as she needed to for the moment?

Kenzie's staring at me, her mouth still in a grin. "Hi," she whispers.

"Hey." I make my voice as soft as hers.

There's a sudden crashing sound, and we both jump. I flick my eyes to the TV screen and remember that the movie is still on. With all my thoughts focused on Kenzie, I completely forgot we were busy doing something else. She gives a little chuckle and turns back toward the television.

I decide to forget about the kisses right now. No sense in pushing the issue. As much as I want Kenzie to beg me to do all kinds of dirty things with her, we just aren't in that place. Not sure when or if we ever will be. This right here, what we're doing? These moments of wrapping my arms around her and getting to hold on all night long? It'll have to be enough.

The movie ends at some point, but I can't say I really know what happened or what the plot was. Kenzie's asleep. I tighten my grip on her—just a bit—and nuzzle into her neck.

"Love you, Sweet Cake," I whisper, feeling like a lucky bastard for being able to tell her my true feelings without scaring her off.

Then I kiss her cheek. The last kiss I'll give her tonight. Though I'm struggling with keeping my eyes open, I almost don't want the night to end. It'll be business as usual with her in the morning, I know it. She'll thank me for a fun night, kiss my cheek, maybe quickly run her fingers through my beard, then head off with a grin and zero idea how much I want her to stay in this house with me.

I can't keep sleep at bay forever. At some point, it feels like I'm starting to doze. My eyes are already closed. I tell Kenz I love her again, though she still can't hear me, and let myself drift.

Chapter 5

Trevor

"You," Lourdes practically growls as I count another bunch of pink geraniums.

Although Lourdes showing up here without texting first isn't new, this is a surprise. I was supposed to drop these off to her in another half hour or so. While I'm glad to see my friend, her tone tells me I screwed up somehow.

"Lourdes," I say, giving her a grin. I can feel that my smile doesn't stretch all the way that it should, and my eyebrows are a little scrunched. She doesn't smile in return. "What's up?"

"Are you seriously asking me that right now?"

Okay. This is the moment I'm supposed to figure out where I went wrong, what I did, so on and so on. I'm not feeling it in this moment. I tilt an untied bouquet of geraniums toward her. "Smell these." Then I give her another grin.

I know exactly what's going to happen next.

These geraniums are some of Lourdes's favorite flowers, for the spicy citrus-like scent alone. This is the first year I've been able to sell any to her in bulk. She should be overjoyed right now.

"Oh my gosh," she whispers. Her eyes close slightly as she breathes in deeply for a moment or two.

"Good, right? Your customers are going to love these."

Her eyes flutter open again. "Trev, you're a genius about a lot of things, especially how to grow the most magical blooms, but you suck at relationships."

Turning away from her, I go back to placing the flowers into the containers. I know what Lourdes is looking for, but I also know I've denied that there's anything between Kenz and me so long that it's easier to go with that lie. "I told you. Kenzie and I are just friends."

In what I know to be a big mistake, I turn again to look at Lourdes's reaction to this. Her tilted head and narrow eyes tell me she's not buying it.

"Two years ago, I would have believed you. Maybe even two months ago. Maybe. But ever since Rhett noticed the way you look at Kenzie—a way none of us really thought about before—I refuse to go back to my ignorance." She pauses like she has more to say but needs a moment, her eyes watching my face.

I'm feeling a little nervous right now. How much grilling is she about to throw at me?

Then she continues. "I heard about that stunt you pulled the other night."

More like a couple weeks ago, but she's been busy. I give her a smile. Can't help myself. I grin like a fool every time I think about that kiss with my amazing best friend. Now Lourdes grins in return.

"Did Kenzie react the way you wanted her to?"

"Yeah. She did." Did she ever. I never thought I'd be able to hold her in my arms like that and kiss her like life or death rested on that lip-lock, and I definitely never thought she'd give as much as I gave her in return or that I'd even hear her give a soft moan in the same moment. I mean, Kenzie moaned because of *me*. Because of something I did with her.

Then I sober, falling back to reality. "But she hasn't mentioned it since then. I don't think it meant much to her."

What else am I supposed to think when she won't talk about it and is pretending it never happened? While my mom would understand, this isn't a topic I'd like to bring up with her after our last conversation. Sure as hell can't discuss it with my brothers, although my sisters are a possibility, especially Jade. Truthfully, I think the best person to have this conversation with is Lourdes, since she actually has a degree in psychology, but I'd like to steer this talk away from my feelings.

"We're best friends, nothing more."

"Like I said, Trev. You are a genius at a lot of things, but you suck at navigating romance and relationships."

While Lourdes is so quick to point this out to me, we both know it's equally true for her. I accidentally let out an audible scoff, and toss a glance her way while I continue packing flowers.

She gives a tiny shake of her head. "Anyway, this isn't about Kenzie. You know what you did."

Now I laugh. Lourdes is definitely in a mood today. "What did I do?" I look up at her, making eye contact.

I can't help but notice her glare, almost as if she hopes it will melt me or something.

"Are you seriously yelling at me about Spence Kirby being in the community garden? That was weeks ago."

She makes a noise almost like a grunt as she narrows her eyes even more. "It was eleven days ago."

This has me taking a break from my work and turning all the way toward her. "Lourdes, I swear, I didn't think it would be a problem for you. I mean, I know you hate him. You have since he left. I just didn't realize you were so hung up on him."

Lourdes huffs and rolls her eyes, but doesn't reply.

Guess it's my turn to do a little friendly scolding. "You counted the days since he's been back in town."

"No, I counted the days since I saw him at the garden. And I didn't even need to count. It was the first of the month."

I raise my eyebrows at her. She might want to convince me that she doesn't care about Kirby, but based on this conversation, I know that's a lie. She's a lot like me in that respect. Love someone from afar and not tell anyone about it.

"Besides, I don't actually know when he came back to town." She pauses again. "But you do."

No reason not to tell her the truth. I nod. "I didn't know how to tell you or even if I should. Like I said, you've told all of us over the years how you didn't care one way or the other about Spence." Then I let out a sigh, because I really should have known better. "I guess I should've listened to Kenz when she told me to tread lightly with this."

Lourdes lets out a hard sigh of her own. "It sucks having the whole town know details like this. It seems like everyone knew about him returning before I did. As much as I hate the gossip mill . . . I mean, *someone* could have told me. Given me some time to prepare."

"From what Spence said, it was a rushed, well thought out decision."

"Whatever that means."

I don't normally push like this, but Lourdes was the one to open this can of worms. "Are you going to mention the fake dating?"

"Seriously?" She groans, clearly unhappy. "I never know who believes Mrs. Hasse and is in agreement that it must be real and who knows the idea of Spence and me being in a real relationship again is complete horseshit."

I don't buy that. Not now. By the look on her face, I think she's aware that I'm catching on. "I'm not one to judge. Since you don't believe my denials—"

"As well I shouldn't," she interrupts.

"Right. Well, I don't talk about this with anyone, but I've been in love with my best friend for forever, since the moment her loser husband left her years ago."

"Honesty, Trev. That's what we're going for, right?"

I nod. I loved Kenzie long before that. Lourdes gets it, but I can't say that part out loud. Best to just skip it. "I'm too much of a coward to risk telling her how I feel. I'd marry her today if she'd let me."

"I know." Lourdes's voice is soft. Kind. "Next time, just please give me a heads up before inviting any more of my ex-boyfriends to my garden sanctuary."

"Do you have any other ex-boyfriends?" I don't say this to be an ass. It's a genuine question, because while I've seen Lourdes date, I've never known her to be in a relationship apart from Kirby.

"You know what I mean."

Since I do, I give her a grin.

"Let's get these geraniums finished," she continues. "Then you can show me how the begonias are turning out."

Not long later, on our way to the begonias in a partially shaded nearby part of the farm, Lourdes turns to me and says, "We're quite a pair, aren't we? I'm in love with a man I'll never get to be with again, and—"

"I thought you didn't care about Spence?" I can't help but interrupt, feeling a little bad about putting her on the spot.

"You told me your truth. I'm telling you mine."

I nod. "Fair enough."

"So. I don't get to be with the man I love because *reasons*, and you're too afraid to try with the woman you love."

After giving her a few minutes of quiet, I say, "You know, you can be with Spence if you still have feelings for him. There's no way he'd turn down the chance for a relationship with you."

She shakes her head. "Trev, he betrayed my trust. There's no coming back from that."

"Okay. I get it." I decide to let it go. "After the begonias, I have a surprise for you."

"Which is what?"

I chuckle. "You really like being prepared for and in charge of everything, don't you?"

Lourdes shrugs. "Being taken by surprise in my life has often equated to losing someone or something. It's never a good thing."

I think Spence coming back could be a good thing for her, if she'll allow it. "Well, I can promise you this is a good one."

The begonias look perfect, according to Lourdes, as do the daisies and the zinnias. We have one last flower to stop at, and quickly, since I know she needs to get back to her shop. I hear she's lost a worker or two, and her work hours are growing by the day. I lead her to a spot on the farm I've been keeping her—and most everyone else—away from the past several months. When I checked here yesterday, I knew it was finally time.

"Oh, Trevor," Lourdes whispers as soon as she sees it.

We stand in front of Bernhardt Farms and Orchard's newest flower field.

"Heritage roses." Her voice is still a hush.

I hold in a small laugh. I knew she'd love this. Kenzie has already fawned over it several times now and warned me Lourdes would probably pull a Lucy for a moment and do this jumping squeal thing. Lourdes has so far proven her wrong, but I can't say I'm surprised. I never told her I was planting these. This journey to get the damn roses to grow and flourish and just plain cooperate hasn't been easy on me or the two members of my staff I hired specifically for this part of the farm.

Lourdes takes in the cream, soft pink, and golden-yellow blooms.

"Just a few to start," I say. "But now that we know what we're doing and what this land is capable of, I think we'll have a lot more color options next year."

"Own root?"

I knew she'd ask this, and I knew it wouldn't take long, either. Of course Lourdes the florist wants to know if the root systems of these roses have been grafted with others or if they grew all from their own.

"Yep," I reply.

She instantly turns to me. "How many other floral shops know about these? Did Jules put her order in yet?"

Now I really do laugh. "I promise, you're getting first dibs. But some of them aren't quite ready."

"No worries. I'll need them for as long as you can supply them. Women go crazy for antique roses." She pauses, then looks from the blooms up into my face again. "You really do know how to surprise a girl in the best way. You need to use that skill on Kenzie. Show her how much you love her. Tell her. Wow her. Just don't be an idiot and pretend there's nothing going on."

"Again I say, you can be with Spence if you still have feelings for him. Don't pretend you feel nothing for him when he's around. Take your own advice."

She rolls her eyes, and I know we're done discussing relationships. Time to get back into farmer and customer mode. Lourdes places a huge order, to be delivered incrementally over the next several weeks, with caveats allowed for demand and/or rose conditions, though I don't foresee anything bad happening to them.

Lourdes eventually heads back into town. I, meanwhile, go over to another part of the farm to check on the progress on one of our barns. Our large east barn sat here for many years, not being used for anything, not even storage really. Dad had had a few antique tractors parked in here, but after he passed, Mom had those moved down to her section of the farm, in a barn behind her cottage.

After once hearing Kenzie gush about how romantic it would be to have weddings in this barn if it were cleaned up—since a lot of people do that now—I decided to have it completely renovated specifically for it to be an event space, complete with a fancy floor and chandeliers. The older, smaller part will be for ceremonies, and the grand open space will be perfect for receptions. Well, according to Kenzie, as she mapped it all out in her head while we walked around and avoided giant cobwebs.

The cobwebs are long gone, and I think I can honestly say this barn has never been cleaner. This is yet another space that almost no one else has seen. Not even Kenzie. I want everyone surprised by the results, though they all know it's happening. Polly has been keeping track of it with photos and blogs and social media posts, but it's been a few weeks since I let her in here either.

As I stand in this barn, I imagine Kenzie being the first person married here. Well, Kenzie and me being the first couple married here.

It's all I want.

It's all I can see.

But it'll never happen if I can't ignore the doubts and fears and tell her how I feel.

·❤·❤·❤·❤·❤·

Happily squished.

That's what I feel right now.

Kenzie's asleep, having missed most of the second half of our movie double-header. She often goes to bed too late, wakes up really early, works at the diner for many hours, takes care of Hayzel and herself and her apartment, and still finds time to work out for hours in addition to spending time with me and the rest of her friends and family. It's a wonder she ever has any energy.

So here we are on my sofa, her back to me, her perfect ass close against me, but not so close that she might feel something I don't think she wants. I've had to shove my own ass as deep into the back of the sofa as I can. But I get to lie here on another sleepover night with my arms wrapped around the woman I love, and chaste or not, I'm not complaining.

It would be nice to have some more room, though.

We've never gone up to my bed before. I didn't think Kenzie would ever be okay with that. And while initially, I used to offer her the guest rooms, I quickly realized she didn't want to sleep alone. But now? Now I think it's time to see what Kenz thinks about sleeping in my bed with me.

"Sweet Cake," I whisper near her ear.

She doesn't stir.

I bend a little closer, so the tip of my nose is touching her cheek. "Sweet Cake," I whisper again.

"Mm?"

I keep my voice soft and tender. "Hey. Wake up. Let's go to bed."

"Wha—" she starts to ask, but then also starts to go back to sleep.

I shift my top arm so I can give her hip a gentle squeeze with my hand. Her eyes open.

"Hey," she whispers drowsily.

"Hey. Let's go to bed. We'll have more room up there."

Kenzie turns a little to glance at our positions on the sofa, then moves her eyes up to meet mine. "Okay."

"Okay?" I can't hide my surprise, though I think maybe I should.

But she nods. "Yeah. Let's go."

She moves to get up, only I stop her, shifting so I'm up on my feet before her. Then I scoop her up in my arms. Well, I try to, but sleepy Kenzie is a little squirmy. She shifts, and before I know it, her legs are around my middle. She nuzzles her face into my neck and wraps her arms around me. I hold her up, trying to keep my breathing steady, and carry her to my second-floor bedroom without slipping my hands down to her ass.

Once in my room, I gently deposit Kenz onto my bed. I assume she's just going to fall right back to sleep, only she sits up when I'm about to walk away to go brush my teeth. When I look back at her, we make eye contact. Then she lifts her top over her head, tossing it toward the plush chair I have in the nearby corner.

I've never actually seen Kenzie in her bra before. I mean, I've seen her in bikini tops, which is basically the same thing, and I've seen her bras when she's doing laundry, but the two have never been together like this before. It's a black satin one, fitting for having been under her dark green tank top. While I'm still stunned that the woman I love is sitting in my bed in her bra, she lies down on her back, lifts her hips, and removes her leggings. She's now only in her bra and black lace thong.

I can't speak. I'm trying to, but my mouth has gone dry and no words will come out. I don't even remember what else I was going to do.

Kenzie lies back down and starts to cover herself with my light comforter. "I hope this is okay," she says, indicating her body and lack of clothes. "I don't feel like putting my pajamas on. They're all the way downstairs."

Is her bag a lot closer than she's making it sound? Could I offer to get her pajamas for her? Could I offer her some of my clothes? All yes. Am I going to say or do any of these things? Hell no.

"It's okay. No big deal," I manage to reply, hoping I sound casual and not at all the way I feel, which is in shock and incredibly turned on.

Only some tiny scraps of fabric are keeping her from being completely naked in front of me. Is it a hardship for me? Definitely not. It does bring about a bit of a problem, however. Normally, I sleep in just my boxers, but taking my jeans off at the moment is probably not a good idea.

Teeth.

That's right. I was going to brush my teeth. I decide to stick to that plan, hoping I'll have settled a little before coming back in here. The whole time I'm in my attached bathroom, all I can think about is my almost-naked best friend in my bed. I don't take long in the bathroom, either. All of me is eager to return to Kenzie.

When I do, it looks like she's already asleep. I strip to my boxers and slide in bed on the opposite side of her. Then I scoot toward her until I'm close enough to hold her again while still leaving a gap between our lower halves. It's so freaking hard right now to not give in and just beg her for what I want, but I can't. Better to close my eyes, will my heart and my breath to slow down, and try to sleep.

Eventually, I open my eyes again to find the sun's rays peeking through the window. It's early as far as I can tell, but not too bad. Kenzie shifts a little. Her body is completely up against me now. I have no idea how or when that happened and what she's noticed of my current predicament.

She turns her head and smiles. "Hi."

"Morning, Sweet Cake."

To my surprise, she rolls her whole body to face me and snuggles up against me, skin on skin just about everywhere our bodies could touch, once again completely against each other. Then. Oh then. This gorgeous woman tips her chin up and lightly kisses my lips.

If ever there was a sign, this has to be it.

I go for it, gently pressing my hands into her back and claiming her mouth like it belongs to me.

She doesn't push me away. She doesn't pull away from me. In fact, she kisses me with as much intensity as our diner kiss. I slide one hand down to her hip and remember she's still in just her thong.

Without thinking, I grab hold of the tiny strap and give it a tug, not off her, just a pull that tells her I want more if she's interested.

Kenzie surprises me by moving her hands from my face to my chest, then down to my abs. She slides the tips of her fingers under the waistband of my boxers. Then she pulls away from the kiss.

"You okay?" I ask.

Only she doesn't answer. She actually gets out of bed.

Shit.

I freaked her out. I know I did, especially because she's getting dressed now.

"What's going on, Kenz?"

Her leggings and top are already on. She moves to head for the door. I crawl to the edge of the bed and stand on the floor. But her feet haven't taken her far.

"Kenz?"

"Nothing," she replies with a light laugh. Her cheeks are pink.

"Is it bothering you that we came up here?"

"No," she answers with a shake of her head.

I push a little further. "Is it bothering you what we just did in bed?"

"No." Her voice sounds genuine.

I watch her face and her eyes, trying to gauge her reaction. When I move closer to her, she doesn't step back or pull away. Something's going on with her, and I can't figure out what it is. The only thing I can think to do is try one more time, hoping she'll either give me what we both want or tell me she has no interest.

Slowly, deliberately, I place one hand on her waist and one on her neck under her hair. She neither moves nor speaks. Bending toward her, I move my gaze from her eyes to her mouth, back and forth, drawing closer and closer. Our lips just barely graze, but she moans. It's that soft, sexy, "I need you now" kind of moan.

Time to go all in.

Chapter 6

Kenzie

MY BEST FRIEND'S LIPS brush against mine. He pulls back for a second before returning to me, our lip-lock tender, but also frantic. Trevor kisses me like he won't be able to breathe without it, like he needs me to give him the strength to face the day. Like this is the only way to get it.

I'm filled with the same heady energy. This right here? This kiss? It feels like it's lifeblood.

He slips his hands just under my tank top, still down at my waist. I caress my hands over his bare back, skimming along each muscle, each of us slowly stroking the other as we get greedier and greedier with our mouths.

But when we slow down and part slightly in order to catch our breaths, I pull away, then step aside.

Trevor puts his arm out, wrapping his hand around the post of his gorgeous antique bed, stopping me in my tracks. "What are you doing?"

"Going to get Hayzel," I say, almost with a laugh. Our weekly "we are only friends, so no hanky panky" sleepover—though a little different than usual since Hayzel's at Trevor's mom's house instead of my parents'—is sadly over once again. Morning usually has me reluctant to leave. But with what just happened . . .

I don't want to go, but I can't stay.

I can't think.

I just need time to think.

I've already changed into my clothes. A shower can wait until home. Trevor has a spare toothbrush here for me, but that can wait until home, too, especially since I haven't had coffee yet. I keep my voice breezy as I continue, doing my best not to wither under Trevor's serious gaze. "I'm sure your mom's exhausted by now. Hayzel is a lot more intense than Wyatt."

"First, Hayzel feels as much like a grandchild to my mom as Wyatt, and she never gets tired of either of them. You and Hayzel are both important to Mom. Remember when you stayed with her when Hayze was a baby and your parents' basement flooded?"

I nod silently. Deb has always been so kind and supportive.

"Second, Kenz . . ." This time, Trevor almost gives a bit of a laugh. "Why are you trying to run off?"

"I'm not."

"Yes you are. Listen, something very important just happened, and we have to talk about it. We just made out."

And there it is. That part I can't seem to wrap my head around. We've done this before, true. I wanted to do it before and after that first kiss. But now that it's happened for a second and third time with our bodies fully pressed into each other? I have no idea what to do with it.

"We did," is all I can say in reply.

Trev steps closer. He takes his hand off the post and rests it on my right hip. I think my body is melting there now. Pretty soon, I'm going to be a puddle of love-struck, yearning, steaming-hot goo, unable to tell this amazing man anything about it.

"You and me," he says. "We kissed like that's the only way to live. Again. And again."

"I was there," I whisper. Somehow, my hands have ended up in his hair, at the base of his beautiful neck, slowly gliding around on his skin.

His dark eyes deepen to an almost inky black. He closes them for just a moment, his hand tightening its grasp on my hip. The force of this has me sucking in a breath. I let it out just as quickly, trying to loop his short but just barely long enough hair around one of my fingers. Trevor's other hand is now at the back of my neck, his fingers fully wrapped up in my blonde tresses.

I have no words. Just so much longing. Our faces are only inches apart.

Trevor's voice is raspy when he speaks again. "We've been best friends for years. Almost Hayzel's entire life." He pauses, and he's quiet for so long, I begin to worry that something might be wrong. Then he adds, "I love you."

Now this is something I can work with. Something familiar and comfortable and soothing to my soul. I smile. "I love you, too."

But Trev just shakes his head. "No, Kenz. Listen to me. For once when I say this, *listen* to me. I. Love. You."

Chapter 7

Trevor

"Like . . . like, what kind of *love*?" Kenz asks, but I know she knows. She's stalling for time to think. This happens when she isn't ready to say more, needing information first. Kenzie usually isn't one for rambling.

Gently, I tug a few strands of hair. "Deep love. Real love. In love with you love."

She's about to stutter out another question. I can see it on her face, in how she moves her mouth, and hear it in the way she keeps taking breaths in and letting them out in short staccato.

"I fell for you when we were kids, when I didn't know much about love except that being around you made me happy and I wanted a whole lot more of that in my life. I knew I would truly love you one day when we were teenagers, if you'd only give me the chance. I fell in love for real as your friend, spending every day with you and it still not being enough."

Kenzie's motionless, letting that sink in. Well, I hope that's what she's doing anyway. I stand here quietly, giving her the time and space she needs. But she's taking an awful lot of time. Maybe the best thing to do is let go and step back. My arms ache to hold her again. I already miss her hands in my hair.

"You want to date me?" she asks eventually.

I shake my head, then put a hand up to let her know that wasn't a no because her nervous expression worries me. "I know what you look like before you've showered or brushed your hair. I know what kind of attitude you have before coffee. I know how your voice sounds when you're sick or haven't slept in three days. Not once have I ever forgotten an important day for you or for Hayzel."

It looks like she's tensed up from this, but I have no idea why. We've danced around this topic too long. "I know exactly what kind of man you need, Sweet Cake. I know exactly what dating you would be like. So no, I don't want to date you. I think it's safe to say that we are well beyond dating."

Her eyebrows scrunch together.

"The combination of the two of us together is not casual dating material. We are full-fledged relationship material, whether you realize that or not."

Her shoulders drop down a little, but I don't think it's a bad thing. I think it's her relaxing. "You want to be with me?"

"Kenz, I've wanted to be with you from the moment I met you," I remind her.

"Yeah, but that's crazy. We were twelve."

I laugh. "Yeah, well, twelve-year-old me knew adult me would still want you."

She smiles.

"We've said 'I love you' to each other every day for about ten years. In all that time, I've meant it as a friend, yes, but more than that, as a man deeply in love with you."

She's still quiet. I wish I knew what she's thinking. Then she says, "I never knew."

"I'm good at hiding it."

"Too good." She shakes her head a little. "Trevor, I wish I could say I've been in love with you all these years. I've loved you deeply, but not in that way."

My heart, stomach, hopes, everything drops.

Except she's still smiling. In fact, she steps closer to me, taking my hands and placing them on her hips again. "Not the whole ten years, anyway. It's recent. For the last few months, I've wondered."

"Wondered what?" I can't help but ask. I think I really need to hear her say the words. "What's recent?"

"If you could ever see me as more than just Kenz."

"You're not just Kenz. Never have been. Never will be. You're not *just* anything. You are everything, Sweet Cake."

She grins, and with it, a pink blush spreads over her cheeks. "Will you promise to call me Sweet Cake even if you're mad at me or we're fighting?"

"Always. You will always be Sweet Cake to me." I squeeze her hips like I did a little while ago, and she does that sexy gasp like she did before. "You still want to leave?"

There it is. That feeling of her grabbing hold of me, her fingers in my hair, her eyes on my mouth. She does a little jump, and suddenly, I'm holding on to her ass and thighs, keeping her close to me and not on the floor. She pulls herself tighter to me, sprinkling light kisses all over my neck, her legs wrapped around my middle. Then I'm carrying her to my bed, and this time, we are definitely not in here as *just friends*.

When I lay her back on the mattress, she keeps her legs around me, holding me to her and on top of her.

"You ready for this?" I ask, my hands paused at the hem of her shirt.

"More than."

We both lean so she can lift off the bed. Within a few seconds, I remove both her shirt and her bra. She scrambles to carefully pull my boxers down my legs. I step out of them and return to Kenz, who's already working on her own bottoms. Another moment, and suddenly, I'm naked with my best friend for the first time.

Holy shit, she's gorgeous.

I mean, she's always gorgeous no matter what. I've just never seen her so flushed and pink and breathing heavily in anticipation of what I'm going to do to her. What we're going to do together.

Though I return us to the position we were first in on the bed, me on top of her, I hold still, nuzzled against her cheek.

"What are you doing?" she asks with a slight laugh.

She can feel how much I want this.

"Taking a moment. Enjoying the feeling. Letting it sink in that this is really happening. I love you, Sweet Cake."

"I love you, Trevor," she whispers, her voice reverent, but also giddy. She turns and kisses the part of my neck that meets my collarbone, then gives it a little suck.

There is no freaking way I can hold in a satisfied groan. And we're off, kissing, caressing, appreciating every part of each other. Everything is too fast and too slow and so damn perfect. I never knew she could sound like this or breathe like this or move like this or say my name like this. All the things I've dreamed about for years. All the things I've longed for.

When we're both so spent we can barely move, we lie facing each other, my hand on her back, hers on my chest.

"I don't think twelve-year-old you anticipated that," she says, chuckling.

I laugh, too. "Twelve-year-old me didn't know most of that existed, and rightly so. Seventeen-year-old me, however . . . We fulfilled about half the fantasies he had of you."

She raises her eyebrows. "Only half?"

"What can I say? Teenage me had a lot of time to come up with as many fantasies as possible."

My girlfriend gives me a grin. "Guess we'll have to work on the other half."

Leaning closer, I kiss the center of her breastbone. "I'll do anything you want, Sweet Cake."

"Anything?"

Her tone catches my attention. I look up in her eyes again, my hands starting to wander. "What do you have in mind?"

"I can't deny I've come up with quite a few fantasies of my own the last couple months."

"Oh yeah? Did I satisfy any of them?"

She nods quickly. "But I have a few more up my sleeve."

I bend and kiss her body again. "Sweet Cake, you aren't wearing any sleeves. You aren't wearing anything." I move a bit and kiss another part of her. I'll kiss every single centimeter of her if she'll let me.

"Anything else you want to do with me while I'm temporarily not wearing anything?"

No woman has ever had me ready again this soon before, but then, Kenzie is far from being just any woman. "Am I allowed to—" I stop both my words and my hand a moment, lifting my hand from her hip, then whisper the rest in her ear, making it as tantalizing as possible. "Or do we have to have an official date first?"

Kenzie's already grabbing my hand, hovering it over the place I mentioned to her in a hush. This has me grinning a wide, giddy smile. "I think it's a requirement to do that at least twice before leaving the bed for the first time," she says coyly, slowly batting her eyelashes before biting her bottom lip. It's the first time I've ever seen her intentionally flirt with me.

"At least twice, huh? Funny. I thought it was supposed to be five times. But you would know more than me, right?"

She laughs. "I did say *at least*. There's definitely wiggle room."

"I've got some ideas if you're in the mood for wiggling."

Now she laughs harder and gives me a saucy smile before planting my hand where she wants it.

We'll have to have our official first date in here, because we are never leaving this bed.

Chapter 8

Kenzie

"I HAVE NEWS," I begin tentatively. This isn't a conversation I ever planned on having, but in this moment, I really don't know why. I've wanted this to be my reality for months now. Why am I not better prepared?

I didn't expect to do this at my parents' house either, but Mom asked Deb to bring Hayzel over so they could still see her even though she couldn't stay last night. Trevor and I were a little too busy in bed for me to give more than a short *I don't mind* reply to both Deb's and Mom's texts.

"What's up?" my daughter asks, her demeanor telling me she's not really worried.

She's such a sweet kid, often seeing the best in people and situations. This must not seem like a tense moment for her. Not that it is for me either. I just wish I had practiced what to say.

Mom smiles at me, gently urging me on. She already knows. I had to tell her when I called to say that I was coming over to speak with Hayzel, but that Hayzel was still going to stay with them the rest of the day as planned.

"So you know Trevor?"

Hayzel laughs like this is the most ridiculous thing I could've said, which it kind of is. "Obviously."

"Right." I laugh, too. "Well, what would you say if I told you that Trevor has a girlfriend." Then I hear how that might sound to her, especially since my mom stands behind her doing this panicky, frantic waving thing.

My daughter's eyes grow wide as she finally slows down enough to look over at me for more than half a second.

"Me, I mean. I'm his girlfriend. Trevor and I are dating." Damn, I am completely fumbling this.

Only it doesn't seem to matter. Hayzel's face turns rosy as she squeals in delight. "What? Mom! That's so cool!" She runs over, barreling into me with a giant bear hug. "Can I go use Gramma's nail stickers?"

I laugh again. "As long as she said it's okay, I'm fine with that."

Hayzel runs off, leaving Mom and me in the living room together.

"And you were worried." Mom chuckles.

"It's a big deal. Trevor and I have been friends her whole life. She's never seen us together in a romantic way. I thought the news of us dating would be a hard shock to her system."

"Oh, come on, Kenzie." Mom shakes her head with a smile. "You two love each other. That's what Hayzel sees. That's what makes her so happy. The fact that you and Trevor make each other happy." She pauses. "You nearly freaked her out telling her he had a girlfriend without context. I swear that child was about to burst into tears any moment."

Maybe not so dramatically as Mom made it sound, but I have to agree.

"Are you two spending the day together?"

"He has some work to do around the farm, and I have a hair appointment. I'll go over to BFO later, and we'll probably have dinner before the Starlight Festival."

"A working date?"

"I know, but I think it'll be fine." I give Mom a grin. Then I think for a moment. "I've only told you, Charisma, Edin, and Lucy so far. Trevor told his mom and his siblings. How long do you think it'll be before the whole town knows?"

Mom shrugs. "Who knows? If you wanted to keep it to yourselves for a while, you didn't have to tell anyone except Hayzel."

I nod, knowing what she means. Real love is precious. What Trevor and I have, especially so. "We discussed it and agreed that we're okay with people knowing right away. No sense in hiding it. He'd literally stand on top of the diner and shout it from the rooftop if he could."

Now Mom gives a soft smile, but I don't really think it's for me. "Your dad and I have that kind of love. Hold on to it, sweetheart. It honestly doesn't matter how long you've loved each other. Now is your time together, and time is a rare, precious thing. Don't waste it." Her wistful tone tells me she's thinking of Dad's heart condition.

I lean close enough to pat her hand a moment. "We won't. I promise."

Chapter 9

Kenzie

"What would you like this time? Want to shake things up and go blue or pixie or shaved off?"

I make a horrified sound, and Fig—the owner of Frances & Fig Hair Salon, who is actually both Frances and Fig—laughs with a grin. My stylist Iris sucks in a breath.

"Don't you dare," she scolds me, her tone severe.

Now I laugh. "Don't worry. I don't think any of those are quite my thing."

"If you ever decide to switch it up from boho to punk, Iris is your girl."

Iris, meanwhile, relaxes. "Trim today? A few inches?"

"A few inches and some pretty waves, please. I have a date tonight."

"Oh, that's nice," Iris says. She sounds only mildly interested.

So the news hasn't spread far yet. I wonder if she knows about Trevor's feelings for me. Iris is Dottie's daughter and therefore Trevor's cousin. We make small talk about the dry heat we've had in our area recently while Iris washes and conditions my hair at one of the sinks toward the back, along the left wall. Once we've made it to her chair, she drapes a cape over me to protect my clothes.

"Thanks for getting me in on such short notice, by the way." It's early afternoon. Trevor and I reluctantly found the willpower to drag ourselves out of his bed this morning, and I've missed him ever since. It's an emotional ache as well as a physical one.

"Oh, no problem." Iris smiles and reaches for a comb. "Mom giving you a hard time at the diner?"

"Never. She spoils me."

Iris gives a soft sigh. "I wish she could start her own place. Run it the way she wants."

"Yeah, I get that. Your mom is the best. But she likes Francie, and she's happy where she is." Though Francie might have the same name as Fig, she runs the diner quite differently than Fig runs the salon. Most notably, Francie doesn't joke around with us and our customers the way Fig does. That has always bothered Dottie, who likes to have fun with all of us, but it doesn't bother her enough to make her want to leave.

"Besides," I add, "Dottie pretty much runs the place anyway. Francie's never there."

After a while spent discussing Dottie's plans to convince Francie to turn a barely used storage area into extra seating—which one would think shouldn't take much convincing at all—and the new cakes Knox has been teaching me, Iris suddenly says, "Can I tell you something?"

"Of course," I reply with a startled laugh.

"I about fell over when Mom told me the story of Trev kissing you a couple weeks ago."

I can't help but laugh again. "Iris, I swear, no one reacted. Not a single one. It was like they didn't care."

"Kenzie, I guarantee they were all dying inside trying to hold in all their cheers that were ready to burst out."

"Or their shock."

But she laughs at me. "Oh, Kenzie. You were the only one who was surprised by that kiss."

So she does know. This makes me smile.

"I think it's my turn to tell you something," I say, lowering my voice conspiratorially.

My trim is done and my hair dry. Iris is about to move on to creating soft, flowy waves, in keeping with my boho style, but also more polished than how I normally look. I know Trev has seen me at my worst and my messiest, but this is our first official date. It doesn't matter that I technically have to work the booth for Button's Diner at the festival. It doesn't matter that Hayzel will be around a lot, even if she is staying with my parents for the weekend.

This weekend marks the start of Trevor and me. The start of *us*. I want to make an effort. I want him to know and to hear and to see how important it is to me.

Iris patiently waits for my news.

"That date I have?"

"Mm-hmm? What about it?" Once again, her tone is kind and agreeable, if not a little uninterested.

Can't say I blame her. As far as everyone knows, Trevor and I kissed once and never did it or even discussed it again. "It's with Trevor," I whisper before she picks up the hot styling tool.

"What?" she shrieks. She's so loud, all the other people in here turn and look at us.

I kind of chuckle, but Iris isn't ashamed in any way. "You're going on a date?" Her voice is squeaky. "That's amazing!" Then she kind of does a little jumping up and down thing.

"Don't tell me everything if there's nudity involved in any way because he's my cousin, so that's just gross. But tell me everything!"

She already knows about the movie nights, the ones that I've sworn for months were strictly platonic. All I have to say is that last night was movie night again, and Iris nods like she understands completely. I tell her about making out—minus the details that are only for Trev and me to know—and how Trevor declared his love this morning. Iris squeals again.

"I knew it. I *knew* it. I'm so happy for you two. The whole town will be."

The entire town might be, but honestly, I'm so happy I don't care either way. So long as this doesn't become a pink ribbon for Lorelai/blue ribbon for Luke situation, what the town thinks doesn't matter much. But I suspect Iris is probably right.

"So what's the date?" she asks in an excited tone, beginning the first curls.

Ha. I was right. She didn't like the idea of me dating someone if it wasn't Trevor. "Why did no one tell me before that everyone thought we should be together?"

"You know how it is in this town, Kenz. Gossips with heart. We're very proud of that title." Iris moves on to the next small section of hair.

"I know, I know. I just wish, since he and I weren't smart enough or brave enough to see it or do anything about it, that someone would have at least mentioned it by now."

She laughs. "Nope. You two were on your own. We knew you'd figure it out eventually."

Then I tell her about Trevor wanting to attend the Starlight Festival with me. "I still have to work the booth, but I think I'll be able to carve out some time to spend with him, just us."

"Hayzel going, too?"

"She's so excited. When I talked to her this morning at my parents' house, she practically screamed the way you did."

"I told you. We've all been waiting for this." Iris pauses her words, but her hands keep the curling iron steady. "Can I ask you something, though?"

"Of course."

"Not that I'm saying this would ever happen. I don't think this is even in the realm of possibility. But what would happen if for some crazy reason you and Trevor don't work out?"

I don't answer. I don't really have one. It just feels like a given that Trevor and I will last.

Iris continues. "Just that you haven't really dated since Cal left. You go on dates, but nothing ever evolves into a relationship. You always said you were waiting for Hayzel to be older before trying anything like that. So what happens with your friendship with Trevor if you break up? Would that mean you'd see less of him? Would Hayzel see less of all of us, too? Because you've got such a great kid, Kenz. You're both like part of the family to us. We'd hate for you to pull away if your relationship ended."

"Honestly, Iris, I don't see that happening. Not even because I'm so blissfully happy with this new shiny relationship. I know sometimes a thing that feels like it'll last forever gets destroyed. I know this. So while I'm certain Trev and I are going to work out, and while I'm also certain that this conversation is probably completely unnecessary, I also know that I adore your family. I'd never be able to take any of you away from Hayzel, Trevor included."

I hope she knows what I mean. A breakup with Trev would be absolutely devastating, but then losing the entire Bernhardt family on top of it? I don't think Hayzel and I could do that. We'll always love them and want to be around them.

"Anyway." Iris brightens. "No more doom-and-gloom talk. You are in a brand-new relationship with your best friend. That's definitely something to celebrate."

It absolutely is. I shake away the dark cloud that threatens to ruin my good mood. "No more talk of breakups and potential goodbyes. Only happy things. Like my first official date with Trevor." Now I'm the one who's squealing.

I still can't believe it. I knew I wanted that kiss to turn into more. I hoped for it so much. We're finally here, and I want to jump up and down and dance and throw confetti everywhere. Be my own personal one-woman parade. Though I guarantee the rest of the town would join me, or they will once they know.

Trev and I have a *date* tonight.

Look out, Syracuse Falls. You have no idea what's headed your way.

·❤·❤·❤·❤·❤·

"Why did I think this would be a good date?" I ask Trevor as I serve yet another slice of pie to a smiling customer. Though I smile in return, I really would rather not be here, at the Button's Diner booth handing out pie, ice cream, and other sweets to Falls residents and guests as each and every one of them asks about our dating status, congratulates us on our relationship, or both. "I wanted to enjoy the Starlight Festival with you."

"What are you talking about?"

I scoff, motioning to the busy street and the clean but cluttered booth. "This is in no way enjoyable for you."

Trev sits near me, as he has for the last hour. Hayzel's here, too, proudly wearing both vinyl gloves and a hairnet she begged me to buy her even though I told her she just needed to keep her hair up and back and not touch it when serving food. This is her second year helping, and for some reason, she decided she needed to "look the part better."

"Don't worry about it, Sweet Cake," Trevor replies. "It's still a good date. I love getting to spend time with you, wherever we are."

Hayzel turns toward him. "Me too?"

He gives a kind chuckle. "You too, kiddo." Then he returns his attention to me. "Besides, you've gotten a couple breaks."

"Five minutes each, and the festival doesn't last long. We might not get to see everything."

"It's the same thing every year, Mom," Hayzel explains wisely, as if she's an absolute expert.

Trevor and I can't help but laugh. "She's right, you know," he adds.

She is. I do know this. And it isn't like Trev and I haven't experienced this entire event together many times in the past. This is just the first time we've been here as boyfriend/girlfriend. I tell them so. "I wanted it to be special."

I sink down on my chair next to Trevor but don't get to stay that way long. Three more customers come up, looking for the chocolate cherry pie we ran out of ten minutes ago. Well, ran out of minus one slice I'm saving for my friend Gwenn, since she should be here soon with her husband Rhett. She's allergic to the apple, our other biggest seller, so I always make sure her favorite is on hand.

When this group of customers receives their goodies, pays, and leaves, Trevor sidles up to me where I stand by the cooler checking supplies. I glance behind us and notice that Hayzel has busied herself with organizing the wrapped utensils in the basket, ready to add more up front when needed. Trevor places his hands on my hips, conscious of the fact that we can't really get any closer than this. "Everything with you is special, Sweet Cake."

Dottie strolls up, her face scrunched. "Why are you here?" she demands.

I lean back and look toward Trevor, but while his hands are still on me, his eyes are on his aunt. So I glance back at Dottie. Her focus is on me.

"What?" I ask.

"You're not supposed to be working."

"Yes, I am. I volunteered, like I do every year."

She shakes her head before I even finish. "I told Jacqui to cover this for you."

Now I laugh. "Dottie, I'm fully capable of working and dating at the same time. Besides, as long as Trevor's not in the way, I didn't think you'd mind."

Her face immediately softens. It's several moments before she speaks. "Well, it's about damn time."

"Language," Hayzel corrects from behind us. She likes catching Dottie with her curse words, ever since Dottie promised her a dollar for every one after a rather colorful complaint about a customer when she hadn't realized Hayzel was within hearing distance.

"Put it on my tab," Dottie jokes.

"You still owe me from two times before this," Hayzel reminds her, now done with her utensil task. She steps closer to us. "Anything else I can do?"

"Go have fun," Dottie tells her with a grin. She glances over at us, too. "All of you. Don't hurry back. The booth will survive without you."

Trevor gives my hips a squeeze, then starts to head out, Hayzel following behind.

"What's going on?" I ask Dottie with a whisper-laugh.

"You two have pined for each other long enough. Go enjoy your date. First of many, I suspect."

"Me too."

We both smile.

As Trevor, Hayzel, and I wander around town, we run into Dom and Charisma. After chatting about this year's fest and when the next family dinner will be, they ask Hayzel if she wants to hang out with them for a little while.

"You don't have to do that," I tell Dom in a hush.

He looks like he's about to say something I might not like, because Charisma places her hand on his arm for a moment. "Don't worry about it. You two go have fun." Then she gives us a smile.

Charisma and I share a hug, then the three of them head off to the face painter. No doubt they'll move on to the carnival games. Trevor and I head the other way, strolling past the Button's booth.

"I thought I told you to go have fun," Dottie practically harrumphs at me. For only being my mom's age, she often sounds like a grumpy old man when she's mad. Then she looks off into the distance, motioning to something behind me.

I turn and see she must mean Dom and Charisma. Her next words prove me right.

"What is it with you girls not knowing a man is in love with you?"

Trevor laughs. I roll my eyes. "I can't do anything about not having noticed Trev's feelings before now, and I especially can't do anything about my asshole of a brother and his friendship with and attraction to Charisma. Maybe it's his fault, not hers."

She opens her mouth, her expression telling me she's about to refute this, when I add, "Anyway, you're one to talk."

Dottie bristles.

"Come on, Dottie. Sal Leggero. That man drinks more coffee than is safe for humans just to see you every day."

"I believe I did the same thing," Trevor says near my ear.

"I know," I tell him before turning back to his aunt. "You pointed that out to me about Trevor when I didn't know what you wanted me to see. Why couldn't it be the same for you and Sal? And before you speak, anything you say is probably true of both situations."

"I'm too old to fall helplessly in love and marry." She smirks, like she's totally won.

I ignore this. "Sal doesn't think so. Think about it." I start a list, keeping count with my fingers. "Sal has had decades to tell you but hasn't, as of yet. He doesn't flirt or show a romantic interest, yet you're pretty much the only one he ever talks to or even looks at. You only see him as a friend, or so you say. Shall I go on?"

She waves me off. "Quit harassing me about that man. Go on and get out of here. Go enjoy your boyfriend and forget that us old folks have less need for that consuming love you and Trevor feel."

This breaks my heart to think about, especially since both Dottie and Deb are widows of relatively young ages. Not the kind of something sisters want to bond them together.

"Dottie, no matter your age, you're never too old for love. Just because you lost yours once doesn't mean you can't find a new one. Not a replacement for the husband you lost years ago. Just something different. Whatever kind of love you want to have with Sal, I promise you he'll be interested. Don't discount that."

Chapter 10

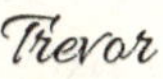

"Can't believe Hayzel's staying somewhere away from home again," Lucy says to Kenzie through the phone. "Last night at Mom's and tonight at Deb's."

Kenz has their call on speaker so she can keep rummaging through my cabinets for a snack. I know she'll go back to the cheesy crackers she's picked up, considered, and set down at least five times. They're her favorite. Despite her protests that she likes the spicy-mustard pretzel twists just as much, in the end, she'll combine the two in a bowl, but the pretzels will remain uneaten. At least by her.

"Yeah, I know. But it's summer. She won't be able to do that much once school starts. And it's nice for her to spend so much time with you, Mom and Dad, and Deb."

"You and Trevor are taking full advantage of all the naked time right?"

I laugh, and Kenzie turns around to smile at me. I've been standing next to her, leaned against the counter, waiting for her to decide what she wants to eat for our temporary downtime.

"Hi, Trevor," Lucy says in an embarrassed tone. "Could've told me I was on speaker, Kenz."

Kenzie laughs now, too. "Would that have been as much fun?"

Lucy's silent for a few beats. "You're naked right now, aren't you?"

We are indeed, but I don't think Kenzie will tell her that. She and I both attempt to hold in our laughs. I feel her doing that more than see it, as I've wrapped my arms around her now, trailing a line of kisses on her neck and shoulder in hopes that this will speed up the snack decision process.

"Okay. Go have lots of amazing sex with your hot boyfriend, don't tell me anything about it, and we'll talk later," Lucy tells her. "Love you, sis. Bye, Trev."

After saying bye in return, Kenzie ends the call and swivels around to face me.

"Crackers and pretzels?"

She nods. "And some cheese cubes. We need extra protein."

"Any particular reason why?" I ask, my tone flirty, my hands brushing her hair off her shoulders.

Her eyes are dark, and she's doing this slow blinking. I'm glad to see it isn't only me feeling heady and a little love-delirious. We've only been together for a few days. I'm almost afraid that at any moment, she'll suddenly decide she doesn't actually want to be in a relationship right now.

"I have plans for us."

"Oh yeah?" I take her arm in my hands, lifting it up to my lips. "Something requiring lots of energy and stamina?"

Kenz gives me a slow grin. "Only one question, though."

"What's that?" My words are muffled against her skin.

"Which part of the house do you want to start in first?"

I look around the kitchen. "Too hard in here?"

She glances down at a particular part of me. "The perfect amount. Just that I thought we could make it a race. Whoever reaches another room first gets dibs."

"On?"

Her smile grows as her eyes peruse my body again. "Anything they want."

I take a few moments, leaving her in suspense. She's watching my face and my eyes, clearly anticipating what I'll say next. "And the snack?"

Now she laughs. "You really want to eat right now?"

I lean forward to her ear. First, I give it a soft kiss. Then I whisper, "Who says we won't? But that's the wrong kind of snack, and we're in the wrong room." Before she can jump into action, I kiss her neck just under her ear and take off for the other side of the house.

Kenzie follows after me, laughing and squealing the whole way.

♥ · ♥ · ♥ · ♥ · ♥

Hours later, Kenzie and I are now in my bed. I'm on my back, one arm under her pillow, her blonde hair cascading down to it. My other arm is curled up so my hand rests on my stomach. I can feel myself dozing off, yet I'm alert enough to hear Kenz give a soft sigh.

I love that sigh of hers. It's something I never heard from her before until we made love for the first time. Learning this about her has been more than exciting. There are so many new things I've discovered. All the ways Kenzie is seductive and spicy and skilled. All things I could only dream of before.

She's on her side facing me, not a single scrap of fabric or gap of air separating us. One hand is under her head, the other on my chest. Slowly, softly, Kenz pins her bare body against my side, adding pressure to our already naked contact. Then she lets out that sexy sigh again.

Another moment, and she's sliding up a bit, then back down. We are still skin on skin, close enough that I can feel her breath on my chest start to quicken as she glides her body up and down against mine.

Yep. I'm awake now.

I let her enjoy herself for a few minutes. Let her enjoy what she's doing to me, with that satisfied moan she gives off. Then I roll, scooping her under me. Within moments, we're kissing and touching and making love again. I want to see how many of those amazing sighs I can get out of her.

I lose track after nine—also because she's drawn several of them out of me, as well.

·♥·♥·♥·♥·♥·

"Oh my gosh, you're family-dinner official!" Lucy squeals when Kenzie, Hayzel, and I walk up to the Larkins' back patio.

"He's been to family dinner many times," Kenzie reminds her.

"Aunt Lucy, didn't Pete come to family dinner when you two weren't dating yet?" Hayzel asks.

Most of us know the real story of Lucy and Pete now, but that's not something for Hayzel to be aware of. I don't think she's even paying much attention to the conversation since she just ran over to sneak a cookie from a platter on the table without waiting for Lucy's reply.

Lucy doesn't seem to mind being corrected. "Whatever. You're official, and I love it."

"Me too." Kenzie squeezes my hand.

When I look over, she gives me a big smile. Kenz lets go when Pete walks over so he and I can shake hands in greeting. I do the same with Dominic and Kerrick, Kenz and Lucy's dad. Nadine, their mom, pulls me in for a hug with a slight chuckle.

"There's our Trevor," she gushes. "We're so happy to have you here!"

"Mom," Kenz says, her sharp tone telling us all she's a little annoyed. "He's been here many times."

Nadine pulls back from our hug and rolls her eyes at Kenzie with a laugh.

Everyone else might be brushing away Kenzie's protests, but I understand where she's coming from. She's avoided serious relationships for many years. We both have. While she's been in love with me for a while and I've been in love with her since forever, this is still so new. I think her family is making this all a much bigger deal than Kenz is comfortable with.

"So what's on the menu?" I ask, knowing it's the perfect distraction for this family.

Dom immediately brightens. "Dad and I went with a barbecue marinade for the steaks."

I look over to Kerrick, expecting there to be more to this story. This is routine for Kerrick and Dom. Over the years, Kerrick's played this running joke on Dominic. Dom's always desperate for Kerrick's grilling recipes, and Kerrick likes to draw out the time before actually giving the recipes to him. Recently, Kerrick has allowed Dom to cook with him, but inevitably, there's some kind of surprise in store for Dominic.

"Well . . ." Kerrick starts with a grin.

Dom immediately turns to him. "What did you do, Dad?" he asks, hands on his hips.

Kerrick and I both laugh. No one else is paying attention to this conversation, otherwise they'd be laughing, too, or at least trying not to.

"Now, you see, I thought barbecue was an excellent idea."

"It was. It is. We agreed on it." Dom's clearly still annoyed, but by the look on his face, I think he knows something's up.

"We did, we did."

"We made the marinade together yesterday before I left. All you had to do was put the steaks into it."

Kerrick gives a little chuckle with a sly look, just for a fraction of a second. It's only noticeable if you know him well. Then he looks at his son innocently. "You're right. But then I thought—"

Dom storms to the patio door and inside the house. Pete comes over and asks me how the summer harvests are going. A minute or so later, Dom returns from the house, his hands holding some foil-covered dish that's been opened on top, a bit of the foil peeled back.

"What's this?" he asks Kerrick.

"There are barbecue steaks in the fridge," Kerrick tells him with a grin.

Knowing him as I do, I can see Dom's trying to keep his cool, but he's also trying not to laugh. This really is an all-the-time thing.

"Right. I saw those. What are these?" He pulls the foil the rest of the way off the dish, releasing the aroma of mustard and something sweet into the air.

I glance over, seeing steaks soaking in a yellowish-brown liquid. Is that apple I'm picking up? Whatever it is, it smells delicious.

Kerrick smiles in my direction. "I just thought we could have something apple in honor of Trevor here."

Dom's mouth remains flat. "He's been to family dinners before."

"Thank you!" Kenzie exclaims, vindicated in her assertions. "That's exactly what I told them."

"It's a great little marinade," Kerrick continues, jokingly ignoring all of this. "You'd probably really like it."

And here it comes. Part two of Kerrick's teasing. Once there's a menu change or we've started to eat Kerrick's wonderful creation, Dom immediately wants the recipe so he can re-create it at home. Only Kerrick makes him wait almost until dinner is over, leaving hints and red herrings along the way.

"Seriously, Dad?"

"Oh no," Charisma says in a laughing tone as she walks out from the patio door. She eyes the dish in Dom's hand. "What happened this time?"

"Dad made a different recipe, and Dom's pissed," Kenzie tells her, walking over to greet her with a hug. "By the way, you didn't tell me you'd be here."

Charisma laughs. "You and Trevor at your first official family dinner? No way was I missing this."

Kenz looks like she's about to correct her, too, but I step over and wrap my arms around her. "It's okay, Sweet Cake," I whisper in her ear. "Let them be excited for us."

She relaxes into me. "I'm excited, too, you know."

"I know." I kiss the side of her head.

Dom and Kerrick gather the remaining ingredients and supplies they need for the grill. The rest of us find seats around the patio, in the sitting area near the outdoor dining table. Kenzie and I are on the love seat together, our thighs and arms touching. I shift so my arm hangs comfortably around her shoulders. Nadine asks about the corn roast my family is hosting at the farm in a couple weeks. I can tell she's a little surprised by this.

"It's so close to the time you have to prepare for Apple Fest," she says. "We know how busy and stressful that time is for you. Was the corn roast your idea?"

I don't really want to put all the blame of this idea on my sister, but Polly was the one to suggest it. Mom and Dad had corn roasts often back in the day, but it's been many years since BFO held one, especially with me doing most of the work for Apple Fest, which is at the end of August.

"Dijon makes an excellent choice for mustard," I overhear Kerrick say to Dom as they both man the two grills off to the side.

"So it's Dijon?"

"Now, I didn't say that," Kerrick replies with a chuckle.

I turn my attention back to Nadine. "We wanted to bring some nostalgia back from when my dad was still alive. Let our customers and our town enjoy things from Dad's time."

"That's so sweet of you all. You know, your mom's a strong one, but I bet she'll be overwhelmed with emotions the day of."

I nod. Kenzie reaches over and pats my leg. I know she's feeling sad for me and my family, too, especially when I look over and see her face. As much as I appreciate their sympathy, it's not something I want to think about or explore more. I lean to the side to kiss Kenzie's temple before turning back to her mom again.

"I'm sure Mom will," I tell Nadine, "but right now, she's happily organizing the workers, finding the perfect location, and basically just throwing all her energy into this new project. Of course when this is over, and Apple Fest is done, there'll be another new project to do."

"And that's in addition to all her work around the farm," Nadine says.

For a moment, I turn toward Kenzie and give her a proud grin. I carry the grin as I turn back toward Nadine. "Mom actually asked Kenz to help with the corn roast."

Then I glance at my girlfriend again. She looks like she wants to wave this attention off, wave off how proud we all are of her. Kenzie's been getting more and more work like this. People asking to hire her to work on engagement parties, weddings, even as a local liaison for a couple corporate events.

"Well, is the beer only in the mustard, or is it in the marinade, too?" Dom asks from over by the grill, his voice steady but also strained.

Most of the others ignore this, knowing it'll probably take all evening for Dom to get the recipe. I can't help but listen. Kerrick loves his kids to no end, but man, he loves teasing them sometimes, especially Dom. It's all in good fun, though, and we all know it, Dominic included.

I know this for sure when Dom says, "Don't worry, old man. I'll just wait until you take your after-dinner nap, then I'll steal your phone and check your search history."

Kerrick only laughs. "Is that so, son?"

"You had to get your inspiration from somewhere."

His audible frustration, mostly evenly mixed with amusement, has me looking over.

Kerrick gives him a big smile. "I told you, it was partly because of Trevor. You see, when I was a kid, my grandpa used to make this roast—cheap, cheap cut of beef, but then it all was back then."

"Did it include Dijon mustard and beer?"

"No, no. He never would have sacrificed his beer for that, and he was a yellow mustard man all the way."

Dom rubs his forehead roughly, his eyes temporarily closed. "So the point of this story is . . ."

"It's all part of that recipe. I'm getting to it. Just have patience. You see, when I was a kid . . ."

He continues as Nadine rolls her eyes, and Pete looks glad it's Dom getting joked and not him. Can't blame him, though I've been at the receiving end of Kerrick's teasing before. We all have. It usually ends with smiles, hugs, and laughs between us. I do have to say Dom tends to have less patience with his dad than the rest of us. Probably why he gets it the most.

Kenzie leans her head against my shoulder. I pull her a little closer and kiss the side of her head, mindful her family is watching us. Like, literally watching us. Every set of eyes on this side of the patio is on us, excluding Hayzel's, but I doubt it really means much to her. Not in a way that would have her observing us with the rest of her family.

"What?" Kenz asks with a chuckle. "It's just a corn roast. I'm sure Deb will want to do most of the work anyway."

They keep looking at us the same way.

No one even bothers appearing guilty. In fact, most of them smile.

"Is this not about the party?" Kenzie asks.

"We're just so happy for you two," Lucy gushes.

"It's taken such a long time for you to get here," Charisma adds. "I thought it was never going to happen. That Trevor would never tell you how he felt."

"Oh please," Kenzie argues. "You of all people should understand."

A particular look is shared between the two that I understand, having discussed Charisma's possible feelings for Dom with Kenzie, and Dom's interest in Charisma with him on separate occasions. I'm maybe one of the few people who's heard both sides with a certainty that tells me it's most likely only a matter of time before those best friends become a couple as well.

"So, three weeks to plan a big event, huh?" Pete asks, breaking the awkward silence.

"Yeah, but Mom gets a thrill out of it."

"It's a challenge, but doable," Kenzie says. "I've helped women throw parties, even engagement parties, on short notice like that. With the right resources, which Deb definitely has, it shouldn't be too bad."

When the steaks are done, the salads are gathered, and we all sit at the table set by Hayzel—who earned extra screen time for doing so. She's staying here tonight, so she'll probably get a lot of screen time if she asks for it anyway, but Nadine and Kerrick do their best to respect Kenzie's wishes. They all spend plenty of time outdoors, too, especially with as much as Nadine likes to garden. She's actually on the community garden board of governors with me, my mom, and Lourdes's mom, as well as a couple Mackintoshes and a few other town residents.

"So Dad," Dom says, and most of us turn to look his way. He still hasn't gotten his full recipe from Kerrick yet.

"Yes, son?" he asks innocently, only his smile slips into a smirk.

"The apple. It's BFO's cider, right? I know you guys keep a stock of that in the basement freezer."

"Could be." Now Kerrick pretends his pasta salad is the most interesting thing he's seen in a long time. This could only mean he's trying to be nice and not laugh as loud or as hard as he has the urge to.

"It could have been apple slices or chunks, couldn't it, Uncle Dom?" Hayzel asks.

Dom gives a tiny shake of his head, but it isn't at Hayzel. He just knows what's coming.

"Or apple cider vinegar," Charisma tells him.

"Or applesauce." Lucy's addition.

Even Pete decides to get in on this. "Juice is an option," he adds with an innocent grin.

"You know, Dad could've chopped up some apples, run them through the blender with some cider and vinegar, and put that concoction in the marinade," Kenzie tells Dom with a shrug.

I almost want to tell the guy to concede this round, but that would be pointless.

"Grampa, you're still going to give Uncle Grumpy his recipe, right?"

Dom looks almost shocked, and turns to Hayzel. "What did you call me?" But his voice is nowhere near harsh.

Her cheeks burn red with embarrassment anyway. "That's what Aunt Lucy called you the other day."

"Oh, she did, huh?" Dom turns to his little sister.

"You thought I forgot about Lucy Goose, didn't you?"

He rolls his eyes. "It's been almost a year. It really bothered you that much?"

They faux bicker for a little while as the rest of us eat and try not to laugh. By the end of the meal, Dom does indeed have his recipe. He was right about it being our apple cider. Finding that out elicits a groan, but he thanks Kerrick all the same with a happy grin.

That doesn't happen often from Dom. If he smiles, it's usually best to remember it, because chances are, it might not happen again. Of course, that's more for anyone not at this family dinner. Lucy and Hayzel are correct. He's definitely a grump, but he also loves his family—and Charisma—more than anyone else.

We all say good night, then Nadine promises to drop Hayzel off at home once Kenzie's done with her shift at the diner tomorrow. Kenzie and I walk hand-in-hand to my truck. When I move to open the passenger door for her, she puts her hand on my arm and pulls me in for a kiss.

"No need to make out right here," Dom says as he passes by us on the way to his pickup truck. "You have two kid-free homes to choose from. Go make out there."

"Your place or mine?" Kenzie asks me with a wink.

"Sweet Cake, I'll go wherever you want so long as I get to be with you."

"Don't be gross," Dom calls out, still in the mood to tease someone else.

We laugh.

"Yours," I tell my girlfriend, catching her gaze. "Not often you get to be as loud as you want there."

"Still have neighbors." But she giggles.

"Oh, trust me. With how good I intend on making you feel, I'm sure they'll understand."

Chapter 11

Kenzie

FOR THE LAST TWO weeks, Trevor has spent a lot of time with my daughter and me, both together and separately. I've helped with the corn roast and Apple Fest the Bernhardts are working on as much as possible, but it's still a lot of responsibility for Trevor, in addition to all his other work. No matter what, he always finds a way to share quality moments with us, even if it's only for a little while.

Family fun time has been a regular thing for Hayzel, Trevor, and me, but in the past, the "family" part of it just naturally included Trevor without a thought. Hayzel never corrected anyone when they assumed Trev was her dad. He and I never did, either. But now that we're officially a couple, considering Trevor in "family" outings to mini golf or outdoor laser tag or the zoo has me thinking maybe I should ask if he actually likes that label.

"Of course I do," he tells me the morning of the Bernhardt Farms and Orchard corn roast.

It's early Saturday. Hayzel spent last night at my parents' house as usual, and I spent the night in all degrees of nudity with Trevor at his house. I have today off, allowing us to spend as much of the morning together as we can before he gets called in to start checking that everything's set up right. Polly's texted at least three times, even though most of the staff hasn't even arrived for the day yet.

She already sent photos of all the sites to me and gotten my approval, but since Trev's the boss, all the final decisions rest on him. I really hope he likes what we've done, especially the secret executive decisions I made that Deb and Polly paid for without question.

Trevor and I are cuddling some more before he goes to see what his sister wants and I go get Hayzel to bring her back here for both the setup and party.

"I just don't want you to think I'm assuming anything."

"Sweet Cake, I'm in love with you. Assume whatever you want. You want me to be part of family fun time—like I always have been? Yes, absolutely. Let's keep doing that." He gives me a loving grin. "Family fun time with my family tonight. You ready for that?"

"Oh yeah." I smile in return. "Your relatives have never intimidated me in the least. I've adored them for years. And now that you and I are dating? Sometimes I feel like they might break into a chorus of cheers at any random moment."

He laughs. "That would be weird."

"Weirder than no one reacting to our first kiss in the diner?"

"That really was strange, wasn't it?"

"Either way, at least people have left us alone, and we haven't been bombarded with opinions."

When his phone beeps again, we reluctantly get up and head down to see what Polly thinks is so urgent. I have to say, it looks fabulous around here. The tractors and wagons for the wagon rides are in their staging area. All the outdoor games I suggested to Deb are in a play area, both for kids and grown-ups. The space for the pony rides is ready, though the ponies won't be here until later, when Hudson Mackintosh brings them by. Honestly, the ponies were possibly the most expensive part of this whole party.

There's a huge section roped off, full of waiting grills to roast the corn. The food tents are up, with tables and chairs at the ready. Deb and I already gathered all the plastic table covers, utensils, cups, and whatnot. There will be a staff to serve each guest their choices for barbecue, corn, drinks, and desserts rather than making this potluck style since I suggested some might be uncomfortable with it if it's more of a buffet kind of thing.

Most people in this town couldn't care less, but I don't want them getting any negative reviews from the certain few who would bash this for less. It's been difficult enough explaining to those few that the Bernhardts can't put all of this on for free. And really, one dollar for entry that gives you access to everything: all rides, games, entertainment, food, etc.? You can't beat that. Plus, the BFO market will also be open, so guests can purchase and take home some of those yummy treats they'll get to sample in the tent.

When I'm heading out to go pick up Hayzel, I pass the truck bringing in the mini train ride for the kids, which Deb came up with and Polly balked at—mainly due to insurance and safety issues, though neither are actually a problem. As I wave to the driver, I just know this is going to be an amazing day.

I stop to fill up my car since my tank is a little too low for my comfort. The light on the dash tells me so. Before exiting my car, I quickly text my mom.

On my way. Just at the gas station.

Once that's on its way, I send another text, this time to Trevor.

Miss you already. Today is going to be fantastic! The town will love it. And if diner talk is accurate, I'd say get ready for a bunch of city people, too, because all our visitors have talked about for the last two weeks is wanting to come back for this.

It'll be a great day. Warm and sunny. Can't beat that.

Don't be nervous. People are going to love it. Your dad would've, too. Love you.

Then one more text to Deb, Trevor's mom.

I just want to say again how wonderful everything looks. It's going to be so much fun for your guests!

Thanks, sweetie! For the compliments and all your help :) My son is so lucky to have you in his life.

He and I are both lucky in that regard!

I fill my tank and go inside to pay and also buy a couple cheese Danishes to share with Hayzel.

"Well, good morning, Kenzie," I hear from a voice I'm pretty familiar with.

It's Mrs. Morek, my eighth-grade math teacher. I turn to greet her with a grin. She smiles in return.

"Good morning! Already finished with your walk?" I ask. Mrs. Morek is one of the ladies around town who like to walk together every morning through the neighborhoods. She's also one of the notorious Syracuse Falls Gossips With Heart.

"We decided to have another go 'round near the garden and the park, with everything in such full bloom." She pauses. "So how are things with you and Trevor Bernhardt?"

I laugh. Can't say I didn't expect this. "Things are going very well."

"Good, good." Her grin holds, but there's something in her eyes. "Trevor goes to the diner a lot, doesn't he?"

"He does."

"Right. So when is your next date?"

I wish I could figure out what she's trying to get at. "Today, actually."

"Oh, the corn roast. You know, Della and I were just talking with Deb a few days ago. I heard it's really going to be something fantastic." Another pause. "So how many more dates do you think you and Trevor will have?"

Wait, what?

Did she just ask me if we have a breakup date picked out?

And the strange thing is, Mrs. Morek isn't the first person to do this.

"As many as we want," I say, trying to bring my smile back in a way that looks natural, even though I kind of wish I could tell her what I really think, which is that it's none of her business.

"Right. Good for you. I mean, I've always liked the diner's pies better than the ones at Bernhardt Farms, so there's that. Well, you take care, Kenzie." Then she walks away like we just had a completely normal conversation.

It's the same thing as what the others did: ask about our relationship, ask how long I think we'll be together, and say whether they tend to go to the diner or BFO more.

Oh my gosh.

I thought I lived in a town of Babettes and Miss Pattys.

Nope.

I live in a town full of Taylor Dooses.

Later in the evening, after a highly successful corn roast, during which my daughter made new friends, Nadine hugged Deb as they both cried over Phil's loss, and Polly watched every activity like a hawk lest someone get hurt, Trevor and I curl up on the grass away from the remaining guests still enjoying the lawn games. Hayzel's asleep on one of his blankets nearby, having exhausted herself today and not having slept much last night.

I finally have a chance to tell Trev about my conversation with Mrs. Morek.

He laughs.

"It's not funny," I counter. "It seems like everyone in the Falls is afraid we might split up and divide the town. They're all acting like Taylor Doose."

"Sweet Cake, I assume I'm the Luke in this and you're Lorelai."

I nod.

"Listen, we are not characters in a show."

"A really good show."

He chuckles. "I get that. *Gilmore Girls* is a really good show, but it's not real life. These people here in the Falls? They won't divvy up our town with pink and blue ribbons. And so what if they do?"

"It's driving me crazy. Can't they just let us enjoy our relationship? It's still so new." This is one reason we've spent more time in Syracuse instead of the Falls. No nosy neighbors harassing us about, well, *us*. "Has this happened at all to you?"

Trev's quiet a moment or two. "Kind of. I guess I don't pay much attention to it. They all wanted us to be together so badly. Why would they also plan on our relationship ending at some point?"

"Maybe they thought we were too stupid to see what was in front of us all those years, so they also think we're too stupid to make it last."

He pulls me closer to him, his strong, steady arms wrapping around me. "They're wrong, Sweet Cake."

I hold his arms with my hands, tightening them a little, relishing in this cuddle. "I know. They are wrong. Even though it took me forever to see that you loved me, that just wasn't the right time for us. We love each other now. We're *in* love now. So long as neither of us gives up."

"I don't see us doing that," he says into the back of my neck. I let go of his arm so he can brush the hair aside and kiss my skin.

"Me either," I say, turning to face him. His dark brown eyes catch my gaze, and we both smile.

"Then we're good."

Chapter 12

Kenzie

MY HAIR WHIPS AROUND in my face, making it a little difficult to see as I grab my bag out of the back seat of my parked car. Even with the wind, the warm sunlight and blue skies make this a wonderful, gorgeous August day. And since I just dropped Hayzel off with my parents, I have the whole afternoon to myself. Knowing my family the way I do, Lucy or my mom will ask if Hayzel can stay at one of their houses after their lunch and movie day together, which means I'll have the rest of the night to myself, too.

Trevor's been so busy today with the continuing harvests of the tomatoes and sweet corn. Running a farm is hard enough, but managing all the different sections of the farm—the fields, the apple orchard, the flowers—when several different things are ready for picking at the same time seems like it could be overwhelming. Good thing Trevor's a pro at this. Though if anyone were to ask him, he'd never own up to it.

He's so incredibly talented—at everything, really, but especially how he runs Bernhardt Farms and Orchard. Yet he's so hard on himself about it. He never feels like he's good enough, even when he's doing the best damn job anyone could. He succeeds where others would certainly fail, but he doesn't see it like that. Trevor still has this little voice in his head saying he should have done it differently or better and so on. I've tried my hardest over the years to get him to see how amazing he is at everything he does.

This wasn't the life he planned for. Trev actually has his bachelor's degree in communications. He worked at the news station in Syracuse for a few years, before his dad died and left Trevor in charge. Out of all the Bernhardt siblings—Trevor, Jade, Dawson, Polly, and Lennox—Trev was probably the one who wanted it the least, and yet he excels at the job.

That's the thing about him, though. Trevor would do anything and everything for his family. They are the most important people to him and always have been. Giving up his dream to run the family farm sounds like a recipe for disaster, but not for Trev.

He'll be exhausted when he finally drives over to the main house, the one he grew up in that is now his since his mom moved into one of the smaller cottages on the property. Surprising him with dinner is hit-or-miss on these kinds of days. Trev never knows where he'll be when or what kind of urgent issues might arise. If I do end up on my own for the night, I could always go over there and keep him warm tonight. Tell him it gets awfully drafty in that big old bedroom, leaving him too cold when he's all alone. Not that he'd ever not want me there with him. He always wants me around, even when there's a farm crisis and I'm of no help whatsoever.

I'm practically skipping up the stairs, mentally trying on which new lingerie I want Trevor to see, when my phone rings. Once I look at the phone in my hand to see who it is, and I nearly fall from missing the next step. I'm able to grab the handrail along the wall and remain mostly upright.

My breaths become quick and shallow.

My stomach clenches several times.

My chest starts to hurt.

It's like I can feel every drop of blood exiting my upper half, almost encouraging me to faint onto the floor. I already dropped my bag, which is now several stairs back. I can't see it. I can't tear my focus away from the screen as my phone continues to ring.

I could never forget this number.

I've never forgotten who this number belongs to.

Then the screen changes.

He got sent to voice mail.

Meanwhile, I'm frozen, only partially standing. Mostly leaning by this point.

Cal.

My Callum.

Only he's not mine anymore. Hasn't been since he walked out when Hayzel was a baby, sending me a short text that said simply, *I can't do it.*

Cal called me.

I can't see any evidence of it now, though. My phone screen is black again.

Oh shit. Wait. He's calling again.

I press the green Accept button, only no words come out of my open mouth.

Nothing.

Not even the sound of my breathing.

If I don't say something soon, he'll hang up.

But I can't force my voice to work. I can't clear my throat. Everything feels stuck.

Finally, in the softest of whispers, I say, "Hi."

When I don't hear anything back after a few seconds, I shake my head and try again, louder this time. "Hi."

Of course, my voice is still hushed. I can't find the strength in me to sound bold or confident or strong. I am not strong. Not right now. No. Right now, I'm clinging to the handrail, willing my eyes to stay dry, willing the tears not to fall, willing my legs to be firm. None of them obey. I drop down to the closest stair I can comfortably sit on. My hands have started trembling.

"Hey." His voice is much softer than I expected, like he wasn't prepared for this.

"Hi," I repeat, because my brain isn't working enough to come up with anything else. It's short-circuiting with the knowledge that I'm finally talking to the man I've missed for ten long years.

"Hey. Oh," he practically whispers, drawing out both words like they're too special to be short in this moment. "There's a voice I haven't heard in years."

Part of me immediately wants to say that's his fault.

I've called him at least three dozen different kinds of awful names over the years from all the hurt he caused me. Pain and longing are fully combined in my feelings for him. All of that is absolutely on him. I am aware of this. Most of me knows this, at least. But the rest of me?

Oh, the rest.

The rest is already aching for him, the way I always ache when I think of him.

"I know, right?" I reply. Then I feel like an idiot because it's a pretty lame response. I just can't think clearly. All I have swirling in my head is the fact that this is Cal. I'm talking to *Cal*. Hearing him again, even if only on the phone, is a million times better than I ever hoped and dreamed it could be.

"Wow. This is . . ." Cal trails off.

I know what he's doing. He's avoiding saying anything that might bring his emotions up and out. He never liked getting choked up, even if it was something that deeply affected him.

In the past, I usually let him off the hook. I would change the subject or steer us away from what he was avoiding, while still acknowledging, even silently, that I heard his pain or his love or his joy.

I don't want to do that this time. He clearly has a reason for calling me. I want us both to acknowledge how affected we are by this conversation.

"I miss your voice, too," I tell him.

Cal clears his throat. "Kenzie, you have no idea how much I miss you."

This should be . . . well, I don't know what it should be, but it shouldn't feel as intimate as it does. We're using such gentle voices, gentle tones. It's like his words have become a comfort blanket, enfolding me in tenderness.

It's been so long. I've only heard Cal speak in my memories for the past decade. It doesn't feel fair to have lived all this time without him, and when he suddenly calls, I turn to absolute mush.

"How are you, Zee?"

He had to do it, didn't he? He had to go and call me the name he used to whisper in my ear when saying good night or good morning or when making love.

I can't.

I just *can't*.

It's sensory overload.

It's emotional floodgates and tear waterfalls.

It's us at our high school prom.

It's us on our wedding day.

It's me on the bathroom floor, sobbing and staring at a one-sentence goodbye text.

It's too much.

I. Can't.

"Can't what, Zee?" Cal asks in response to those two words I didn't mean to say, his voice still soft and sweet and soothing.

I wish that voice could soothe everything. Make it all better. I wish Cal would make it all better.

"I can't understand why you're calling." Which is the only thing I'm brave enough tell him.

A few moments pass before he replies, "I want to see you." He clears his throat again. "It's been too long."

"Far too long," I repeat, more to myself than to him, though I'm sure he can hear me. "Why?" I add.

Cal kind of laughs. "What do you mean why? I miss you, Zee. I'm back in town. For good. You are the person I want to see the most. You and our daughter, but I'd really like to start with you."

Oh. My. Gosh.

This is it.

The moment.

The freaking moment I've waited ten extremely long years for.

"No," I say, quieter than I was before.

"What?" Cal does that almost-chuckle again.

"No, you can't come here," I tell him in a panic.

It's a burst of confusion, a shock to my system.

What the hell is he doing calling me *now*?

"Kenzie, I just want to see you. I don't care where. It's okay if you don't want me in your apartment. Name a place and a time, and I'll be there. I'll wait all day, wherever it is, if I need to."

"I have to think about it."

So, so many things to think about. Cal, here in town. Cal, having returned to town numerous times before and nary a word from him to me. Cal, the former love of my life and my once husband calling and asking to see me. *Me*. Telling me *I* am his priority. I haven't been his priority in years.

I am a strong, independent woman who has raised our little girl by myself, scraping by at times, selling off what little valuables I owned, shoving the hurt and resentment down into a little box in my core, ignoring the searing pain of not even being worth one freaking phone call.

And yet.

Here I am on the phone with my asshole ex, and he's telling me I am *finally* important to him again, and all I want to do is sprint to him, which is extremely inconvenient, considering my boyfriend will want to throat punch Cal for this.

I have to talk to Trevor. *Now.*

Trevor.

Shit.

I have to tell Trevor about Cal, and I will, but I also have to tell Cal about Trevor.

But how? Like, literally *how*? If there were anyone around, I'd ask them for advice, even Mrs. Fraber from 2E, who pulls on both her ears whenever she hears an ice cream truck and always smells like Swiss cheese potpourri.

There's something you need to know. Only I can't say it.

I'm dating Trevor Bernhardt now. Definitely can't say that either.

"Take all the time you need, Zee."

You have to stop calling me that. I can't think with you calling me that. "I can't think while on the phone with you," I say, unable to speak the words I need him to know.

"That's all right. I'm not going anywhere. Call me whenever you're ready."

"Okay," I whisper in reply. Then I stare at his number on my screen. I can't bear to push the button that will end this call. I just can't do it. He's right here—so to speak—in my hand and my ear. I've waited forever for this to happen. What if we hang up and he disappears again? What if this is it? If this is all I'll ever get? I can't do it.

"Zee? You still there?"

I breathe a heavy sigh. "Yeah. I'm here."

"Hey, it's okay. When you're ready to talk again, I'll be here. I promise."

"Okay," I repeat. I shakily end the call this time, without even saying bye. I can't say bye. Last time, it was apparently supposed to be goodbye forever, at least on his side. I can't go there right now.

At least ten more minutes pass before I'm able to pull myself up off the stair and drag myself the rest of the way to my apartment. I'm weeping like someone just died. Thankfully, none of my neighbors have seen me. I sink into the sofa, forgoing the tissues I wanted to dry my face with. It's been months since I've shed any tears over this man, yet here I am. Crying is the only thing I can do.

My vision blurs as my eyes fill and empty. My body shudders. The skin under my eyes is raw and sore from all the rubbing I've done. All of my skin must be so red, I bet I look like a lobster. Yet I cry more.

Lucy texts me, but I ignore it. Charisma calls, but I send that to voice mail. Trevor texts me, but I ignore that, too. Then I remember I was going to surprise him. I had all those wonderful plans before.

Before.

One phone call, and I'm a wreck.

That was never supposed to happen.

I was an absolute mess when Cal first left. I cried to Trevor. I cried to my parents and Charisma. Not my siblings, just because they were still young. Eventually, though, I learned fortitude. I learned how to push the thoughts of Cal to the back of my mind. I learned how to do what I had to on my own. Raise our daughter, work a full-time job plus a part-time job, as well as anything I could get on the side just to have enough money to pay the bills.

I became strong and resolute. I was determined to hate him. He was never going to make me miserable again.

Only I still cried over him. I still missed him. I just learned how to space those moments. I never fully fell apart. I didn't allow myself the luxury of letting it all out, of releasing the sad energy. I would cry just a few minutes, then suck it up and carry on with my day.

Now I know that was not the greatest idea. I have far too much built up inside me, and it's turned into thunderous rapids and demolished dams.

Trevor texts again.

Tomatoes are done. Polly's pleased with the numbers, which gets her off my back. I'm happy, too. How would you like to help me celebrate? Clothing optional.

Not too tired?

Never too tired for that

I tell him I'll ask my parents to keep Hayzel. He and I will have to be alone for me to tell him about Cal. There's an incredible amount of potential for it to devolve into a disaster of a conversation. Question is, do I still wear the sexy lingerie under my clothes? Will Trev be insulted if I tell him I'm thinking of meeting with Cal, then hoping for sex after the conversation about him is over? I have no idea.

Thing is, I still want to give Trevor the good surprise. He deserves it after working so hard at BFO. Maybe this talk about Cal can wait a day. It's just one day.

When Trevor eyes me with a wolfish grin before stripping the new lingerie I wore for all of seven seconds off me, I think I've made the right choice.

Just one day. I'll tell him tomorrow.

Chapter 13

Kenzie

OH NO. No, NO, no. This is not good. Cal in the diner?

I can just see it now. Dottie would throw him out, and if she somehow didn't, Knox would. And Trevor? Oh gosh. Trevor's there every day, at any and all hours, depending on our schedules. He could show up at any point for breakfast, lunch, dinner, coffee, or his staff's daily pie treat. Cal in the diner is the worst idea ever.

I can't let Cal keep distracting me and taking up all my thoughts, but I also need to figure this out. It's been days, and I still haven't found the courage to bring this up with Trevor. I was only supposed to wait one day, not several. I know he's going to flip out, though. Maybe not outwardly, and certainly not to or at me, but he'll rage inside. Cal is the last person in the world Trev would ever want me talking to.

It's so awful keeping this to myself. They all know he's in town, but not one of my three best friends has any idea Cal contacted me. Neither does my family. They all think it's the same as every other trip he's had here, where Hayzel and I somehow don't exist.

How can I tell any of them that I desperately want to see him? That now that a meeting is finally an option, the world would always feel off-kilter if it never happened? I doubt any of them would understand. They'd probably judge me, or at least question my decision-making. No matter how much they all love me, allowing Cal back into my life would be seen as an awful mistake by all of them.

I get another text.

Cal

> Whatever you want, Zee. Always.

> But I won't promise not to scoop you up if I see you around town.

He adds a winking emoji.

And there's the problem right there. Because while I'm seriously conflicted about setting up a meeting, if I happened to bump into him at Mickie's Grocery Mart or even the gas station, I'd most likely sprint to his arms.

·♥·♥·♥·♥·♥·

"You've got a visitor," Dottie whispers to me as she passes by me with a tray of food for her table on the other side of the diner.

I whip around, terrified that Cal showed up after I told him not to. I find Lucy, her smile faltering as she scrunches up her face. I let out a quick breath, allowing myself to close my eyes for a moment.

"What's going on?" she asks, sounding closer.

After opening my eyes again, I motion for her to sit at a nearby empty booth. She obliges, but never stops watching my face for longer than half a second.

"I'm okay," I say once she settles in her seat. "What are you doing here?"

"Meeting Lourdes and Gwenn. Kenzie, I know I'm stating the obvious, but you don't look like you're okay."

I nod. "I know. It's just that something happened, and I don't know what to do about it." I take a breath. "When Dottie said I had a visitor, I thought it was someone else."

Lucy's eyes go a little wider. "I hope not Trevor, because you did not look happy to see whoever it was you expected."

"No, no. Definitely not Trevor."

As my little sister patiently waits for me to continue, I think about all the times this conversation would have been different. Luce and I have had so many ups and downs in our sisterhood. I'm so glad we are finally in a place where I believe I can trust her enough to confide in her.

"Cal called me," I whisper, unable to make eye contact. Not just yet. I need to let her feel all the emotions she's going to feel without my hopes and fears being pinned on any of them.

When I finally hazard a glance at Lucy, she isn't moving. She almost looks frozen. "Luce? Say something please. It's never good when you're quiet."

"I'm going to gloss over that, since this is a serious, emotionally-charged moment. What do you mean Cal called you?" Her voice is steady, not giving anything away. My sister, the hopeful romantic, trying to keep herself calm and impartial has me more than uneasy. I would rather she burst into a speech on why it is or isn't a good idea.

"He's back in town. Not sure for how long," I add before she asks.

"I knew he was in town, but him calling you? That's new. That's big."

The bell dings on the door, and within moments, I see that Lourdes is here. Once she walks over, I give her a smile. Well, I try to. It doesn't feel like my mouth moves at all.

"What's going on?" Lourdes asks, unintentionally echoing my sister.

"Cal's in town," Lucy tells her.

Lourdes moves her eyes to me. "I'm guessing there's a reason this is a discussion. Did he contact you this time?"

She is actually the queen of remaining impartial to any kind of news. Usually anyway, though I know having her own ex back in town hasn't been easy on her emotions. Lucy's trying to learn how to stay as calm and collected as Lourdes often is, but in this moment, looking at my sweet sister's face, I can tell there's something big she's struggling to hold in.

"He called. Asked to come over. I told him no." I give myself a moment before continuing. "Then he asked to meet me somewhere—anywhere—so we can talk. Even suggested coming here to make it easier for me."

After a few beats, Lourdes asks, "What are you going to do?"

I shrug. "Hell if I know. I'll figure it out, I guess. And I won't let him see Hayzel yet. That much I do know. He can't come here, either."

"Kenzie, coffee?" calls Roy, one of the local farm workers—someone I grew up with, and a diner regular.

He often doesn't mind waiting for his coffee. Usually, he ends up getting it at the counter himself. Lots of our regulars do when all the servers are busy. Today, though, Roy doesn't seem like he wants to do either of those things.

"Be there in a minute," I call back with a wide smile. Roy doesn't know it's fake. Then I look to Lucy and Lourdes again.

"What about Trevor?" Lourdes asks.

I shake my head. "I don't know. Cal coming home was always my hope. This should now be my dream come true, only life changed in his absence. Time moved on. I moved on."

Trevor—my best friend and now *boyfriend*—chooses this moment to send me a text. I hear his special tone coming from my phone in my right pocket.

"No matter what you do and who you pick, just be careful," my sister tells me as I debate taking a break so I can check Trevor's text.

"I agree with Lucy," Lourdes adds. "I understand what it's like to have a great love return from the past. There are complexities you can never fully prepare yourself for. Just . . . make sure you know how to keep your heart safe before you dive into anything."

I give them a small smile. "I will. Don't worry."

"And Kenz?" Lucy says. "If you decide not to see Cal, don't let him pressure you into meeting anyway."

"He wouldn't," I respond straightaway.

Lourdes and Lucy give me solemn expressions in return.

Reluctantly, I add, "I won't let him. I promise."

Finally, after at least forty-five minutes of nonstop work thanks to a large, super nice, but very needy group of out-of-towners, I'm able to read the text from Trevor.

Miss you, Sweet Cake.

I have to tell him. There has to be a way to do this and not continually panic, unable to say what I need to say. I don't need flowery words. Just gentle ones.

Miss you, too. Call you tonight when Hayzel goes to bed?

Got a long night ahead of me or you know I'd love to talk to you. Tomorrow? Oh, by the way, Freya said the chocolate pie from this morning was an excellent choice on your part. She's tired of me not buying enough of those apparently.

LOL I'm glad, and tomorrow's perfect. Love you.

Love you, too. See you in the morning

One more day is good. It's one more day to ready myself for what promises to be an awkward, awful, but necessary conversation.

Chapter 14

Kenzie

IT'S GOING TO BE *okay*, I tell myself. It's my new mantra, at least as far as this Cal situation is concerned. But maybe Trevor won't see it that way.

We're snuggled on my sofa, both having worked twelve-hour days. Hayzel's sound asleep in her room. I still haven't mentioned Cal to him yet.

"You okay?"

Lying isn't a good option. "Why do you ask?"

"You're hands are trembling." He holds me a little tighter. "Cold? Something wrong? What's going on?"

This feels like a face-to-face moment. A conversation when we need to make eye contact. I reluctantly move out of his arms and turn toward him. "Yes."

"Yes what?"

I swallow, but it mostly feels like it's air. Almost makes me choke. "Something's wrong. Something happened. I've been trying to tell you for the last five days, I just . . ." I shake my head at this thought. "You're going to be pissed."

His curious expression darkens. "What happened? Did someone hurt you? Are you okay?"

"Nothing like that. Just . . ."

I thought I panicked at seeing Cal's number on my phone, but that was nothing compared to this. Though my panic is ramping up, Trevor seems to be calming down, clearly reassured that I'm physically okay.

"Cal called me," I finally whisper.

"What?" It sounds almost garbled. "What do you . . . how did . . . what are you talking about?"

"Cal. He called me," I repeat. "He's in town again. For good this time, he says. He wants to see me."

Trevor is more than alert. He's practically ready to jump up and do I don't even know what. He looks like he's about to start sweating at any moment. "Hell no. Absolutely not. That's not happening."

"Are you telling me not to go or simply suggesting it?"

He gives his head a shake. "I would never make decisions like that for you. I just thought you and I were finally working toward a joint goal. You and I together forever."

"We are. This doesn't change that."

"Sweet Cake, you're an intelligent woman. You know this is a terrible idea."

"I agree, but also . . ." I can't say the words out loud. Not to this incredible man, whose eyes are already showing the hurt and the fear I've been worried about.

"You need this, don't you?"

I nod, teary.

Trev heaves a long sigh. "In public. With witnesses." He scrubs a hand on his face so roughly, I'm surprised this action doesn't make his skin red. Then he says, "And me."

I'm already waving my hands at him in opposition. "No. No way. You two hate each other. You'd kill him before he'd even have a chance to say hello."

"I do hate him. Always will. But I suspect that if I try to keep you from doing this, it's only going to make things bad for you and me."

"Trev, I promise, you have nothing to worry about."

"I trust you, Sweet Cake, but I'll never trust him."

This is going exactly as I expected, yet I still can't seem to calm my body down. After wiping a few stray tears that fall, I say, "Problem is, I think those two things go hand-in-hand right now."

"No, they don't, which is why I'm going with you no matter what."

Chapter 15

Trevor

Heirloom roses were supposed to be the death of me. That's what Polly said.

Well, maybe she said they'd be the death of her from all the stress, and she'd be the death of me if I didn't sell enough of them right off the bat. None of that worried me. I knew these beauties would grow well and sell well, and they have. Not only has Lourdes put in historic-sized orders, other florists in the area are clamoring for some. All that research and study and practice has paid off.

It's time to gather more for Lourdes, who honestly can't stop raving about these soft-pink ones I'm about to harvest for her. Harvesting heirloom roses is slow, deliberate, careful work. None of them should be shaken or jostled or mishandled in any way in order to keep them as close to perfection as possible.

A UTV comes to a stop nearby, but I can't look away from my work. I can hear it's Lennox and Dawson, though.

"Hey." I greet them without looking up, and they greet me.

"What's up?" I ask.

"Can't we just hang out with our big bro for no reason?"

"Nope. What is it?"

They're too quiet. When I hazard a look over at them, I can tell by the way they're looking at each other that they come bearing bad news. "Will one of you just spit it out?"

"Hoffman's back in town," Dawson finally says.

I gently set a rose stem into the box on the ground next to me, then turn to my brothers. Of course. They corner me when I can't stop and can't freak out. "A little late with the news, Dawse. Kenzie already told me."

"Did she also tell you he has a new job in the area?" he asks.

"Meaning he plans on staying here for good?" Lennox adds.

"And get his wife back?"

When I dart my eyes up to Dawson's face, he knows he screwed up. "Sorry. Ex-wife. But that's the story, man. The whole town is talking about it."

"When have any of us given a shit what anyone in this town thinks?" I ask.

"Never," Lennox replies as I return my focus to the flowers. "But this has to be a big deal for Kenzie, which makes it a big deal for you. We wanted to see if you were okay. Both of you."

I take a moment, letting my hand with the clippers relax. These gloves make me a little sweaty, but they help a lot in preventing thorn pricks. "I can't speak for Kenzie on whether she's okay. I'm not. I'm pissed. He has no right to come back like this. Calling her after all this time? It makes me think he's up to something more than that."

"Want me to look into things?" Dawson offers.

"No," Len and I reply in unison.

"The last thing you need is an accusation that you're using your office for illegal purposes," I add.

Dawson laughs. "Come on. It's a village job. Not like I'm governor or something."

"No thanks. I can handle this. Just want to get this whole stupid meeting over with."

"What meeting?" Len asks. His voice is curious, but also concerned.

I don't bother looking up again. "Kenzie and Cal."

"Wait. You're letting that asshole see her?" Dawson asks.

"I can't control her any more than I can control either of you. But I'll be there with her. She'll cry, he'll be a jerk, and it'll be over soon enough. I can take her home, hold her and comfort her, and then she'll know she never needs to see him again."

"And if it doesn't actually work that way? Or if she runs into him in town?"

I ignore this. My voice is hard when I reply. "I'll take care of it. Everything will be fine."

They let me get back to the rose harvest in peace, except there's no longer peace to be found here.

Chapter 16

Kenzie

I'M NEVER ONE TO be on time.

Honestly, I have such impeccable timing that I'm always five minutes early. Somehow, though, with all my nerves, arriving five minutes before Cal didn't feel like enough. I open the door to Capelli's half an hour early, hoping this will be plenty of time to steady my nerves. Trevor won't be here for a while, but that's okay. It's probably better I chill out before either man shows up.

Only Cal's already here.

I see him at a table toward the back, the front of the restaurant too busy to have any open spaces. His gaze catches mine. Holy crap. He looks ten years older, but also exactly the same. Same sandy-blond hair. Same pale green eyes. Same beautiful, cool and casual smile.

He's quickly on his feet and heading my way.

Then I notice it.

His bare hand.

He never removed his wedding ring when we were married, and he took it with him when he left. I just . . . why is it such a shock to my system to see that particular finger bare now?

Before I can react, he reaches me and scoops me up into a bear hug, his face snuggled in my neck.

"Kenzie Hoffman, you need to marry me again," he whispers, and suddenly, it's like we're twenty-two, when he said that to me every time he held me.

I wasn't ready to hear those words again—ever.

My knees would have buckled, but Cal already has me up off the floor, his body—his muscles—taking on all my weight with ease.

"What do you say, Zee?" he asks, enveloping me in warmth.

What do I say?

We're already married, I always laughed.

Cal usually laughed in return. *So? Marry me today. Tomorrow. Next week. I'm in love with you, and you're in love with me. We need to celebrate this shit every day.*

I have no words right now. I obviously can't do our old bit.

He tightens his grip on me. My feet aren't even touching the floor. Cal has me up on him, my chest against his. "I missed you so much," he whispers in my ear.

It takes all I have to not let a sob escape my mouth.

My ex snuggles even deeper into me. I can't tell where I end and he begins.

This isn't right.

I know that.

I *know* it.

But what I feel?

I feel like this should have happened years ago, but I also feel like maybe this shouldn't have happened at all, and I don't know how to reconcile those two things. All the while, the familiar scent of Cal's cologne—one I used to sleep every night and wake up every morning surrounded by, safe in his arms—fills my lungs, adding to the headiness of this moment.

"What the hell are you doing with my girlfriend?" Trevor's voice booms next to us.

Cal and I both flinch at the sound, but he doesn't put me down or drop me or release me in any way. In fact, he actually squeezes me a little harder, just for a moment, before carefully setting me on my feet. The only reason he lets go is because I pull away first.

I turn to Trevor, able to muster a smile. "Hey. I got here early. So did Cal. I'm sorry I didn't call you." Can he hear the shakiness in my voice? Because I sure can. And the panic. I'm not one to freak out, but this is definitely an extenuating circumstance. My boyfriend found me in what I guarantee looked like a loving embrace—because it was. I don't know what to say to him.

His steely gaze is not on me, but my ex-husband. "I asked you a question, asshole," Trev says to Cal.

This is the exact thing I was afraid of. Fists are going to start flying at any moment, I just know it. I can handle blood, no problem. But seeing it coming out of the two men I love the most would be far too much for me.

"Trev—" I start, but Cal just laughs and puts a quick hand up to me, like it's okay.

"How you been, Bernhardt?"

"You're not seriously asking me that question, are you, jackass?"

"How many times are you going to insult me in front of my wife?" Cal responds, and I about fall over in shock.

It's been ten years since I've heard him call me his wife. It's been ten years since I was his wife. But those words still hold extraordinary power over me, whether twenty-five or thirty-five.

My wife.

I grab hold of Trevor's arm for support.

He finally looks at me. "Hey," he says, his voice soft. "You okay?"

I nod. I mean, what else can I do?

"She's not your wife anymore," Trevor huffs, eyes on me, his words meant for Cal.

Cal does that almost laughing thing again. Something I would have found completely irresistible when we were together.

"So long as she hasn't remarried, she'll always be my wife."

Okay. Time to go. This was a *very* bad idea.

"Who the hell do you think you—" Trevor turns toward Cal, but I pull him back. He refocuses on me, not finishing his sentence. "What do you need?" he asks me softly.

"We have to go," I whisper in return. "I have to get out of here."

Though I'm whispering, Cal can still hear me. "Please don't leave, Zee. Send Bernhardt away and stay with me. We have years to catch up on."

Trev and I are still watching each other.

"She'll call you some other time," Trevor tells Cal before leading me out of the restaurant and onto the sidewalk.

"That was . . ." he begins, but he doesn't say more.

I don't know what he's thinking. I can't look at him. I'm not sure I'm really looking at anything. Not enough to see things clearly. Only as much as I need to so I can walk on my own to . . . wait. This isn't my car.

"Why are we at your truck?"

"You really think you driving right now is a good idea?"

"I'm fine," I lie.

My boyfriend shakes his head. "Don't do that. Don't tell me shit that isn't true. I know you better than anyone. Kenz, what just happened in there shook you up. More than you're willing to admit? Fine. I'll say it for you. Let's just go somewhere, the two of us. Give you some time to clear your head and straighten things out."

I nod. "All right."

Once we're in the truck, Trevor pulls away from the curb. We arrive at his house a few minutes later. Well, I know it's been a few minutes, but I didn't notice any of them. I didn't notice anything on the drive over. All I keep thinking is, *What have I gotten myself into?*

Chapter 17

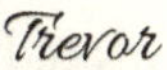

KENZIE'S BEEN QUIET SINCE we left Capelli's.

She's sad. I know she is. And I know it's so much more complex than just her feeling sad, but that's really the gist of it. She's feeling so many emotions right now, good and bad. Mostly bad. I can see it on her face. Despite me being here with her, she's withdrawn into herself. This happens sometimes, but it's been many months since the last occurrence. Maybe a year.

I thought she was starting to finally let him go. I thought she was ready. If I'd known this was going to happen, I absolutely would've still kissed her, but I would have been better prepared for what was to follow.

It's a good thing Hayzel is still with the Larkins and will be until at least tomorrow afternoon. I texted them before heading to Capelli's, asking Nadine to keep her for a few more hours than she was supposed to. Of course, she happily agreed. From what she told me, the three of them are having a lot of fun. I'm glad for that.

What I'm not glad about? Anything that's going on with my girlfriend in this moment. She has her arms wrapped around her legs as she sits on my plush sofa, gaze unfocused on something near her. Why does that jackass still affect her like this? Why have I had to swoop in and heal the broken heart that he caused for the past ten years? I'm not complaining about being there for Kenzie or for taking care of her. I just hate the emotional damage he leaves her with.

What about me? What about my love? All the years I've been by her side no matter what? Through every problem, complication, crying fest, and so on. Why is Cal apparently still more important to her?

I stand from my chair, unable to stare at my silent, sullen girlfriend anymore. I'm her best friend, too, and I know one thing she always wants in times like this. I head to the kitchen and start the kettle for some tea. She usually goes for a lavender Earl Grey when stressed and chamomile when she wants to relax in general. It's often rose hibiscus when she wants to be in a happier mood, but I'm not sure which one she'll want this time. I fetch the box from the cabinet with all the options inside, thinking that letting her choose is probably best.

After pouring the hot water from the steaming kettle into a mug, I place the mug, the box of teas, a spoon, and a jar of Kenzie's favorite orange blossom honey on a wooden tray she forced me to buy a few years ago, carrying it all to her in the living room. She hasn't moved, not that I expected her to.

I place the tray on the coffee table in front of her, but she gives no indication of wanting any. Instead of returning to the chair, I sit on the sofa next to her, resting one leg on the seat and turning my body so I face her completely.

"Big day," I say as gently as I can.

She nods.

"Maybe . . . maybe it wasn't such a great idea. Meeting up with Cal."

But she balks. "It's fine. I'm fine."

"Sweet Cake, what did I tell you about lying to me? You've never been dishonest with me in the past. Don't start now."

Kenzie sighs. "I just, I didn't anticipate all . . . *that*."

I soften again. "Maybe there's a reason it was so hard. Maybe he should have stayed gone. He doesn't need to be here. He doesn't deserve to see you. He doesn't deserve you at all."

She doesn't reply. Only looks at me, then away. Her gaze re-centers on the tray of tea things.

"Which would you like?"

"I don't care."

I'm sure that's not true, but I don't fight her on it. Instead, I put some chamomile in the mug to steep. This makes Kenzie smile. Well, at least I did one right thing today, in her eyes anyway. I know going to the restaurant was the best decision for all of us. I don't even want to think about what he might have manipulated her into had I not been there. I wasn't even late, yet there they were. My girlfriend in some asshole's arms.

Correction: *the* asshole's arms. The guy who used to tell me every time he was going over to her house to talk her into having sex with him, just because he could sleep with her and I couldn't. The one who hated her looking my way, even to smile and say hi, so much that he used to literally take her hand or her arm and pull her away before she noticed me, of course laughing and smiling the whole time like it was some cute joke on his part. Then he'd come after me later. With every hit, he'd spit at me that I had no right to Kenzie's attention.

That jackass never deserved her time, attention, or love then, and he sure as hell doesn't now. I can't believe we're still in this place where he has the power to make her cry. Which gets the gears in my brain going.

I stand, offering her a hand to help her up. She rises to her feet without question. "Should I bring my mug?" There's a glimmer of naughty hopes in her eyes, but I won't screw the sadness out of her, if that's what she thinks.

Well, not yet.

When we make love later, I want it to be because she wants me, not because of how he's made her feel. I want to make her happy in a way that has nothing to do with him. Besides, with as upset as she is at the moment, I'm afraid she might cry, which would make us both sad.

"You'd probably like having it," I reply to her, motioning to her tea.

Hand-in-hand, I guide her out the front door. We follow a grassy path from my yard, taking a shortcut to one of her favorite places on the entire property. It's part of my homestead, yet not too close to the house, giving us privacy from any of my family who might come looking for us—which they always seem to—and also away from any farm visitors who might end up lost somehow.

Farther down the grassy path, other walkways split off, some lined with stones to our other gardens, albeit with locked gates—again to keep wandering BFO guests out. Some are gravel—with more gates—and lead to other parts of the farm. But Kenzie and I stay in the soft grass, still barefoot from having been in the house. We wind up in a secluded little nook surrounded by dogwood and crabapple trees. Kenzie curls her legs up under her on the sage-green outdoor sofa, one she easily convinced me to buy a few years ago.

This garden, nestled away from the rest of the world, is the same garden I brought Kenzie to when she showed up on my front porch in tears two days after Cal left her. I was the first person she told after her parents and siblings.

She hadn't even told Charisma at the time, which was a big deal. The fact that Kenzie somehow knew I'd understand how difficult it all was for her—when she'd barely been able to talk to me much before then—wasn't lost on me. Maybe all my efforts of showing her I cared without being able to say it subconsciously registered in her brain. I didn't know. I simply sat in the grass with her and held her as she wept.

That was the day we became best friends. That was the first day since I was fifteen that I allowed myself to have hope when it came to her. Hope at least that I could be in her life, loving her in any way she'd let me. The strength she showed that day and every day after was such an inspiration, even if countered by the heartbreak I witnessed from then on.

She's always liked the gardens here at BFO. When I opened up a few of the ones down by the orchard and the sunflower maze, Kenzie had no idea I did that because of her. She'd talked about how sad it was that no one really got to enjoy the gardens since my family rarely went down to them. For the most part, only Kenzie and I, and our full-time gardener, ever saw them before that point.

Kenzie also inspired me to have the barn renovated to use as an event venue. I'm not sure if that one's occurred to her or not. That she's the reason I moved forward on the idea. It's all part of a plan, but it isn't time for revealing this yet.

"So," I begin, sitting close enough to have my hand on her thigh, but not so near that she might spill her tea, "things are a little different now."

She nods.

"I won't demand anything of you. I trust you not to do anything physical with him. But he's back in town. He actually contacted you this time. You've seen him. What does this mean for you going forward?"

"I'm not going to leave you for him, if that's what you mean." Her voice is soft, not accusatory or hurt. Simply reassuring.

"I believe you. But he clearly wants more of your time now. He wants more of you."

"You said he doesn't deserve me or my time."

"He doesn't. I still stand by that. But I know him. He's going to push to get it anyway."

"He hasn't demanded anything of me, Trev. He hasn't pushed."

"Not yet."

She sighs, then takes several slow sips of tea. We're quiet for a really long time.

"How would you feel if I said I wanted to see him again?"

And there it is.

"You can do whatever you want. I just want you to be cautious for yourself. Your mental and emotional health. Also for your daughter."

"And for us."

"Absolutely. I won't deny it. The idea of you being around him makes me sick."

We fall into another lull. Honestly, I don't feel like replacing the silence with words. Anything she's going to say will be about Cal. He's the last thing I ever want to think of or talk about. Yet here's my girlfriend wanting to spend time with him.

"This is bullshit," I mutter.

"Trev, you know I need this."

"No," I correct her. "I know you needed to see him, which you've done. One day. One moment. Why should he get more than that? Why do you even want more than that?"

Her eyes are glassy. A few tears splash down onto her cheeks. "Ten years, Trev. Ten years of waiting and wondering. One moment is not enough."

"You seriously think he's trustworthy?"

"I think I deserve the chance to figure that out. Hayzel hasn't even seen him yet."

"Sweet Cake, if he's still the prick he was back then, she doesn't need to know anything about this."

"Hey, look at that. Something we agree on." Kenzie gives me a soft smile, but it quickly disappears. "How will I know for sure if I don't talk to him or see him again?"

Damn it. "I hate this."

"I know. I sort of do, too." Her voice gets a little shaky at the end.

"But you're also really happy." I don't like having to say these words out loud.

"Happy. Confused. Still angry and hurt. So many emotions and feelings I can't name at the moment. Things I can't define or describe right now."

I nod. "I will tell you this: If he calls you his wife one more time—"

"He won't," she interrupts quickly. "I'll remind him that he and I were done long ago."

However, she doesn't sound too confident about this.

She silently finishes the rest of her tea. There isn't much else either of us wants to say. I shift my hand off her knee, draping my arm around her back. I just can't believe it. Over twenty years later, and that asshole is still trying to take away the person who means the most to me.

Chapter 18

Kenzie

THOUGH I KNOW IT'S only been a day since I saw Cal, I don't understand why I can't get that man out of my head. I was so distracted at work that Trevor actually had to ask for his cake instead of me offering it or just bringing it out to him. I know he knows what's going on with me, but neither of us really wants to discuss it.

Once again, our Friday night looks different than usual. Hayzel's home, since my dad isn't feeling well. Mom's not worried about it being his heart, which is a relief, but it's still enough of something that Hayzel can't go spend the night there, Since Hayze isn't going to my parents' house, this means I'm not going to Trevor's. I asked him for a movie night with the three of us, but another "emergency" popped up at the farm. I swear, as much as I love Polly, she definitely has a flair for making things sound much more dramatic than they really are. And while it isn't a true emergency, it is something Trevor has to stay there and help fix.

My phone beeps with a new text as I stare into the fridge, wondering if I should scrounge something together for dinner or order out. I guess I've been too busy with everything going on that I haven't made a trip to Mickie's Grocery Mart in a while. After another moment or two, I close the fridge door and check my message.

Cal

Home tonight?

It's only been one day, but then, it's already been a day, and I want to see him again. Maybe it's too much, too soon. I'm about to tell him so, when he texts again.

You two hungry? How's pizza sound for dinner?

Pizza always sounds good, but maybe now isn't a good time.

Maybe?

Does this mean I should head back down the stairs?

Stairs? He's here?

I don't read his words in a snarky way. Nevertheless, they still bother me.

What's going on?

Thought maybe you and I could catch up and I could spend a little time getting to know our daughter.

I'm completely unprepared for this. Cal wasn't supposed to meet her until I was ready. Though I guess I might never have been ready for this. I don't really know. But I'm standing at the door now, hand poised above the handle. If he senses that I'm here, he doesn't let on. Doesn't call out to me or text me. The next move is mine. He's waiting.

I open the door, and the first thing I see is Cal's wide smile. "I'm glad you still know when something's too good to pass up."

I grin in return, but before anything else is said, something important needs to be done. "You weren't supposed to just show up like this."

His smile slips. "I'm sorry, Zee." He pauses. "Would you like me to go?"

"Actually, yes. Just give me about twenty minutes or so to talk with Hayzel, okay? She needs to know you're coming over to hang out and why."

Cal's grin is completely gone now. "She doesn't know who I am?" His voice isn't terse. Quite the opposite. But it is a little raspy, like this knowledge hurts him.

"What was I supposed to do, Callum?" Now I realize we're still standing here having a conversation with my door open. "Why don't you just let me text you in twenty or so minutes. Okay? I can't just have you waltz in here and surprise her like this. It's going to be a shock."

"It'll be a shock no matter what, but with me here, I could at least answer her questions."

"That time will come. Just not in this moment. If she's not comfortable with this, you can't come back. I need to know that you understand."

"I understand." He gives me a sad smile, then turns and heads toward the stairs.

After shutting the door, I check on Hayzel, who's in her room reorganizing one of her shorter bookcases. She looks over at me with a grin.

"Hi, Mom. I know it looks like a mess, but I promise I'll get it all put back together. I just thought, what if I alphabetized in rainbow order? So, all the reds would be alphabetical, the oranges, the yellows. All of them. It's going to take a little while, though."

I smile in return. "Sounds like fun."

Then I join her on the floor, sitting cross-legged like she is. I've practiced what to say to her about Cal for years just in case he ever bothered to contact me. Now, though, all those words have fallen away like my brain is a sieve. I absently pick up a book from the blue pile and flip through it without seeing any of the pages.

"We make a good family. You and me. We're a good team."

"Of course," Hayzel readily agrees. Her focus is on the stack of red or mostly red books in front of her.

I wish I didn't have to do this so suddenly. And I know Cal's right that finding out about her dad being here will be a shock no matter what, but I'm just not ready for this, and I don't think Hayzel is either. Problem is, it wouldn't feel right keeping this information from her. I never mentioned him visiting town in the past because he never called me. There was no need for her to know then.

It isn't like she doesn't know anything about him, though. She's seen pictures of him from back then, heard lots of stories, even compared her own photo to his to see what of her takes after him. I know she's smart enough to comprehend how crushed I was when he left, but we've been really happy, the two of us girls on our own, despite our struggles. Cal not being here never felt like much of a loss in her eyes. Maybe to her, it won't seem like such a big deal to meet him now.

Only one way to find out.

I toss the book aside, then pick up another one just to have something to nervously fidget with. "There's someone else in our—well, *your*—in your family who hasn't been here in a really long time."

She doesn't even take her eyes off of her books. "Gramma and Grampa don't come here much, but we go to their house all the time. We see Uncle Dom and Aunt Lucy all the time, too."

"You're right. We do." This is harder than I expected, and I expected it to be a lot.

"Who else would be here?" she asks before I can think of what to say next.

Time to rip the bandage off for me while being as gentle as I can for my sweet daughter. "Your dad's back in town," I whisper.

Hayzel doesn't look over at me. She doesn't stop what she's doing either. "Has he never come back before?"

I can't say for sure someone hasn't mentioned this situation to her before. I never have, but that doesn't mean she hasn't found out somehow. This isn't something I ever wanted her to know. It isn't like you should ever say to your kid, *"Hey, your dad's in town, but he has zero interest in seeing you."* Regardless how of true that might be.

"He wants to see you," I tell her, deflecting away from that sticky question. "To meet with you. Spend time with us as a family."

"A family?"

This is the hard one. Trevor's always been like a dad to her. I've wondered countless times how she would react to her actual dad coming back this way. "You don't have to consider him family if you don't want. You don't even have to call him Dad if you don't want. You can call him Cal if that feels more comfortable to you."

She's quiet, and I can only assume she's pondering all of this. I have no idea how strange this must be to her. Even with my guesses, those never compare to a real situation. We sit in silence for a few more minutes.

Then she says, "I think I'll call him Cal to start with, and see how I feel after that."

"All right. That sounds like a really good plan." I pause, giving us both a few seconds before my follow-up question. "Do you think you might like to meet him?"

She nods. "I think I would."

Wow. Okay. Deep breath. "When do you think you might like to do that?" I don't want to tell her he's waiting for an answer. This has to be when she's ready, on her time frame, not his.

Hayzel shrugs. "I don't care. Whenever."

My tween is so wise and kind. She's trusting me with this, and I'm having to trust Cal. If this goes to shit, I think I really will finally hate him for good. This cannot go to shit. "There's zero pressure, okay, sweetie? I want to make that very clear."

"Okay, Mom. But really, it's okay. I don't care when."

"I think he's free if you want to see him today," I reply slowly.

"Like, now?"

Immediately, I shake my head slightly. "Doesn't have to be. He mentioned being available for dinner, but only if we want to. We don't have to."

Finally, she looks up at me. I can't read the expression in her eyes, but her face is a little pinked. "I think I'd be okay with that."

I give her a warm smile. "Okay, sweetheart."

"Will you text him and let him know?"
"You bet."

> Hey. You can come back now :)

Hayzel's okay with it?

> Yep. Just please don't screw this up.

> And don't make her hug you or call you Dad. This is all on her time frame, not yours.

Noted. I wouldn't force her into anything anyway.

And thank you, Zee.

See you in a few minutes

He arrives soon as promised, still bearing all the food he bought as well as the board game. I take everything from his hands, setting it all on the coffee table for now. It's been fifteen minutes since he was here last and everything's getting colder by the second, but something more important needs to happen before we eat.

Hayzel stands next to me, then in front of me, leaning back. I wrap my arm around her shoulders. "Hayzel, this is your dad, Cal."

Cal smiles warmly at her. There's so much genuine love and kindness on his handsome face. "Hi, Hayzel. How are you?"

"I'm good," she whispers. "Hi, Cal."

To his credit, he doesn't flinch. "How do you feel about fist bumps?" he asks.

She smiles and puts a fist out. After they do a quick fist bump, he asks her, "How do you feel about pizza?"

"Love it!" Hayzel exclaims. "Let's eat! I'm starving."

I hand her the bag that I assume has breadsticks and sauces while Cal picks up the pizza boxes. It's a small apartment, so I have to make this fast and quiet. With my free hand, I reach out and grab Cal's arm.

"That went really well," I tell him with a smile.

He beams, his smile so much like our daughter's. "Thank you," he says again, before planting a short kiss on my cheek and guiding me to the kitchen for dinner.

·♥·♥·♥·♥·♥·

It's well after bedtime, but it doesn't make any sense waking Hayzel up just for her to go back to sleep a few minutes later. She can brush her teeth in the morning. I scoop her up from her little nest she made on the floor during our viewing of the princess movie *Enchanted*—after she won two rounds of the strategy game Cal brought—and carry her to bed. Cal fixes her blankets before I get there so it's all ready for her. Once I've tucked her in, Cal and I return to the living room.

"Can't believe I missed all this," he says, his voice thick, his tone soft. He gives a slight shake of his head. "I missed everything."

I match his muted tone. "You did." Now is not the time to scold him or make him feel bad. I wait for his reply.

"Hey," he says, his voice still quiet, "you think maybe I can stay tonight?"

How does this man hold the ability to send me back in time so often? Because I swear we're eighteen again, and he's asking to stay the night with me while my family's out of town. I let him then. I can't now.

"That's not—"

"I don't mean in a romantic way, I promise," he quickly interrupts.

I pause, letting him add more information if he so chooses.

"Just that it would be easier for me to stay. It's already so late," he continues. "And this way, you and I would have more time to catch up, just us."

It's the *just us* that's the problem. I can't say I'm not tempted, though. I would love to have hours alone with Cal to talk things out. To ask questions and get answers. But letting him sleep here wouldn't be right for me or our daughter. She literally just met him. There's no way she'd be comfortable waking up to find him still here.

"Why don't you come back another day, okay? We can catch up later. If you're staying in the Falls, we'll have plenty of time."

He nods. "Can I call you tomorrow?"

"Of course." I lean up and over to kiss him gently on the cheek. Then we walk to the door together.

Once he smiles and leaves, I lock up and head to bed.

Chapter 19

Kenzie

IT'S A LONG DAY at the diner, from early morning until afternoon, but at least the lunch crowd includes Trevor. He eats his favorite meat-loaf sandwich, gets a slice of carrot cake to go, and leaves with two bags full of chocolate cherry pie for his staff. My feet ache and the waistband of my new black leggings is a bit too tight in the hips, digging into my skin. Definitely not a pair I'll wear again unless I can stretch them out a little.

My mom called this morning offering to take Hayzel since Lucy couldn't. Dad still wasn't feeling well, but whatever's wrong with him isn't contagious, and Hayze really wanted to see her grandparents, so I let her go. I'll have to text Mom later to find out when exactly Hayzel's coming home. For now, I want to bask in being in our home by myself for a little while.

When I pull into the lot of my apartment building, I see that Cal's car is here next to the spot where I usually park. Only he's not in his car. Why would he be here anyway? I didn't invite him over. I made sure to tell him I had to work today.

Do I expect to find him in my apartment? Not even a little, yet that's exactly where he is.

I yelp. "What are you doing?" I ask, then need to catch my breath from him startling me.

He was on his phone, but now he sets it down on the table, next to where he sits on the sofa. "I've been thinking. You're my wife, Zee."

"Not anymore," I reply quickly.

"You know what I mean. You and Hayzel are my family. I belong with my family. I know it might take some time getting used to each other again, but it's worth it."

"What are you saying?" I ask, narrowing my eyes at him.

"I'm staying."

I can't help barking out a laugh. "You can't be serious."

Cal only blinks at me.

"No, you're not. You can't live here. How did you even get in?"

"The hide-a-key. Which, by the way, isn't safe, Zee. I don't like worrying about strange people breaking in here."

"Like you?"

"Not funny. You and I were married. You know me."

"Correction: I knew you. It's been a decade since we've spoken. We never even caught a glimpse of each other since then."

"I'm still the same guy."

That's what I'm afraid of.

"That key is for emergencies, Cal, not you thinking you can waltz back into our lives on a whim."

"You think this was done on a whim? I haven't stopped thinking about you for months. I got a new job nearby. I sold my house. I'm here now for you. Permanently."

"And yet you never asked to be in here."

"This is a bit extreme, I admit. I get it. But Zee, you were always my world before. That never should have changed. I never should have changed that. I want to fix what I screwed up."

"It's too late, Cal. I'm with Trevor now. You can't live here."

"I'm not leaving."

"You always stayed with Leo when you came to visit. Stay there with him this time, too."

Cal stands and steps closer. "Zee, I miss my wife."

"You have to stop calling me that. Trevor will kill you if you call me that in front of him again."

"Anyway, Leo's wife doesn't want me there anymore. They're fixing that room up because her parents are coming to stay for a few months, I guess."

"So you have nowhere else to go?"

"I'm in the place I want to be."

I know what I should say to this, but the words won't come out of my mouth. I don't like the idea of him being stuck with no options. I want to help him any way I can. Of course, this is a really stupid idea of his, and it might blow up in both our faces if I let it happen.

Cal speaks before I have a chance to. "Listen. I still have a few more things at Leo's house that I need to bring over. That'll give you a little more time to get used to the idea of this." He kisses the side of my head. "Be back soon." Then he's gone. He left all his luggage here, over by the hallway, I now notice.

I drag myself to my bedroom, hoping to nap for a little while, or at least lie there racking my brain on what to do before I have to tell Trevor what's happened. But by the time I reach my doorway—eyeing more of Cal's suitcases, which he left in my bedroom—I know that I have to tell Trevor now. There's no way this can wait.

"Hey, Sweet Cake. Miss me already?"

I smile, though he can't see me. "Always." Then I pause. How the hell am I supposed to say this?

"Mom!" Hayzel calls from the other room.

Guess my parents decided to bring her home early.

"In here, sweetie," I call back.

"Gramma and Grampa leave already?" I ask once she's in the room with me.

She nods. "Grampa's doctor appointment got moved up. They couldn't stay, but they said hi and they love you. Gramma also said she'll talk to you later."

"What's going on?" Trev asks. "Need to call me back?"

"No. No, it's fine. Hayzel just came home." I wait a second. "Hey, Hayze, why don't you go find a snack in the kitchen? I think there's still some egg rolls left over from the other night. You can warm them up in the microwave."

She happily walks off. I quietly close my door. "Listen. Something happened today," I begin.

"Okay, now you're scaring me. What's up?"

I tell Trevor what Cal did.

"Be there in a minute." Then he disconnects.

Chapter 20

Kenzie

"WHAT THE HELL ARE you talking about?" Trevor demands after I close the door behind him. He steps into the living room, then rushes down the hall to check the bedrooms. "Where the hell is he? And who the hell does he think he is?"

"He's not here," I say, repeating what I already told him on the phone. "And be quiet. Hayzel's home. You know, you didn't have to rush over."

"The hell I didn't." Now he hurries back into the living room and over toward the kitchen.

"Trev. Cal isn't here. It's okay. Stop stomping around."

"I'm not stomping," he snaps, "but I am pissed. Who does he think he is? He can't just move in here. You're not married anymore. Even if you were, he still can't live here. He left. He has no say in any freaking thing you do anymore."

I can handle this. I can handle Cal. Trevor's presence will only make the situation worse. Cal's probably going to be back soon with food once he has all the rest of his stuff. He texted with the promise of a meal for Hayzel and me.

"How does it not matter to you that he has nowhere else to go?"

"Where does he stay every other time he's been in town? Where did he sleep last night? He can go there."

"He says he can't."

"Why are you being so lenient on him?" My boyfriend catches my gaze with his eyes and doesn't relent. "You should have him arrested. He forced his way into your home."

I shake my head and break the eye contact. "Why are you being so hard on him?"

"I was okay with you having lunch with him, not living with him."

"You were absolutely not okay with me having lunch with Cal."

"Okay, no, I wasn't. That doesn't affect this. He has to go."

"He doesn't have any place else."

"Fine. He can stay with me."

I'm already laughing. "Right, because that wouldn't end with either of you punching the other in the face or anything. Or you kicking him out after an hour and him still needing a place to stay."

"I have three floors, including five bedrooms. The one on the third floor is perfect since it has a mini living space in addition to the en suite. He wouldn't be in my way, and he could use the smaller staircase that I never use. I work long hours. He and I would never have to see each other."

My laugh lessens, then dies a swift death. "Trev, no. No. It would never work. You and I both know that. You'd still have to share the kitchen, the breakfast nook or the dining room, the laundry, and the mudroom. So many parts of your house would be taken over by *Cal*."

Trev shudders.

"See? Not only that, I'd be there with you. I stay with you every time Hayzel's sleeping over somewhere else. What if you're upstairs and Cal comes down for a drink of water, only I'm in the kitchen for the same reason. Then you wake up to find me gone and come looking for me. You'd flip out seeing him talk to me. At least if it's him and me here and not in your house, I can just as easily rebuff him without worrying that you'll be in a fight or have a coronary or something."

"Without me around, can you guarantee that he'll listen to your refusals?"

"Yes, I can. He'd never force himself on me."

"He wouldn't, but he also knows how to wear you down. I'm not letting you live with the guy."

"Hi, Trevor," Hayzel says as she walks into the kitchen. She throws away an empty chocolate-bar wrapper, then gives Trevor a quick hug. "Did you hear about Cal?"

Trev nods. "Yep. But don't worry. Your mom and I are taking care of it."

"Uh, no, *I'm* taking care of it. I don't need your help for this."

Trevor eyes me for a few silent moments, then turns to my daughter. He gives her a bright smile. "Hey, go pack a bag, okay? Big one, lots of clothes."

Hayzel grins and agrees right away. She runs off, presumably to her room. Trevor heads that direction, too. I follow. He stalks into my room, walking over to grab one of my suitcases out of my closet. Immediately, he starts filling it, pulling my tops and dresses from their hangers.

"What are you doing?"

"You don't want to make him leave? You don't think he should stay with me? Fine. You and Hayzel are not staying here."

I watch him shove my clothes, jewelry, even picture frames into both my suitcases. Now he's reaching for my duffle bag. "Again I say, what are you doing?" I ask when he has my bag almost completely full and is spinning around, almost like he's looking for something. He has to walk around a few of Cal's bags, kicking one out of his way. Then he "needs" to kick another one, too, apparently.

"And yet you think him staying with you could actually work," I say with an eye roll.

Trev ignores this. "You have any more bags or suitcases? Any boxes?"

"Why won't you listen?"

No answer. He just keeps searching through my closet and looking under my bed, though the only thing under there is a few small totes of my winter clothes.

"Can I empty those or do you need them?"

"Trevor, look at me," I say by way of reply.

He finally does.

I give him a look that I know expresses what I'm thinking. My head is tilted, my eyebrows are high, and my mouth is scrunched to the side.

"What?" he asks innocently.

"Oh, come on. It'll be fine. I know him. I was married to him."

"You haven't seen him in ten years. You *don't* know him. Not anymore. He could be an entirely different person from who he was then. No way am I letting either of you stay here with him. If you won't kick him out, you're staying with me."

"Yes!" Hayzel exclaims from the hall.

I didn't even know she was listening, though both doors are open. "No, we're not," I call to her.

Hayzel grumbles something, but I can't really hear what.

I turn back to Trevor. "We can't do that."

"You can't stay here, Sweet Cake." Trev emphasizes every word. "You knew him back then, but Hayzel doesn't know him at all. He's just some strange man to her. One dinner together and the knowledge that he's her biological father isn't enough. She'd never be comfortable living with him."

"What's the verdict?" Hayzel asks from the doorway, but already I can see her scooting back, closer to her own room.

"You ladies are moving in with me," Trev tells her.

"Temporarily," I add quickly, but Hayzel's already gleefully on her way to finish packing.

I look over in time to see Trevor dump all the rest of my jewelry into my duffle bag, including items I haven't worn in ages.

"What are you doing?"

He doesn't reply. Now he shoves my shampoo, conditioner, and hairbrush into my toiletries bag. The bottles are still a little wet from my shower this morning, but he shoves them in anyway. He does the same with my toothpaste. When he's about to put my toothbrush in, I stop him, grabbing it from his hand. This doesn't deter him.

"Trevor," I whisper-yell.

Okay. I think he's intentionally ignoring me at this point.

I motion to the empty jewelry box. "Do you seriously think he's going to steal from me?"

"Ten years, Kenz." He doesn't elaborate, but I don't need him to.

"Spence was gone from Lourdes's life for ten years, and she would never think to hide her valuables from him."

"Because at his core, Spence is a damn good guy. Cal is a ticking time bomb. We have no idea what he's thinking or what he'll do next or when he'll disappear again. He never once paid you any type of support money. What if he never had it? What if he owes money to some really shady people? It's possible. Can you honestly tell me you trust him with your stuff?"

"What are you suggesting?" I ask, unwilling to argue the point at this moment, because, yes, I think I can trust Cal not to steal from me. Trevor is definitely in a mood, though. "It isn't like I can pack up my whole apartment." Then I look at the toothbrush in my hand and replace it in the cabinet. Trevor comes behind me and takes it back out, putting it in its travel case this time before it ends up in the bag he holds.

"Why not?" His tone is snarky and sharp.

I hold in a sigh. "I can't take the television. Or any small appli-ances."

"Fine, but the jewelry and anything else that's portable is coming with. I don't care whether it feels warranted or not."

He turns toward the hallway. "Done packing, Hayze?"

"Not yet," she calls. Her voice sounds hurried, like she's running around her room, which she probably is.

"Want to help me finish packing your stuff?" Trevor asks me.

No, but I think I have to. "For starters, I don't think I'll need this." I pull out a navy-blue bridesmaid dress I wore in a friend's wed-ding two years ago. After replacing it on the hanger, I start to refold everything Trevor shoved into my larger suitcase to make room, but he stops me.

"There's no time. Just deal with it as is. Try to make it work." Then he leaves the room.

"Where are you going?" I call after him.

"We can't forget Cinnamon and all his stuff."

"Trevor's right, Mom," Hayzel says as she enters the hallway, her arms full of stuffed bags. After setting them down, she heads back into her bedroom. "We can't leave Cinnamon here. Cal doesn't like him."

"That's not entirely true," I say, only . . . well, I think it is partly true.

When Cinnamon meandered over last night to say hello and sniff Cal, my ex definitely didn't seem interested in giving him a scratch behind his ears. He also scooted Cinn away from him with his foot at some point when Cinn was walking around underneath the table. That's enough to make Hayzel worry about the cat while we're gone.

Guess we're all going with.

I make sure I have all the clothes and toiletries I'll need, then I check with Hayzel to make sure she has the same, plus any extras she might want. Of course, if we forget anything, I can always come back and get it. Really, though, I don't see this lasting very long. Cal will find a new place to live soon enough. I believe that.

When Hayze and I carry all our bags and cases to the living room, we see that Cinnamon is already in his carrier. Trevor has boxed up his treats, food, and toys.

"Ready?" Trev asks.

Instead of answering, I turn to my daughter. "Why don't you go check your room one last time?"

She huffs but quickly runs back down the hall.

"Are you sure this is a good idea? Me moving in with you?"

"Not just you. But you know this is necessary." He pauses a moment. "I know it feels like rushing into something in our relationship that you're not ready for. You're welcome in my home, always, but if you won't stay with me, at least stay with my mom or with Polly."

I gaze into my boyfriend's eyes, thinking of all the years we were solely best friends.

"We'll stay with you," I tell him, my voice soft.

The three of us load up my car and Trevor's pickup truck, letting Cinnamon ride along with him. Then we head over to the farm. Once everything's unloaded and piled up in the large entry way and Cinnamon is freed from his carrier to explore the house and reacquaint himself with his siblings, Trevor leads us upstairs.

"Which room would you like, Hayzel?" he asks.

"Can I have any room I want?"

Trevor gives a little laugh, knowing full well where this is going. "So long as it's not mine, yes. You can."

She jumps a little into the air, then takes off down the hall. "I call dibs on the window seat room!"

Now I laugh, too. "She'll probably sleep on that window seat if we let her." Then her words really hit me. "Wait. She said dibs. Does that mean she thinks I'm staying in one of the guest rooms?" Only now I realize this is a little presumptuous. "Sorry. Am I staying in one of the guest rooms?"

Trev steps closer and leans in to kiss the tip of my nose. "Don't apologize. And you can stay wherever you want. Whatever you're comfortable with for both you and your daughter. I will never make you sleep in my bed if you don't want to."

"I want to. Always. I'm just . . ."

"Nervous."

I nod.

"I get it. This is a big step, necessary or not."

"You wanted full-fledged relationship. Now you've got it." I pause. "What if it turns out that it's not actually what you want? What if I drive you so crazy or you get sick of me?"

He's already shaking his head. "None of those things are possible."

But I don't listen. I can't. My brain won't let this go. "What if you decide I'm not the woman you really want? What if I'm too loud or intense or emotional or negative? What if morning me is too much of a turn-off? What—"

"Stop, Sweet Cake. Just stop. All those what-ifs? They don't mean anything. You will never be too much of anything for me. I love you. Every part, even the messy ones." He stops a moment. "If at some point we decide we aren't ready to live together yet, and you for some reason haven't kicked Cal out, then we'll figure out a plan B. Right now, this is where you belong. But I'm confident this is going to work. It's going to be okay, Kenz. You'll see."

I blink several times, fighting off the extra moisture in my eyes. "I love you, too."

Trevor smiles. "Good. Now let's finish getting you moved in."

Setting up Hayzel's new room takes practically no time at all, in good part due to the fact that she's so happy to be here, she's willing to do most of the work herself in record time. Every item in her bags has a new home within half an hour. Trevor even found extra hangers for her to use.

Getting my stuff set up in one of the other guest rooms—except for the essentials I'll need while actually sleeping in Trevor's bedroom—takes a lot longer. I also mentally make notes about how early I'll have to wake up and even how late I'll have to go to bed sometimes just to be able to appear as though I've been in the spare room the whole time.

When I slip a few negligees and other pieces of lingerie into a drawer Trevor emptied for me in his bedroom, I take a quick glance over and catch the saucy gleam in his eye.

Naked sleepovers for the two of us every single night? Yes. Please.

Chapter 21

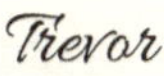

"Hello," Polly calls out. Sounds like she's at the side door, in the mudroom.

"Hey, Polly," Hayzel shouts, running in that direction.

I follow, my walking pace steady, not bothering to catch up. They meet me in the kitchen.

"Hi," Polly says, her face shiny from this new makeup or lotion or something she's been wearing. Kenzie said it's some kind of gel. I don't know. I just know it makes my sister's face look a little funny, not that I'd tell her and hurt her feelings. "I saw Kenzie's car pull out of the drive a little bit ago. What's going on?"

"We moved in," Hayzel tells her in an excited burst.

Polly's eyes widen, and she looks up at me. I give a tiny head shake.

"Hey, Hayzel, how would you like to hang out with me and Wyatt today? I'm going to pick him up from Jade's in a few minutes."

"Can I, Trevor?"

"Let me ask your mom."

Hey, Polly asked if Hayzel can spend the day with her and Wyatt. Is that okay?

Sure! Something normal will be good for her.

Sounds good.

"Your mom says it's okay," I tell Hayzel.

She smiles. "I have to go get that book I wanted to show Wyatt. He'll love it." And off she runs for the stairs.

"All right. What's going on?" Polly demands in a loud whisper.

I quickly explain the situation.

"Shit. I knew it was bad by the way you tore out of the drive onto the main road."

"Yeah. I didn't have time to explain to anyone."

Polly's silent a moment. "Kenzie went home already?"

"She said she wanted to confront Cal."

"But now they're in her apartment alone, which is exactly what he wants."

"Okay, you know what? You all need to stop listening to the damn gossips," I say in a harsh whisper. "I trust Kenzie. She'll yell at him, then she'll come back here to me, and that's it. So long as he's there, she'll be here. There's no reason to worry."

Not that I *entirely* believe it, but now is not the time to delve more into this.

We can hear Hayzel's quick feet on the stairs, so we immediately shift into a short discussion on revenue from the corn roast and how everyone wants us to host one next year. Since it was mostly her idea, I'm not surprised how interested Polly is.

"See you later, brother," she tells me with a grin.

"Bye, Trevor."

And off they go.

I hope Kenzie's right. I hope this day isn't too crazy or jarring for Hayzel. This is just how it needs to be.

While I could talk to Mom about this, knowing she'd be a great listener and would probably have some good advice for me, I don't think now is the right time. None of this has fully sunk in yet. My girlfriend lives with me, only because her ex-husband forced himself into her apartment and her life. Not the way I ever saw our relationship heading. Living together? Oh, hell yes, but not this soon and not these circumstances.

I can't just sit around here waiting for Kenz to come back. There has to be something I can do to get all this energy out.

> Hey, Mom, you still want that rickety, rotten shed of Grandpa's torn down? The one in the far northwest corner?

> Sure, if you can get to it. Probably will need the track loader just to make it through the brush.

That's not a bad idea.

I get the loader, some thick gloves, a few chains, and a fully-charged cordless saw, then head out to rid myself of these stupid worries, as well as the farm of that broken down shed, whichever comes first. If I end up pulling a few muscles in the process, so be it.

Chapter 22

Kenzie

I DON'T KNOCK. WHY the hell would I knock? This is *my* home, not his.

"Are you out of your freaking mind?" I yell when the door has barely shut behind me. I don't know where Cal is, but I know he's here. I saw his vehicle in the parking lot.

He comes strolling in from the hallway that connects to the bedrooms. This is only a two-bedroom apartment, and I think it's safe to assume Cal won't be sleeping in Hayzel's room.

"No. Nope. Not happening. You can sleep your stupid ass on the sofa," I tell him as I storm past him to my room.

There, I see he's already made himself at home. His stuff is everywhere. In my dresser drawers—based on the open ones—in my closet, on my nightstand. He even put a pillow on my bed, on top of the red, orange, and magenta quilt I bought at a flea market seven years ago because it reminded me of my great-grandma's when I was little.

"What do you think you're doing?" I whip around to face him, knowing he followed me in here. "You barely met Hayzel last night."

"I don't need to meet my own daughter."

"Yes, actually, you do. More importantly, she needs to meet you. She needs to get to know who you are as a person, let alone as her dad. That takes time. You cannot just show up and announce you're going to live with us. What kind of shit is that? Who does that, Cal?"

"I am sorry about how this is affecting Hayzel. I would never want to do anything to hurt her. But the rest? You want me to be sorry about coming here for you, but I'm not. How many times do I have to say it? I want to see you, Zee. I want to be around you, and this was the best way I could think of to do that. Our family needs to be together again. We missed out on so much. I missed out on that, and before you bitch me out, I know that it's my fault. I was stupid and scared, and I ran. I get it. But I'm here now to fix things."

"This isn't how things get fixed."

He tilts his head a little. "You didn't say things can't get fixed."

He's right. I didn't. My reply just slipped out without me thinking much about it.

"Does this mean there's a possibility?"

"Of what?" I ask, because I need more time to steady my thoughts and my heartbeat.

"Of getting back together? Will you consider it?"

"No, of course not."

But Cal smiles that half smile I love. "Okay, Zee."

Shit.

There's so much trouble coming my way.

Chapter 23

Trevor

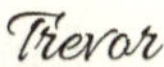

WHY IS THIS PART of the freaking zucchini field going to freaking shit? I really don't understand. Not that I have anyone around me to answer my questions. I sent the few workers who were over here away to any other part of the farm. I really didn't care where they went. But when I hear the familiar rattle of the truck Dawson only uses at BFO, I know exactly where my employees ended up. Or with whom.

"Who ratted me out?" I ask without turning around.

More than one laugh is my answer. Now I swivel to face my siblings. All four of them.

"Seriously?"

Dawson's still laughing. "Dude, you basically threw them off your lawn like a grumpy-ass old man."

"That's not what happened."

"Then what did?" Polly asks. "Why did Mom send us out here to yell at you? Because I have important work to do."

Len rolls his eyes. "Right, because the nutritionist doesn't."

"You've been out of town for two weeks for some horse thing," she nearly growls in return.

"Doesn't mean I'm not important or not needed. I'm always on call whenever my clients need me, which is almost constantly."

"Not really." Polly's never bothered to hide her annoyance at Len's ever-increasing arrogance. This is no different.

Honestly, though, I wish they'd all shut up and go away for a while. I need peace and quiet. I need to purge myself of this stupid anger before it really starts to freak me out.

"Actually, yes." Len turns to her, hands on his hips. "I'm always on their minds."

Before Polly has a chance to snap back, he adds to me, "What's going on? This about Hoffman again? I thought you were going all zen with that shit or getting him kicked out of town or something."

I glance around at my siblings. "Really? None of you gossips told him?"

They all pretty much just shrug and mumble half-hearted replies. I catch Len up on what's been going on.

"Which is a pretty damn stupid thing to be mad about," Dawson says when I'm done. "Now your girlfriend's living with you. How is this a bad thing?"

"You just don't get it, Dawse."

"I do. I would almost kill for the woman I love to want to live with me."

There's no way I can respond to this. Dawson doesn't talk much about still being in love with Ruby Sutherland, the woman he dated in high school. She left during college but came back a few years ago to base her interior design company in our hometown, moving it from Los Angeles. Though they fight constantly, I do know he'd jump at the chance to have her so close.

I mean, hell, he's the reason they fight so much in the first place. He often says something totally dickish to her just so she'll yell at him. Conversation is conversation in his mind, even if she's pissed at him.

"I don't think you get it," Dawson continues. "You're the one Kenzie will be spending all her time with."

"I don't know," Jade says.

When I turn to look at her in surprise, I see I'm not the only Bernhardt sibling to do so.

"Kenzie's independent. I'm guessing she'll still want to go back to her apartment a lot," Jade reminds us.

How right she is. I just know it.

"She's going to spend a lot more time with him by default than any of us think," I predict.

Unfortunately, there's not a damn thing I can do about it, except maybe figure out a way to get that asshole out of town and out of her head like Len suggested. Cal shouldn't exist to Kenzie anymore. Good riddance, truthfully. I almost wish I could scrub her brain clean, leaving no traces of him.

I'm at the zucchini again today, only this time, I haven't dismissed my workers in a cloud of frustration. Simon and I are about to discuss harvest times for the salvageable ones, when I get a text from Polly.

Pollywog

> Rumor has it Hoffman's here.

> He's here or are people just telling stories for the hell of it again?

A few minutes pass.

> He's here. Looking around the market. Let him buy something first before you go yell at him.

You seriously think he's going to buy anything here, Polls? Not likely.

Just don't do anything dumb

After shoving my phone back in my pocket, I tell Simon to text me in an hour so we can finish setting up the schedule for the zucchini. Then I hop into the UTV. I've no idea where I want to go, but I do know I should probably avoid the market, and not because Polly said to. Simply because facing off with Hoffman is not a good idea.

I'm not the terrified kid I was back then. He doesn't scare me now. In fact, based on muscle mass, I'm a little bigger. I might be able to take him. I just don't want to. I've never been a fighter. My anger from what he did to me never turned me into a fists-flying rage machine, which is something I was so afraid of that I sought counseling in my early twenties.

Somehow, I end up at the market anyway. I park, then stare at the building. Not going inside, but I don't want to just sit here either. In the end, I decide to wander over to the empty picnic table area and take a seat. I brought my water bottle with me, so at least I have something to keep me occupied.

Obviously, Cal finds me. It's not hard. I'm visible from a few of the market's windows.

"What's up, Barnyard?" he begins, and already, I'm wishing I could get to my feet and leave.

But I won't. I hold steady, sipping my water and looking as relaxed as possible. While I don't reply, I give him a hard stare.

He does that stupid half-chuckle thing. "Hey, sorry, man. Old habits." After a moment, he continues. "What's up, Trevor? How've you been?"

"Good."

I'm not watching him. Don't really feel like looking at him, but I can still see in my peripheral vision that he's moved a little closer. Then he steps back again.

"Farm looks good."

Should I point out that he's never even been here before? Against my better judgment, I glance over at him. He seems uncomfortable and out of place, but that's to be expected, I guess. Then he looks like he's going to say more but stops short.

When he does this again, I ask, "What's going on, Hoffman? What do you want?"

Though he opens his mouth, he doesn't speak. Just gives a small head shake. "Nothing, man. See you around."

Once he's gone, I sit here wondering what the hell just happened. I expected an argument or a fight about Kenzie. I expected him to be a total and complete jackass like usual. I wasn't expecting him to be nervous. This definitely throws me off.

But you know what? Screw that guy.

I never cared what he thought or felt before.

Sure as hell not caring now.

Chapter 24

Kenzie

"WHAT THE HELL IS wrong with your town, Kenz?"

"What do you mean?" I ask Edin, stifling a yawn. It's no use. It also doesn't help that she knows what I'm doing anyway. Not easy to hide facial features on video calls unless I pull the phone away, and then she pesters me with questions of what I don't want her to see.

"How can you possibly be tired? Didn't you say you slept, like, twelve hours last night?" Then she gives a sly grin. "Oh wait. You spend every night with Trevor now. Is that what you meant by 'sleeping'? Because all you had to say was, 'My sexy boyfriend and I were busy all night long.' I'd totally understand. You know that."

I wish I could laugh. "I haven't been sleeping well. Fitful nights. Dozing at work. No energy to work out. Trevor made me go to bed right after dinner." I stifle another yawn. "Anyway, what's wrong with the Falls?"

"Oh, that. At least five people have suggested I make tomato soup cupcakes, just in the last hour. There have been twenty-three suggestions in the past two days. Yes, I counted. What's up with that?"

Now I laugh for real. "Mrs. Abernathy made them every August for her son's birthday, even when he moved away. Mrs. A died last year. Knox won't make them for the diner, and Capelli's has never served cupcakes. With your brand-new bakery, you're the next best thing to Mrs. Abernathy."

"Oh. Now I feel like shit for bitching about them behind their backs."

"It's okay. They'll do something different next month to annoy you, and things will be back to normal."

Edin laughs in return. "Very true." She pauses. Her facial features almost dim a little. "So this lack of sleep. It's because of Cal." This is not asked as a question.

I nod. "He texts me good night, good morning, good everything. He's there when it's supposed to be my alone time in my own home. He always wants to be around me."

"I don't even believe him." She scoffs.

"What?"

"That prick seriously thinks it's as easy as camping out in your apartment so you'll just pick up right where you left off."

I flinch. "It might not be as bad as that. Maybe."

"It is." Edin's clearly confident in her answer. "You're with Trevor. Cal knows this. He just thinks you'll drop everything in your life to take him back, since he's the king and all." She rolls her eyes.

"You don't know Cal." But even as I say this, I have to admit that while Edin has never met him, she definitely knows him. She knows exactly what he's like and how he thinks.

"So introduce me."

I balk with a pitiful excuse all ready. "Edes, you're one of my best friends, but I'm not sure you'll really understand all that is Callum. He's . . . complicated."

"Aren't we all? I don't buy that as an answer. It's just a cop-out. You know that I understand him, and you don't want to admit it out loud. You kind of hate that we both know I'm right."

I try not to break eye contact, but I do anyway, giving myself away.

"Told you." Then her voice and her facial expression soften. "Kenz, this isn't about me being jaded. Cal did an awful thing to you and didn't apologize or try to make it right. Not once. What does that tell you?"

I take a deep breath and let it out slowly. "That maybe I should listen to my best friends more often."

Edin laughs. "I know your friendship with me is different than what you have with Charisma and especially Trevor, but we all love and support you and want only good things for you. Cal is not it."

"You want to meet him anyway?"

"Hell yes!"

♥ · ♥ · ♥ · ♥ · ♥

I didn't have the heart—or the mental strength—to tell Edin no. She wants to meet Cal? Sure. Why not?

Just . . . not right now.

I don't think I have the mental strength for that, either.

Edin won't relent on tomato soup cupcakes, but she did whip up a huge batch of watermelon cupcakes that actually look like sliced watermelon. Her bakery is so packed with customers that I think I'll avoid popping in for now. I have the morning off, having switched with Jacqui so she can take her son to an appointment. Trevor's at work, and Hayzel gets to hang out with her aunt Lucy for the day, before they both head back to school. Cal mentioned going to see some friends over in Marcellus. This is the perfect opportunity for me to finally be alone in my own home.

Honestly, I also want to check on the place, just to make sure he's taking care of everything. To my surprise, when I open my door, I see that he actually is. It doesn't appear that I have to clean anything. There aren't any dirty dishes lying around. No food wrappers. The bed is made, with the top of the quilt folded down the way I like. No clothes scattered about. My entire apartment is neat and tidy.

This is not the Cal I was first married to. This is the Cal I taught.

I can't help but notice that he put his clothes in my dresser drawers, but I can't be mad about that. I'd hate to make him live out of his suitcases.

Now that I'm in here, my bed is calling my name. I love Trevor's antique four-post bed and its super comfortable mattress he bought for it late last year, but right now, I really want to lie down in my own space.

Only this bed is no longer mine. Doesn't matter what it looks like or where it is.

Despite all the pretty colors and patterns, this bed is one hundred percent masculine. Cal's cologne has permeated into every inch of it. With my eyes closed, I'd swear I'm in the bed we shared in our house and not my cute little apartment.

Does he spray the whole bed—sheets, pillows, quilt—with that cologne? Let it soak for a while?

Of course, I'm sure this isn't accurate. It's not even that bad. Actually, it's not bad at all. I always loved this smell. It's so perfectly him. But thinking about the real reason this bed smells like Cal—because he's been sleeping in my space, on my pillow, under my blankets, in the same spot I usually end up—ratchets up my heart rate, and I promised myself I'd work on not letting that happen anymore.

I have to get out of this bed. Only I stay here for another ten minutes before heading to the bathroom to splash a little water on my face. And my bathroom now smells like Cal, too. In here, it's definitely more his body wash, but still emphatically *him*.

I'm walking out into the hallway near Hayzel's room when I hear the entry door close.

"Cal?"

He meets me in the hall near the end of the living room. There's a bouquet of yellow roses in one of his hands and a case of beer in the other. "Hey, Zee."

"Oh hey." Then I shake my head slightly. "I'm sorry, do you have plans? Is that what's going on here?" I motion to the stuff he holds.

"These are for you," he says, tilting the flowers my way.

"You weren't supposed to be here while I was here," I stupidly reply. I mean, it is a valid response because that was technically our agreement, but it's definitely not the thing I want to say. What I really want to say is, *Don't you dare have sex with anyone in this apartment.*

"I know. I'm sorry. But it feels like you've been avoiding me. This seemed like a good way to be able to see you." He looks at the roses again. "Did you think these were for someone else?"

I can't come up with a quick enough or calm enough reply.

Though I expected him to give that little half laugh, Cal silently straightens a little. His voice is rough when he speaks again. "You thought I had a date? Or . . ." What comes after that seems to hit him pretty hard. He narrows his eyes. "You seriously think I'd bring a woman back here? Are you crazy?"

"I'm not actually, but thanks for asking." My acidic tone has no effect on him. "Besides, you're a single guy. Good looking. Fun. Always up for a good time. It isn't unreasonable to think you might date."

"Do you not understand why I'm here?"

His green eyes bore into me, and I falter.

"You are all I want, Zee. I came back to town for you. Not to date someone else. I wanted to be here with my family. That was the whole point. Not for *my family* to live with someone else."

I can't think about that. If I focus on his dating life or his desire for me, I won't be able to speak. "You need a place to stay at night. You have that. Stop complaining."

"Seriously, Zee?"

"You were wrong to assume we'd stay here with you. Hayzel and I don't know you well enough for that."

"But you know Bernhardt?"

"He's my best friend and my boyfriend, as you're well aware."

He grunts. It's definitely one of annoyance. One of those things about him I actually didn't miss. "Charisma's your best friend," he counters.

"She is one of them, yes, as is Edin, who you haven't met. And I'm warning you now. Edin is going to hate you. She already does."

"She doesn't know me."

"She knows enough."

"Why would you tell me something like that?"

I can't help but laugh. "It's good for your ego. You think everyone loves you or should love you. You almost demand it of us. It's nice to know I'm not the only one who gets pissed at you. Also nice to know you have enemies."

"She wants to be my enemy? Fine. The only opinion I care about is yours."

Now I laugh again. "Right. Because you cared so much about that when you left me."

Based on his expression, I know I've wounded him. I didn't expect it to hurt me this much, too. Guess I couldn't hold it in any longer.

"I'm different now. Things are different. I won't be that guy anymore. I'm not. I can promise you that."

"Don't promise me anything," I reply, almost before he's even finished speaking. "It's too soon to know if you'll actually be true to your word."

He tilts his head a little, but remains silent for a few seconds. "When can I meet your other BFF?"

"Tomorrow too soon?" I don't know where that came from. I'd wanted to take a little more time to ready myself, get myself in a calm mindset. This urgency definitely takes me by surprise.

"If it's this important to you? Not soon enough."

And now all I want to do is be a puddle.

I practically am on the inside.

"So what are you really doing here?" I ask, needing this conversation to be far less emotionally charged. "I was supposed to be here by myself. It isn't the first time you've done this."

Cal cocks his head more. "Will Bernhardt not even allow you to be around me without him? What kind of bullshit is that?"

"That's not what this is," I begin. Then there's a knock on the door.

He and I look at each other, both clearly confused. I check my phone. "No one told me they were coming over," I say.

"Me either," Cal replies. He sets the flowers and case of beer on the coffee table before heading over to open the door.

A few of his friends are on the other side of it.

"What are you guys doing here?" he asks, annoyed but still friendly.

"Making up for lost time," one of them answers.

"Plus, Perry's TV went out and the game's about to start, and my wife told us no," Leo adds as the three of them nudge their way past Cal, into the apartment. They've brought pizza, beer, and what looks like a box of cookies with them. Must be Perry's. He always had a sweet tooth.

"Actually, now's not a good time," Cal says, trying to usher them back to the door.

But Leo has already planted himself on the sofa, feet up on the coffee table. At least he left his shoes by the door. "You don't mind, do you, Kenzie?"

I would, but this way, I don't have to worry about continuing my conversation with Cal. I never thought to ready myself for his words. I suppose I either need to find a way to get him to stop saying those things or figure out how to not let them affect me. Either way, right now, I'm taking the out. "No, I don't mind."

Now Cal really looks at me like I'm nuts before turning back to his friends, no longer hiding his irritation. "You guys can't stay."

"Sure they can." I smile at all of them. Only Cal doesn't smile back.

He gently takes my arm, leading me into the hall. "Just a minute, guys." We end up in my bedroom, where he closes the door behind us.

"What are you doing?" I ask.

"We were talking. They interrupted."

"It's okay, Cal. I'll see you tomorrow."

"You're not staying? You can watch the game with us."

His sweet smile and soft eyes are tempting me to stay. I can't believe how much I want to, which makes me feel like shit when I think of Trevor's reaction. He'd never understand.

"I can't," I say with conviction.

Cal nods. "Okay. See you tomorrow."

Chapter 25

Kenzie

HAVING THREE BESTIES OFTEN puts me in an interesting situation, but I've never felt it so acutely as I do now. My ex-husband is back in town. One bestie knows him and hates him. Another bestie knows him, hates him, and—in some ways—took his place. The third bestie hates him without having met him. That changes today.

Well, the not having met him part. I don't control Edin or what she feels, and if she continues to hate Cal after today, there's nothing I can do about that. I just can't believe I'm so nervous about this.

They both gave me the final decision on the meeting place. I chose Capelli's again, wanting to stay in town but also wanting to avoid the diner. There's no way I could ever bring Cal there. Between Dottie, Knox, and my favorite customers, not a single person would let this meetup happen without commenting on Cal's history of being a shitty husband and absent father. Not to mention the fact that the diner is special for Trevor and me. He shows up daily, even if we've argued or when he's swamped with work. It doesn't matter. Trevor's there nearly every single day. He's missed maybe ten days out of the last thousand, only because he was either sick or out of town.

"You ready?" Edin asks before we leave my car.

I picked her up a few minutes ago at the bakery, which she left in the capable hands of her two assistants, Val and Phoebe. "Are you going to clobber him with insults and questions right away?"

Edin waits a few moments, but I know she already has her reply. "Maybe. Are you going to fall into his arms like last time?"

"That was an anomaly," I say, stiffening. Honestly, I have no idea just how much I'll melt if he tries hugging me again. I've avoided all physical contact with him since then, even after he moved into my place.

My bestie smiles. "Then let's go."

Cal's there before we are, like last time. He already has a table, my favorite near a corner in the back. When he stands to greet us, he moves closer like he wants to hug me, but he doesn't reach out in any way. "Hey, Zee," he says with a grin, his voice bouncy in the way it is when he's nervous but happy. Then he looks to my friend. "Hey, Edin. Nice to finally meet you."

"It's too soon yet for me to say the same to you," she replies with an equally wide smile.

"Why don't we sit down?" I suggest, hoping this won't turn into a brawl. Though he wanted to pummel Cal, Trevor would never throw a punch unless absolutely necessary. Edin, however, will absolutely attack with verbal jab after verbal jab when provoked, each as painful as if it were a physical hit.

Cal pulls Edin's chair out for her, motioning for me to wait so he can do the same for me, too. After Zara, our server, takes our drink orders, Cal turns his brilliant smile on Edin again.

"So you're a baker? Do you prefer making things that melt in your mouth or things with a little more bite?" he asks her, his voice smooth and silky.

I know that tone.

Edin gives me a look, but I shrug. That's just Cal. He always sounds flirty. It doesn't mean anything to him. No use pointing it out.

"I'm a baker, yes. I don't have a favorite texture so long as it tastes good. Actually"—she glances over at me—"I just came up with a new blondie recipe using honey to replace some of the sugar."

His smile grows bigger as he leans ever so slightly closer to her, his eyes darting around her face before returning her gaze once more. "A blondie recipe? I've always had a thing for blondies." He gives her a wink, mostly likely in a nod to the fact that Edin's hair is blonde at the moment. "I bet it looks as good as it tastes, too."

Again, Edin scowls at me. I know what she's trying to say. *It's really okay*, I want to tell her.

But then I stop myself.

If there's one thing I've learned being Edin's friend, it's that she knows how to read people accurately. She thinks Cal is doing something he shouldn't right now, based on the way her face scrunches when she looks my way.

I can almost hear Trevor's voice as I think maybe I should try to see this from Edin's point of view or anyone's except mine. And what do I see? Cal's flirting with her.

The once love of my life is intentionally flirting with my bestie right in front of me.

Before I can say or do anything, Edin scoffs, glancing from Cal to me. "Nope," she tells me. "He is not the guy for you." Then she fixes her focus once more on Cal. "Don't you have *any* decency or dignity? You think you can just schmooze everyone? Flatter them into compliance? *No.*"

His mouth practically drops open.

"Let's go, Kenz," Edin adds, scooting her chair back and rising to her feet. She motions for me to stand as well.

"You're not serious," Cal says, looking back and forth between us. He focuses on me. "What the hell is going on? Did I miss something?"

"She's my best friend," I reply as Edin practically drags me up out of my chair. "You insulted both of us."

"What? How?"

I'm standing, but I haven't followed Edin to the door. Something is keeping me at this table, staring into my ex's eyes.

"What did I do?" he asks, standing now as well.

"Seriously?"

"Yes. Seriously. Zee, we were just talking. I don't get what's happening right now."

"You can't flirt with my friend."

He looks taken aback. Literally. He physically moves back away from me, like he's wounded. "I didn't."

Before I have a chance to answer, he adds, "Is that what you think? Is that what you saw?"

I nod, unable to say the words out loud.

"Zee, I swear, I was not flirting on purpose. I didn't even realize I was doing that. I would never do that to you."

I put a hand up to stop him, my eyes watery, burning. Everything burns. It's a consuming, familiar pain. "I can't do this right now. We'll discuss it some other time. I'll see you later, okay?" I don't let him respond. "Please don't follow me out. Order some food. Enjoy your lunch. It'll be delicious like always. I have to go." Then I walk away.

Twenty minutes later, Trevor pulls up to his front porch, where I sit on the swing with a glass of sweetened iced tea, still wondering what the hell just happened.

"Edes texted you, didn't she?"

"His apologies are worthless. Nothing but horseshit. I agree with Edin. You leaving Cal alone in that restaurant is the bare minimum that asshat deserves."

"Since when are you all about revenge?"

"I'm not. You know that. But that guy gets under my skin. There are never consequences for him. What he did to you . . . What he's done to me . . . It's just—"

I take a few moments to really look at my boyfriend. His voice has an odd tone I don't hear often from him. "Are you okay?"

He shakes his head, waving me off.

At first.

Then he focuses his gaze on me before joining me on the swing. I scoot over and allow him to wrap his arm around me. Whatever it is that's going on will most likely require silence on my part. Trevor usually needs a few moments to gather his thoughts.

"I never wanted to talk about Cal's bullying before." He's quiet again.

"No," I whisper in return. "I know."

"Sweet Cake, you need to know just how bad it was."

I give him another few minutes of quietude. In the silence, I'm imagining shoves in the hallways and hard slams into lockers. Things that are terrible, but also things our friends might not have thought much of.

When he still hasn't spoken after maybe ten or fifteen minutes, I brave the question, hoping he's ready for the prompt.

"Please tell me." My voice is softer than a light breeze, yet also as raspy as coarse grit sandpaper on wood. "Name-calling? Pushes? Hair-pulling?" Every word chokes me, but I have to get them out.

"That was part of it, but it was also much worse. He often left me bloodied, bruised. Never my face or arms or anywhere people could see it."

"That's why I never knew," I whisper. I didn't exactly mean to say this out loud.

Trev nods. "Once we were teenagers, Cal used to torment me with graphic details of your relationship with him." He shakes his head like he's trying to rid himself of a memory.

I, meanwhile, am trying to quell my sudden nausea. "He told you those things?"

"It didn't matter how many times I fought back or at least attempted to or told him to shut the hell up. He never relented. His friends might not have physically touched me, but they sure as hell helped Cal get away with it."

I'm both horrified and heartbroken with the truth. It's the hardest thing, trying to imagine my Cal doing something so cruel. But it's also the hardest thing picturing all those moments Trevor was made to suffer.

I set my glass of tea down on the table next to me and wrap both my arms around him, holding him close. "I'm so sorry to make you relive that."

"You didn't. That isn't on you. It's on him. He pushes and pushes and never gives up. You didn't do anything wrong, and you have nothing to apologize for." He has to clear his throat.

"I saw someone for a while. Counselor. Therapist. I worked through it and got over it. But Cal doesn't seem to have changed at all. I don't care how many times he says you can trust him. What has he done so far? He forced his way into your apartment and moved in uninvited. He threatened me. He hit on your friend. He has no idea how to parent your daughter and has no interest in learning the right things to do. He all but ignores her, from what I've seen."

He pauses.

She also hasn't been around him much, but this is not the time to point it out.

"Cal's not a good guy. He's not the guy you want him to be. The one you dreamed of him being for so many years. I realize how difficult it might be to let that dream go after all this time. It feels ingrained into your very being. Those hopes and wishes, those thoughts that permeate into everything. Even if you can only let go of one small part at a time, you still need to release him. Get him out of your head. Don't let him take up any more space or any more time."

"But I see it," I counter. "I see the good in him. He was a bully and an asshole for many years, but I believe him when he says that he's working on himself. Sometimes reactions to people are a reflex, and—"

"Kensington, don't you dare make excuses for him."

Oof. Trevor doesn't use my full name often. Never good when he does. "Listen." I wait a few seconds for both of us to take some breaths and maybe cool off a little. "Since he's been back, he hasn't done the things that you've said. He's been good. He's also trying with Hayzel. He really is. And he's trying to be nicer to you."

"What? By buying some bread from our shop to give to you? Really, Kenz?"

"He came here to talk to you. Maybe he choked. Maybe it just felt too overwhelming."

Trevor turns away a little, looking beyond the house to the side entrance of one of several barns on this property.

"Hey." I say this softly, hoping it will get his attention and tell him I don't want to fight.

He turns back to me, but there's still a fiery anger in his eyes.

"How often has Cal come here to your farm? This trip home, or any other time?" I want Trevor to let this question sink in, let it linger, and really think about what I'm asking.

"Just the once."

But the look on his face tells me he isn't seeing it the way I do. I push on. "And you don't think an apology might have something to do with that?"

"You don't think him living in your apartment, trying to get you back, has anything to do with it? Perhaps rubbing it in my face?"

"Is that what he did?"

Trevor's quiet a moment. "No. But that doesn't mean he didn't want to."

There's no way this conversation is ever going anywhere. Trevor won't listen, and I totally understand why. I can see it from his point of view. I'm just not sure how to get him to see it from mine.

I allow this frustration to push me away, all the home. True home.

I can't actually stay at my apartment, but I can still go there whenever I want. Trevor would prefer that I'm alone whenever I do, but I think Cal and I need to have a conversation.

I use my key to let myself in and find Cal in the kitchen, filling a glass of water from the tap. Upon seeing me, he immediately turns the water off and sets the glass down on the counter. He comes over to me.

"I'm sorry, Zee. So sorry. I hurt you, and I didn't mean to. I offended both of you. If I've hurt your friend, too, I will absolutely apologize to her in whatever way the two of you are comfortable with. I won't make you forgive me, but I hope that you do."

"What happened? I mean, honestly? I know you've always been a flirt. It's who you are. It's what you do. It's deeply ingrained in you. But my best friend, in front of me?"

"I swear, I didn't realize I was flirting. I was just trying to make you both smile. Put us all at ease. I don't know how it got away from me."

"Like I said, that's just you."

"But it shouldn't be, especially if it hurts you."

I nod.

Cal steps a little closer, his hands out, arms spreading open a little, like he wants to embrace me. I slowly walk into his arms, letting him hug me again. We haven't done this since that day at Capelli's. I'm doing my best not to fall at his feet again. Not to melt into goo he has to hold up on his own. Damn. Why does he have to smell so good? Why does he have to hug me so perfectly?

But it's more than that. So much more.

Trevor and Cal both feel like home to me. Trevor is the home that part of me wishes I had years earlier. Cal is the home I thought was lost. Both feel familiar and safe.

"I should go. Or you should. One of us needs to leave," I say, stepping back out of Cal's arms.

"You okay? What did I do?"

"Nothing, it's just—"

"It's just that your boyfriend doesn't want you around me—ever—let alone hugging me. Right?" He scoffs. "What the hell, Zee? I thought you were an independent woman with a mind of your own. Letting Bernhardt make all your decisions for you? That's garbage, and you know it."

Now I huff. "That's absolutely not what this is." I pause at his raised eyebrow. "And so what? How would you feel if the situation were reversed?"

Several seconds pass before he answers. "If you let him hold you the way I just held you while you and I were together? I'd want to bash his face in."

"That's not funny."

"I'm not joking. I was an asshole then, and I absolutely would have punched him for it. You know I'm not that guy now. So if it happened now, yeah, I'd still probably want to. I wouldn't. But I'd want to."

I nod, feeling a little sick to my stomach. I hate thinking about Cal and Trevor's history. "I know. Just, try to see it from his side more often. You can't hold me. You can't kiss me. You can't tell me how much you want me back. None of those things are appropriate anymore."

"I'm a patient man."

"What's that mean?"

"It means, I know at some point, it will no longer be inappropriate. I know at some point, you're going to tire of him. You're going to miss me more than you can stand it."

I already do, I think.

"You'll want to hear those words from me again, Zee. You'll want all the things you say I can't do right now. I guarantee it."

Chapter 26

Kenzie

I'M AT MY APARTMENT again, after running a few errands around town, including stopping at our town's local grocery store for a few snacks and whatnot for Hayzel. She starts cheer camp tomorrow, so I already loaded her new uniform into the washing machine. Trevor's machine suddenly decided to die this morning, and I don't have time to wait for someone to come out and fix it, including Trevor, who's busy with farm stuff right now.

"Hey," I call out, having seen Cal's car out back.

"Hey," he replies from somewhere down the hall.

Hayzel's uniform load should be done by now, but when I get to the washer, I see that it's still running. That's weird. I check my phone's timer that I set. It says I'm early by a minute or so, but that would mean the spin cycle, not the start of the rinse load. Super weird.

Then I see it.

The plastic laundry basket on top of the dryer has a heap of wet clothes in it.

"Cal?"

"Yeah?" he asks, joining me by the closet where my washer and dryer are.

"What is that?" I point to the clothes in the basket.

"Oh. Well, I'm going out tonight, and the shirt I want to wear was dirty. I was going to finish those later."

I spin on my foot to face him. "She needs that for cheer camp tomorrow."

"Like I said, I'm going to put it in as soon as mine's done."

"If it sits wet like that, it might get smelly. Why would you ruin her uniform?"

Cal scoffs. "Relax, Zee. It's okay. I'll wash it next. I just didn't have time to wait."

In a rush, I walk off as I say, "Of course. Cal's time is the only time. No one else matters."

"Hey." He gently grabs my arm. I can't see his face, but his words are soft. "Don't do that. All right? I'm trying. I really am sorry if I ruined anything."

I don't want to look at him yet, but I turn anyway. His grip on my arm is loose enough that it spins with me, so he's still holding on to me. I avoid looking into his eyes. "Okay. It's fine. I'm just annoyed. I want everything to go right for her first day." Now I catch his gaze.

His eyes search mine, but I don't know what exactly he's looking for.

This moment feels too intense. Why do we keep ending up in situations like this? To lighten the mood, I gently tug at his T-shirt. "What's wrong with what you're wearing anyway?"

When he smirks, I remember that I used to do this back then. "Just wanted something a little nicer."

"Hot date?"

His smile drops. "Not funny."

"Wasn't meant to be." I head back to the living room, knowing there's clothes on the sofa that need folded. I saw them when I came in. Cal must have dumped them there.

"You think when I get back, you and Hayzel can come over for a while?"

I shake my head. "I'm guessing it'll be late by then. She'll be in bed, at Trevor's house because that's where we have to live now."

Cal follows me the whole way. "But you can't wash your clothes there? Not that I'm complaining. I'll take all the time with you I can get."

When I pick up the first towel, Cal pulls it from my hands. "I'll do that," he says. "I can clean up my own messes. You don't have to pick up after me."

Then he begins sectioning it just the way I like. The way I showed him when we were first living together. Why does he still do things my way?

This renders me motionless.

It would render me breathless, too, if not for my need for oxygen.

I force myself to check a text that just came in.

Mom

> Don't forget, four o'clock. That should give us all plenty of time to talk and eat, and time for Hayzel to get in bed early enough for a good sleep. Cheer camp tomorrow! Woo-hoo!

> We'll be there! :)

I send a text to Trevor reminding him of the time and asking if we're all riding together.

> Of course, Sweet Cake. I'll be done with work well before then. Love you

"Four o'clock," I mumble to myself as I set a reminder on my phone of when I need to get Hayzel from Jade's house since she's over there playing with Wyatt again.

"What's at four?" Cal asks.

"Family dinner," I reply without thinking.

He sets another folded towel onto the stack he's started, then says, "Let me go, too."

I dart my eyes up at him. "What?"

"It's a family dinner. I'm family. I want to go, too."

"No, you know what? That's not a good idea." I pick up a kitchen towel and fold it quickly then move on to another. "I can't just invite you. Mom and Dad need to do that, and they won't." It's a good thing, too. It would be such a disaster. I can see it now.

Cal pulls his phone out. I keep folding towels and washcloths. Then my phone dings as he puts his away.

I laugh. "Did you seriously just text me?"

He doesn't reply, but his barely there smile tells me he's up to something.

Mom

> Cal is more than welcome to join us, Kenzie! The more, the merrier! We'd all love to see him again, too.

See, everything sounds completely benign with that text—Mom offering an invite to Cal, knowing I see him and talk to him often—until I get to the very last word. "Too." If I grab his phone right now, I know I'm going to find a text to my mom. When I glance up at him, his smile widens.

"What did you do?"

Now he laughs gently. "I just mentioned that it would be nice to catch up with everyone, and going to dinner would give me more time with my daughter." He finishes the bath towel in his hand, the last of the pile, then takes his phone back out. "Canceling my plans right now. Larkin family dinner, here we come."

Chapter 27

Trevor

USUALLY, I LOVE LARKIN family dinners. The laughs, the food, the company. Extra time with Kenzie. It's all good.

Until now.

Because now, *he's* here.

Oh, but he's "family." I forgot.

Seriously, though. Cal stopped attending Larkin dinners months before he left Kenzie. She's admitted this to me. He didn't care enough to ever show up back then. What difference does it make to him now?

Well, obviously, I know the answer to that. Kenzie just doesn't want to see it or admit it.

To top it off, Cal's at Kerrick and Nadine's before Kenzie, Hayzel, and I are, leaving us as the last ones to arrive. Dom, Charisma, Lucy, and Pete are already here.

"There you are," Dom practically barks when we enter the house. It's too rainy for a cookout tonight.

Kenzie pulls her phone out. "What are you talking about? We're right on time."

Her brother scowls at her.

Everyone else greets us with warm smiles and hugs, or handshakes for me from Pete and Cal. He actually has the nerve to shake my hand, and since we're in front of the whole family, it isn't like I can say no.

Hayzel says hi to Cal, but noticeably doesn't hug him. Neither does Kenzie, but I'm afraid that's more for my benefit than anything. Then Hayzel's off to another part of the house, while the rest of us naturally wander to the living room to hang out for a while before it's time for the food to be ready.

I'm worried about Kenzie right now. She's not looking so well. Neither was Hayzel, so I'm not surprised when Nadine comes back from checking on her and announces that Hayzel fell asleep on one of the guest beds.

I turn to Kenzie. "Sweet Cake, maybe I should take you both home."

She shakes her head at me. "I'm okay, and I don't want to wake Hayzel. If she's not feeling well when she wakes up, we'll leave then."

"All right." I kiss her forehead, and she doesn't feel too warm, which is good.

"So, Cal, what was it like being away from the Falls for ten years?" Charisma bores her eyes into him, yet her face is all smiles.

"It was all right. Nice to be home, though."

"Except you're not really home, are you? You're staying in Kenzie's apartment."

"I'm looking for a house," Cal replies congenially, and this is the first I've heard of that. Maybe Kenzie forgot, or maybe Cal never told her, or maybe it isn't even true. It's definitely something we'll have to talk about later, no matter which one is the truth.

The Larkins continue peppering Cal with questions, in a "we don't like you but we'll be civil to you" kind of way, based on their tones. I hate to admit he takes this in stride. I think maybe he's determined to be on his best behavior, even if they are lobbing snarky comments at him left and right.

Hayzel wakes up in the middle of this conversation. Each Larkin chooses a moment to send her on some sort of errand or favor they need, like suddenly, Nadine wants to show Lucy an article from a certain gardening magazine that Hayzel has to sort through two separate bookcases to find.

Once she's gone for the most recent errand of finding Kenzie's old knee-high Halloween-themed socks she bought as a joke several years ago and left here in her old room, Charisma and Lucy continue the game they started a little while ago.

"How's country life again, Val? Or maybe you were living in the country and we just didn't know it."

"Oh! Maybe you were an international spy while you were gone, Mal."

"No, no. I got it. Hal here was an undercover alien who had to return to his home planet before it imploded," Lucy says with a laugh.

Cal hasn't bothered answering. He doesn't look like he wants to punch something either, which is a first for me to witness. Still, I'm sure he wants this dinner to end as much as I do, which, now that I think about it, has me wanting it to last a little longer. Maybe an hour or two more than normal. Let him squirm a little more. He sure as hell deserves it.

Apparently, no one else wants to speak.

Charisma smiles at Cal. "I'm so sorry, Carl. It's not fair to you to harass you like this."

I think he's aware of how sorry she isn't based on the fact that she intentionally flubbed his name again. She and Lucy are having so much fun, I kind of wish I could join in. Kenzie wouldn't like it, though. She's pissed enough as it is.

"So, Trevor, your mom tells me things are coming along nicely with the barn renovation," Nadine says to me.

"Yeah, it's going really well."

"You're still not letting anyone in there?" she asks with a grin.

I smile back. "No, no. Not yet. It'll be an amazing surprise once it's ready."

"What do you think about keeping people in the dark, Clay?" Lucy asks him.

"Oh, Cole would never do a thing like that," Charisma replies with a laugh.

"Will you two stop it already?" Kenzie snaps.

Neither of them looks chastised in any way.

"It's fine," Cal says to her, his voice quiet. Soft.

Why the hell is he talking to my girlfriend like that?

Maybe I was wrong in changing my mind. This dinner shouldn't go on forever. It needs to be over right now.

Only it actually takes another two hours, and since Hayzel was feeling fine after her nap, there wasn't any way I could convince Kenzie that we should leave early.

"See you later, Cam," Lucy and Charisma call on their way out.

If only stupid nicknames and passive aggressive conversation were enough to get rid of this guy. No. Instead, he chose to let every single dig roll off him like it was never spoken. He remained calm. I don't understand what happened or why I'm the one stewing right now, but I do know that this can't last long. Cal will slip up, and Kenzie will see that I've been right all along.

Chapter 28

Kenzie

"Mom, Tay Tay would have a crop top under her overalls, not this," Hayzel complains as she holds her pretty—but apparently not up to her slash Taylor Swift's standards—stretchy white short-sleeved top that goes under her red plaid overall dress.

"Sweetie, Taylor would understand that little girls can't wear exactly what she wears and would also think you look super cute," I remind her for the third time.

Since we might never be able to afford concert tickets, if we were actually able to get access to them, a few moms and I decided maybe having a Taylor Swift party would be the next best thing for the kids. Violet's mom offered to hold the party at their house because they have the most space. I already dropped off trays of food as well as a perfectly on-point cake Edin made for the occasion, complete with spun sugar fringe inspired by Taylor's gold fringe dress.

All the kids are dressing up, and those whose parents say it's okay will also get to wear red lipstick just like Taylor does. I was a little iffy on that part but ultimately agreed to it for Hayzel. The other moms and I worked together, carefully curating a kid-friendly Taylor Swift playlist that they'll listen to, sing to, and dance to.

"Mom," Hayzel says in a whine. She's still gripping the white shirt, perhaps hoping it'll magically become several inches shorter.

"Hayzel, we had a deal. Your shirt has to cover your belly."

We're in our apartment because I forgot to take the cowgirl boots with us. Sparkly ones I actually made with some serious glue and tons of glitter, following a DIY tutorial I found online. They turned out pretty good and look a lot like Taylor's silver ones.

My daughter rolls her eyes. "Fine," she says in a huff.

I head for her open door, grabbing hold of the handle. "Get dressed quickly, okay? We promised Cal we'd spend some time with him before we leave."

"Sure." Short answer, but I understand her annoyance.

I leave and shut the door to give her privacy then rejoin Cal in the living room, only he isn't there. He's in the kitchen with several drawers in one section removed—all but the bottom one—a flashlight in hand. He's leaning over the remaining drawer, which is open, but not quite all the way.

"What's going on?"

"The drawer wouldn't close, so I thought it was jammed, but it opens just fine. I think there's something stuck under or behind it. I don't know. I can't get it to come out either."

"Want some help?"

He glances over at me with a quick smile. "Thanks, but I got it."

I open my mouth to speak, but he immediately looks at me in the silence and gets his words out while I'm still trying to form mine. "Before you tell me that I'm just a visitor here or suggest you ask Joanna instead of letting me do this, I want to say that waiting for Joanna to fix something I'm capable of fixing right now is unnecessary. And while I am technically a guest, I want to take care of your house the way I'd take care of ours. It's the least I can do."

He always did take care of our house. He showed me how to fix things, too, just so I had the knowledge if needed.

I thank him for his kindness, which he replies to with another cute smile. Then my phone beeps with a text. It's Violet's mom, and it's not good.

> Sorry this is last minute, but Violet's not feeling well. Been throwing up off and on for the last thirty minutes. Taking her to the doctor soon. Party'll have to be postponed : (

"Oh no," I whisper.

"What's wrong?" Cal asks. He's suddenly by my side.

Moving my eyes up to meet his, I see that he's worried. "Everything's okay, but Hayzel's party has to be rescheduled. Violet's sick."

Cal relaxes, aware now that it's not an emergency. "Oh. That's too bad. Hayzel will be disappointed, won't she? She's been talking about this party nonstop all week."

"Yep. This is going to crush her."

He moves his arms around me for a quick hug. I appreciate that he doesn't linger. "I know it's sad, but she'll be okay," he reassures me.

While he's right, I hurt for my daughter. One the one hand, sure, it's just a party. On the other, it's something the kids have looked forward to for months. It took a lot of planning and schedule conflicts that needed worked around for this party to even come to fruition. Now Hayzel is all dressed up in her room, excitedly waiting for the time that we can leave, and I have to go let her down.

But she comes into the kitchen before I have a chance to walk to her room.

"Ready, Mom?" she asks with a bright expression.

I step closer to her, at the ready to give her a hug if she needs or asks for one. "Listen, sweetie—"

"No. Don't tell me I can't go," she starts, her panicky eyes searching my face. "You look sad. It's the party, isn't it?"

"Violet's mom texted. Violet's sick and has to go to the doctor."

"So why can't we go to the party when she gets back?"

"That's not really how it works, kiddo," Cal says to her gently.

She moves her watery eyes back and forth between us. "Why? Why can't I go?"

"Honey, she doesn't feel well, and she's possibly contagious. We can't risk that."

"I'm going to cry with Tay Tay," she tells us, teary and pink-faced, before rushing off to her room.

Cal looks at me. "She doesn't actually know Taylor Swift, right?"

I laugh. "No. She's going to listen to her albums." I remind him of the records Trev bought her for her birthday.

Cal nods. I know he doesn't like talking about Trevor, but it isn't like we can pretend he doesn't exist. That could lead to a lot of very bad things. Awful, terrible idea. "Why didn't you let her take them when you left?"

"Didn't think you'd stay here that long."

"Zee, I know you think I'm intruding on your space, and maybe I am, but I'm here for you. Because of you. To be with you. If I leave, I'm afraid I'll lose my chance with you."

"But you don't have a chance, Cal. You get that, right?"

We're both still standing here, staring at each other, his green eyes watching me with hope. It's palpable.

He steps nearer to me, eyes still on mine. I don't move. I don't know what's happening, honestly. Then his hands are on my waist.

I pull back. "This can't happen. I don't want this."

Cal relents. "You do, you just won't admit it yet. I get that we can't be together right now. You have Bernhardt to deal with first. But I promise you, our time is coming. We're perfect for each other, Zee. You'll see." He leans again to quickly kiss my cheek, but lingers this time.

"Callum," I scold softly.

He takes a step back. "No funny business. Don't worry. I got it." But the smile he gives me says that while he'll stay hands-off, he's still undeterred.

His words bounce around in my head the whole way back to Trevor's a little later on. I'm more than a little shaken by them. Hayzel has her records and record player with us this time. Trevor isn't home, I see as I pull the car up near his house. After helping Hayzel carry her albums and record player up to her room, I settle in with a cup of tea in the tiny breakfast nook Trev never really used until we moved in.

It's much different here than at my apartment, but I like it. Not quite fully home, yet.

Only I'm not sure where the *yet* came from.

It's too soon, right?

More things to add to my *What am I doing about this?* list.

Chapter 29

Trevor

"Yes, I can hear myself, Dawson."

"You sure about that?" my brother answers back to me.

I'm hanging out with him at his place in what is considered the center of Syracuse Falls, not that it's busy or highly populated in any way. It isn't. Dominic and Spence are here, too. I get that we're supposed to be watching the game since our actual game got rained out, but all I see is Cal's smarmy face as he worms his way deeper and deeper into Kenzie's life.

"So just kick the asshole out of her apartment already and be done with it. You have a key. Move his shit out when he's gone."

I shift to look at him, my beer bottle in hand since I was about to take a swig. "You seriously think that would be the end? No. I'd be the bad guy. I can't let that happen. I can't have her hating me."

"So what, then? You're just going to sit back and watch him destroy her again?"

Sometimes my brother knows exactly what to say to make me like him the least of all our siblings. "Of course not."

But I have no idea how to stop the train wreck I know is coming our way.

"You're gonna be pissed at me for this," Dom begins, "but I don't hate the guy."

"Says the man who hates everyone," Dawson retorts with a laugh.

"Screw you, Dawse. You know what I mean. He's still here. He stuck around for Kenzie and Hayzel. Like it or not, they are his family."

"Hayzel is," I reply. "Hoffman left Kenzie in the dust on his way out of town. He can eat shit for all I care. He doesn't deserve to have her in his life anymore."

·♥·♥·♥·♥·♥·

It's so good to be home later with Kenzie. Since this is Hayzel's last weekend of summer before school starts, she's staying with the Larkins until the end of the holiday on Monday.

I hoped Kenzie and I would be able to *fully appreciate* our alone time, but the way she's looking at me tells me that's not going to happen. We're sitting on the front porch, on the swing my dad installed for my mom. Kenzie has her feet up, knees up by her chin, facing me.

"What's up, Sweet Cake?"

"You're not going to like it."

"What did he do?"

"How did you know it was about Cal?"

I rub my hand over my face a moment. "Why would it not be? He's determined to make our lives miserable."

She's quiet a moment. "He thinks he and I are a perfect match."

I let out a bark of a laugh.

She scrunches her eyebrows and tilts her head a little. "How is that funny?"

This sobers me. "Wait, you're serious?"

"I don't think it's true."

"Of course it isn't. Kenz, he was never good enough for you. He lied to you constantly. Started treating you like crap toward the end. He was never his true self with you. You can only be a perfect match with someone when you're both honest about who you are."

Kenzie nods. "I know. That's why I want to be honest with you about the things he says and what goes on when I'm with him. I don't want to keep things from you."

I lean closer and kiss the tip of her nose, then move to let a soft kiss linger on her lips. "Which I appreciate."

"I know you aren't happy about any of it."

"I like having the truth."

She and I do end up having some really fun naked alone time, but something keeps coming back to me. It's true that I love her honesty, but all that stuff Cal's been up to? It's enough to literally keep me awake at night.

Chapter 30

Trevor

"THAT ASSHOLE TOLD MY girlfriend they're a perfect match," I say to Lennox a week later as I join him at his truck. I stewed about it for a whole week before mentioning it to anyone. Lennox seems like a good first choice. He also has the coolers we need for the bonfire, full of beer, soda—much to his chagrin—water, no sugar added juice for the kids, and probably a few surprises.

"Hell of a greeting, brother." Lennox laughs.

"I just talked to you ten minutes ago when you texted me from the gas station."

Lennox shrugs, wearing a smirk. "Still. Would it hurt you to be a little nicer?"

"I am the nice one, and everyone knows it."

My younger brother grabs one large cooler, and I get the other. We carry them down to the stone firepit in my backyard. Though it was a warm day, it's turned into a cool night. Perfect for sitting around the fire with friends and family. I already have buns, brats, burger patties, salads, and all the condiments waiting in another cooler, in addition to all the plates, cups, utensils, napkins, and chips on the large folding table nearby.

"So he actually said that to Kenzie, huh?" Lennox asks.

"Yep." I hate remembering it, and I hate talking about it, but I needed to get it off my chest. Lennox just happened to be the first of my siblings who showed up.

He's quiet for a few moments. "What did she tell him?"

"That they were never perfect."

"Nobody is. No relationship is, either. You think she's tempted by him?"

"Who's tempted by who?" Mom asks as she walks up. She rarely drives here, preferring to follow the tree-lined lane she and Dad used to walk between this house and the cottage when he was in better health.

Lennox looks at me for an answer. I shake my head, hoping Mom won't notice, since she's temporarily looking his way.

"Just some friends."

Mom nods and smiles, but I'm sure she doesn't really care. I can't have her knowing what's going on with Kenz. Mom is not a gossip, and thankfully the town's true gossips haven't been babbling much, which means they might not know much, but putting that kind of information out about Kenzie and Cal isn't good for any of us, especially Kenzie. I couldn't care less how anyone feels about Cal. Well, except for Kenz. That's the whole problem.

"Where's Kenzie?" Mom asks as I walk over to the woodpile and gather what I need for the moment.

"Work. She switched shifts with Jacqui again. Hayzel's in the house finishing up cleaning her room. Kenzie told her it needed to be done before everyone got here."

"How does it feel having Kenzie and Hayzel still here?" Mom asks, a glint in her eye.

I notice Lennox is looking over at me as well.

I hope Kenzie and Hayzel never leave, but I won't say that. "It's good." I smile at my mom and brother.

Mom believes me, but I see the obvious doubt in Lennox's eyes, with good reason.

Unwilling to say more, I busy myself with the task of starting the fire. Dawson, Polly, Jade, and Wyatt soon show up within minutes of each other. Our friends—including Lourdes, Spence, Charisma, and Dominic—get here around the same time. It's a full house. Well, full yard. We've got folding tables and camping chairs everywhere, plus a couple picnic tables Dawson and I brought over from our outside dining area at the commercial part of the farm. Hayzel and Wyatt play with a few of the other kids.

It's all laughs and smiles and jokes, exactly the way I want it. I don't want to think about losing my girlfriend—the love of my life—to her ex. I can't bear it. Drinking a little beer and hanging out with the best people I know? That's the perfect remedy to clear out all unwanted thoughts.

Well, it usually is. But when just about everyone's left except my brothers, Charisma, and Dominic, and Hayzel's curled up asleep, wrapped in a blanket on the rocking swing—close enough that I can still keep an eye on her but far enough that if she wakes, she won't hear our conversation—Lennox asks me that question again.

"Do I think she's tempted? I don't know, man. I've been thinking about what Dawse said. I won't stand by and watch him destroy her, but if being with him is the choice she willingly makes—"

"Don't even tell me you'd let her leave you for him," Charisma interrupts, her tone severe.

"How can I stop her? I won't force her to be with me, or guilt her into it like he's trying to do."

She's not happy with my answer but doesn't reply.

Everyone else stays quiet.

I take a deep breath, because not a single person in this circle is going to like what I'm about to say. "If Kenz gets back together with Cal, I'm not sure I could stick around."

"As in?" Dawson ventures.

"The Falls. I'm not sure I could stay here in the Falls."

There's an immediate chorus of exclamations and interjections, just as I expected. I throw my hands up with a "whoa, whoa," hoping they'll stop. They don't.

"You can't leave the freaking farm just because your heart gets broken," Lennox snaps. "Who the hell is supposed to run it if that happens? We all have careers of our own."

"Hey, I had a career, too, and walked away to keep this place in family hands. Not a damn one of you would do that for me? Even temporarily?"

No one really answers.

I look over at my brothers, who sit next to each other. "Thanks, assholes," I scoff.

Charisma speaks up again. "You can't let him run you out of town."

"Listen, if I stay, it would only be for two reasons. This farm, and Kenzie and Hayzel. If I'm the only one who can keep this place going, fine. And I'd never desert Kenz and Hayzel. But don't expect much else out of me. I won't date. I won't want anyone or anything. I'll be a miserable freaking mess."

"And if Cal hurts her again? Because you know he will, whether she leaves you for him or not."

"I'll always be there for her to help her pick up her broken pieces when Cal shatters her. But . . . I cannot bear the thought of her being with anyone but me—especially not him."

"Is there any truth to the rumors that he had someone on the side back in the day?" Dawson asks.

Leave it to a politician—local or not—to bring that up.

"Kenzie never knew for sure," Charisma answers for me.

Dawson's still deep in thought. "Ophelia Daley, right? Leo's younger sister?"

I nod.

"Trevor?" Hayzel's voice is suddenly closer than I'd expect her to be.

Startled, I turn toward her. "Yeah? You okay?"

"I'm cold."

"You want to go in the house?"

She nods, then yawns. I check my phone. It's an hour past her bedtime. I also have a text from Kenzie.

Sweet Cake

Long night. Group of self-proclaimed Mad Hatters that were all too happy to keep buying coffee and pie. Crazy old ladies. I think they had a flask of whiskey they were pouring into their coffees. Dottie and I didn't have the heart to make them leave at closing time lol. Tell you more later. Be home soon. Love you

Home.

I still can't get over that. My home being her home, too. I love it almost as much as I love her.

Love you, too. See you soon. I'll send Hayzel up to bed.

"Bedtime, isn't it?" Hayzel asks. She always seems to read the situations well. Intelligent and wise, just like her mom. Even if her mom is a little muddled at the moment.

"Yep," I say as I give her a soft smile. "You know the routine. Teeth. Pajamas. Bed."

She comes a little closer and gives me a quick hug. "'Night, Trevor."

"Good night, Hayze. Sweet dreams."

She says good night to everyone else, giving a hug to Charisma as well.

"Good night, sweetie," Charisma tells her.

Then Hayzel heads into the house. The group is now standing, gathering chairs and coolers. We already cleaned up all the food mess earlier so I don't have to worry about raccoons or other critters getting into anything. The picnic tables can go back in the morning before we open.

We all say our good nights and see you laters, then I head into the house as well. I've just managed to kick off my shoes, grab a bottle of water, and plop down on the sofa when I hear Kenzie come in the side door, by the mudroom.

"Hey," she says with a tired smile a minute or so later, joining me in the living room.

"Hey." Once she's next to me, I lean and gently kiss the side of her head. "Crazy old ladies, huh?"

She laughs. "The craziest. I'm not sure I've ever seen Knox so nervous before about threats of a customer joining him at the griddle. Of course, they were flirty threats, and she was way more interested in certain skills he has that have nothing to do with his job, but Dottie and I managed to keep her away from him."

I chuckle. "Well, he's only twenty-eight. I'm guessing those ladies were in their sixties."

"At least." She laughs again and shakes her head. "Hayzel go to bed okay?"

"I just came in before you came home, and she'd only been in here a few minutes at best. I was giving her time to get it all done before checking on her."

Kenzie plants a soft, sweet kiss on my lips, lingering for a few moments. "I'm going up for a shower and then bed."

I'm about to tell her I'll be up soon, assuming she'd like to be alone for a while after such a long day, but then she adds, "Care to join me?"

No way am I turning that down.

We make sure Hayzel's asleep first. Then Kenzie and I practically sprint down the hall to our bedroom. It even becomes a race to see who can get naked first. Kenzie beats me by only a few seconds, since I trip up on my socks at the sight of her in all her bare glory, smirking and beckoning me to follow her into the steamy shower.

Dawson's right. There's no freaking way I'll ever be able to stand by and let Cal convince Kenzie to take him back. Maybe I'm just going about this the wrong way. I've tried talking with Kenzie, who still thinks her ex is a good guy now. I know reasoning with Cal is impossible, because he's that much of a selfish jackass that any sign of weakness from me will be considered a win by him.

There has to be something I can do. I just don't know what.

·♥·♥·♥·♥·♥·

The next day, Kenzie, Hayzel, and I are at home, hanging out with Lucy and Pete, who wanted to come over since they couldn't make it to the bonfire last night. We're all out on the back patio, sitting in the "living room" area, as Kenzie calls it. Hayzel's having fun playing with Pete's new dog, Ranger.

I pop inside to get some more iced tea for Kenzie and Lucy. As I walk toward the sitting area, I hear Lucy's voice. "I can't believe I'm saying this, but I want to believe in him. I mean, the hopeless romantic in me just swoons at the idea of him being a good guy and being good for you."

Who is she talking about?

None of them have noticed me.

Lucy continues. "I know he wasn't that great to you before he left. Well, he was, then he became icy and cold. But people can change. Situations can change them. I think he's the kind of guy now that you always wanted him to be."

"Are you kidding me?" I ask, startling all three of them. Hayzel's too far into the yard to hear any of this conversation.

I keep my gaze on Lucy. "What exactly are you trying to tell her?" My voice is firm but not harsh.

"Look, Trev, I was too young to be aware of what Cal did to you. So was Dom. We didn't know that side of him. Neither did Kenzie. We knew the amazingly charming, kind Cal. He's that guy again, but better this time. He's willing to admit his mistakes and work to fix them. He's the guy Kenzie always dreamed of." After a few silent moments, when she seems to realize what she's implying, she adds, "But you're a great guy, too. You and Kenzie are good together."

"Gee, thanks," I can't help but snap. "Good to know you're only slightly hoping she and I will break up so they can reunite."

"That's not what I meant," Lucy replies instantly, but it's too late.

I'm pissed, Kenzie's pissed, and Lucy and Pete clearly feel awkward now. This whole thing does, but I'm in no mood to fix it. Lucy started this shit. Or maybe Kenzie did?

After silently handing Lucy her tea, I return to my place next to Kenzie, giving her the glass of tea I added extra lemon slices to because I know she likes it that way. They both mumble thank you to me, but I don't really acknowledge them. I left a few inches of physical distance between Kenz and me when I sat down, but now that gap feels the size of a crevasse.

Then Lucy says, "I think maybe we should go."

"Yeah," Pete adds. "Why don't we hang out again next week? Dinner? You guys think about it, and let us know." Then they're retrieving the dog from Hayzel and off around to the front of the house to leave.

"Why is Aunt Lucy leaving?" Hayzel asks as soon as her feet reach the steps up to the patio.

Kenz and I still haven't spoken to each other since I came back outside.

"They had some things to do, but they'll come again another day. Or we can go hang out or have dinner with them."

"Okay." Hayzel nods. "I just wish I could've played with Ranger more." She sinks down onto the plush chair Lucy was just in, but it's only a few seconds before she's on her feet again. "I'm gonna go find Cinnamon and Pumpkin. Or Cheddar if he isn't hiding where I can't reach him. Maybe they want to play." And off she goes into the house through the french doors.

"Why did you do that?" Kenzie asks.

"Do what?"

"Why did you attack Lucy like that?"

No way am I addressing that question. I shake my head. "How is it possible that Cal's even more of a manipulative prick than he used to be? How is it that you and your entire family are enamored with him again? How the hell did that happen?" And how is she even entertaining the idea of getting back with him?

"He's not," she replies. "He's a different guy now. Better than he ever used to be. You just don't like him."

"Of course I don't like him."

She huffs, I sigh, and we're silent again.

But I hate the silence. I hate arguing with my girlfriend over some guy who should have stayed wherever the hell he was and never come back here.

"If he was good to you, treated you nice, sincerely and genuinely apologized for the past, made amends with you and everyone else, and all-around was a really good person now, no, I still wouldn't like him."

"That's just it, though," she replies instantly. "He is all those things. He's doing all of those things, Trev. Why do you refuse to see it?"

"Kenzie, as one of your best friends, my instinct is supposed to be me saying I'd be happy for you if you were happy in choosing him. That isn't reality. I'm your boyfriend. I don't want you with him. I want you with me. He will never be that guy you need. I'm that guy."

Kenz shakes her head and sets her empty glass on the table in front of us, having finished the whole thing in all our silence. She won't hear me. Doesn't want to. Listening to me means letting go of something she's held on to for so long. It's painful. I get it. I'm trying to give her time, but it's been so long since she even meant anything to him. I've loved her longer than I've been friends with her. She's been my everything for years.

There shouldn't be a debate. There shouldn't be annoying little sisters telling me that the ex is just as good of a guy as I am. Kenzie belongs with me. We belong with each other. Despite my brothers telling me to fight for my girl, I'm starting to think maybe I'm the only one who feels she and I are destined for each other.

Chapter 31

Trevor

I NEVER COULD FIND any proof of Cal cheating on Kenzie either in high school or in their marriage, not for my lack of trying. Knowing he wasn't good enough for her, I was definitely on the lookout for shitty behavior. He was a shitty human, so it's not like it wasn't in the realm of possibility. But he's also pretty damn manipulative and clever. It would be easy for him to hide if he conned the right people into helping him, especially the women he duped.

As far as I know, Kenzie never thought he slept around. Well, she didn't want to believe he bullied me, either. Of course, I never told her, but I know some kids did. It was a hard thing to hide. I mean, hell, I still have a bone that healed slightly misaligned because of Cal. Never did tell my parents what really happened that time, coming up with a lame excuse I'm sure they didn't believe. After a while, it just became simpler to keep his attacks on me a secret, or so I thought back then. I was honestly sad and ashamed, feeling like I brought it on myself because I liked Kenzie too much.

Obviously, I learned that those attacks weren't my fault, no matter how I felt about Kenzie. It's just a topic that's been bouncing around in my head ever since Hoffman came back.

I text Kenzie. I always text Kenzie when thinking of this because she grounds me. Loving her and being loved by her in return reminds me that I did nothing wrong.

> Miss you

> Miss you, too. I'll be home soon. Jacqui came back early, so I don't need to cover the rest of her shift. Oh, and Mom and Dad asked for a family dinner today

> Cal's invited, too, FYI.

Of course he is, because why wouldn't he be?

Oh, I'm not bitter at all.

Sure.

I hate that he's Hayzel's dad. I think I would have been happier had it been anyone else.

Well, I mean, no, that's not entirely true. Hayzel wouldn't exist as she is without Cal, and no man was ever good enough for Kenzie. Doesn't matter who he was. Wishing it had been me instead does no good, either.

All I can do is suck it up and tolerate Hoffman as best I can.

·♥·♥·♥·♥·♥·

"Why is this happening? Since when does your whole family love Cal?" I ask Kenzie in a low voice.

It's a few hours later. There have been no jokes at Cal's expense. No teasing. No calling him any name other than his own. Zero drama.

What is going on here?

She shifts her head a little as we're snuggled on the outside love seat, in front of the warm fire Kerrick started in the firepit an hour ago. Hayzel, Cal, Lucy, Pete, Charisma, and Dom are playing a board game over by the table. Kerrick and Nadine went inside the house to wash up dinner dishes, refusing help from any of us.

"What do you mean?"

I watch the group play Telestrations.

"What is *that*?" Lucy suddenly bursts with a laugh. She's aiming the drawing book at Cal, this round now over.

"What?" He laughs in return. "It's a horse."

Lucy's still giggling. It's a happy one, not a *let's piss Cal off* one. "That is not a horse! It's a weird cat-alien hybrid. How did any of you get that right?"

Charisma gives a laugh and a grin. "I can see it."

"Me too, Aunt Lucy," Hayzel chimes in.

They continue on about Cal's drawing skills as well as everyone else's. It's a kind, good-natured argument.

"Stop doing that. Stop pretending you don't understand why I don't like this," I tell Kenzie, keeping my voice down so as not to be heard. The group's so loud, they probably wouldn't anyway.

"Everyone deserves a second chance, don't they?" she counters gently.

Sure.

Maybe.

But this guy?

What if the Larkins changing their minds about liking or not liking Cal leads to them second-guessing who they want Kenzie to be with? Lucy's already started. What if it isn't me anymore? What if it's him? Reuniting the Hoffman family—Cal, Kenzie, and Hayzel, all together again. Who else wants that?

This has me on edge. I know Kenzie can feel how tense I am. She starts rubbing my arm that's around her.

"It's okay, Trev. I know you're scared to have Cal in town again, but it'll be okay."

"I'm not afraid of him. I'm afraid of what he'll talk you all into believing."

But she doesn't want to hear this. She shakes this off, reassuring me once again that things will be fine. I wish I could believe her.

Chapter 32

Kenzie

"WHO'S HUNGRY?" CAL CALLS.

I hear the front door close. A minute or so later, he joins me in the bedroom.

"Hey." He gives me a sweet grin before glancing around the room and back at me. "I like the look of you in here."

"It's my room, not the other way around." Of course, it doesn't help that I'm actually sitting on my bed cross-legged, folding clothes of mine I came here to wash and listening to a true-crime podcast.

Cal holds two large paper bags. From the smell of them, I think it's safe to assume he brought home Chinese takeout. I try really hard to not let this remind me of all the times he did that when we were together and too tired to cook. Well, sometimes he used that as an excuse because he liked when I taught him how to use the chopsticks even though he already knew and never used them anyway. I always ended up in his lap, holding his hands in mine while he practiced picking foods up and feeding them to me. Eventually, this led to us eating the rest of our dinner naked after giving in to what all the flirty teasing was leading to.

That cannot happen this time.

It won't.

But I hate how often memories like this come up. The ones where I start to feel sort of heady and wistful. The ones I should never think of again.

"You okay?" he asks.

I realize I've been silently staring in his direction.

"Yeah. Just . . . well, I thought you weren't coming home until later. Back, I mean," I quickly correct myself. This is my home. This is only his temporary lodging. "Coming back until later."

I'm not surprised that he caught my words. He looks a little smug with his happy smile. "I wanted to have dinner at home with my girls."

Yep. He definitely caught it.

"I'm not your girl anymore."

Cal laughs. "Zee, you'll always be my girl."

I choose to ignore this since I just don't have the heart or the energy to correct him this time. "Anyway, Hayzel went home with Lucy after school."

"Oh." He genuinely looks disappointed at this. "What about you? Care to join me, or will I have to eat alone?"

Trevor's still working for the day. He won't text me for at least another couple hours, I think. They're busy harvesting, so one never knows how long that'll take. There isn't anywhere else I need to go. This means I don't have to leave if I don't want to.

"It's just dinner, I promise," he says to my silence. "I swear, I won't try for anything more. Though I really do love seeing you on the bed I sleep in."

"Callum!" I exclaim in mock surprise.

He's already laughing before I finish the second syllable of his full first name. "Sorry not sorry."

"We can have dinner," I finally tell him with a nod. "Platonically."

Only Cal still stands there, watching me lift myself up to my knees on the bed. I know what he's thinking, and he's aware of this, too, because he gives another devilish grin.

"You on your knees is even better."

"Do you want dinner with me or not?" I try to sound mad, but it's not working all that well.

"Yes. I'm sorry. I'll stop." Then he shifts one of the bags to his other hand, leaving one free to reach out to help me down.

Trevor would tell me that I don't need his help. So would Edin and Charisma and Dottie and Gwenn and Lourdes, and on and on the list goes. They'd all be right. I don't need his help. Can I deny wanting it, though?

No, I cannot.

I accept his hand and step down from the bed. While I assumed we'd eat in the living room on the sofa, using the coffee table to hold the food like we used to, Cal leads me to the kitchen. It almost feels fancy eating at a table that was meant for such things. This isn't normal for us.

While I gather plates, Cal places the food on the dining table, then steps to the drawer for utensils. We join each other near the chairs at the same time. It took me so long because I was still marveling at how different this is from our old life. He really has changed over the years. As he serves me my favorite foods, filling my plate and adding the extra sauces I always liked, I stare at him.

"What?" he asks with a chuckle.

There are so many things I want to say. Finally, I settle on thank you.

He grins. "You're welcome."

We silently begin eating our meal.

"How do you like living here?" Cal gestures to my apartment.

"It's nice. Quiet. Good neighbors."

Then I think maybe there's more to this question. "Why do you ask?" I say as casually as possible.

"Just wondering. You always liked our house. Never wanted to . . . well, anyway, I thought maybe looking at houses might be fun."

"For me or for you? Or us?" I ask, though I'm pretty sure I know which one he means.

"Me."

I nod, but then he adds, "For now."

"Forever," I correct quickly.

Cal just chuckles.

I clear my throat, but it's impossible to hold back a grin. "My friend Gwenn owns Rhys Realty. She's the best. She can definitely help you." I take a moment to pull out my phone and text Gwenn's number to Cal.

"Thanks." He gives me a sweet smile.

Time to focus on dinner again. No more cute moments between us.

The fifteenth bite of food I take is just as good as the first. Only I feel my cheeks flush at how happy it makes me that he still remembers my favorites from so long ago. I need to cool down the warmth this gives me. I also can't hold in my urge to say something that's been on my mind.

"You've been here for weeks."

Cal nods, then holds up some of his garlic spare ribs for me to try. I dutifully accept the offer with an open mouth and hold back a short moan at how good the food is. Don't want to give Cal any naughty ideas. Though I think he already has them after watching me part my lips for him like that. His face is flushed and his breath quick.

After I finish my bite of pork, I continue, avoiding the heat coming from both of us. "You've lived in my apartment for weeks."

He laughs. "You said that already."

"I know. I just . . . What are we now?"

"What do you mean?"

"We didn't speak for ten years. We were basically strangers."

He chews and swallows a bite of fried rice. "Didn't really think about it like that, but yeah, I guess we were."

"Okay. So what are we now? Are we friends? Acquaintances? Friendly acquaintances? Friendly strangers? Am I still a stranger to you?"

Cal tilts his head a little, then puts his chopsticks down and focuses his eyes on me. "You're Zee."

"What does that mean?"

"It means you're Zee. My Zee. I don't need definitions or labels for that."

"What if I do?"

"Who cares? Honestly?"

I place my chopsticks on the table, then force myself to look up into his eyes. "That's seriously the answer you're going with?"

"Kenzie, why do you care? You shouldn't. Why do all these little things matter to you so much?"

He takes a breath and speaks again before I've had a chance to regain my composure. It's a good thing I don't get a chance to talk, because I might end up shouting at him. "So many questions, about stuff that doesn't mean anything now. Just relax and let it go." Then he picks up his wooden utensils and eats another bite.

Yep. Still want to shout. But honestly, with his attitude, how much none of this seems to faze him, I don't think continuing this conversation will do any good. I used to be able to relax and let things go. So much so that it became detrimental, yes. This is true. But right now? Right now, I just want to eat a delicious meal and not have my stomach in knots.

I focus only on the food, not ignoring yet not prioritizing my dinner companion. Once we've stuffed ourselves and stored the leftovers in the fridge, Cal gives me a sweet smile.

"Let's go do something. The three of us. When is Hayzel coming home from Lucy's?"

I send my sister a quick text.

Lucy

Hayzel wants to stay the night since I promised her manicures and movies. The new season of that tween cat show came out this week and it's all the kids at school can talk about. Is that all right? We won't stay up too late. She still has spare clothes and toiletries here.

"She isn't," I tell Cal as I text Lucy back telling her that's fine.

"So it's just you and me?"

"You know, I have a boyfriend I need to spend time with."

"Of course you do." His tone is bitter.

I tilt my head at him. "Why are you mad about that? He and I started dating before you returned to town."

"I came back for you, and you chose that asshole over me."

"No, I didn't. I chose Trevor for him and for me. That decision had nothing to do with you."

He scoffs. "Right. Sure."

"Cal, you aren't the you I dreamed of all this time. I wanted my husband back, but that man has been gone for years. Your wife—the version of me you thought you'd get when you came back—is gone, too. We both know this. I've accepted it. Now it's your turn."

"But we're still us. You're you. I'm me. I'm even a better me than I was then."

"In some ways, yes. But in others, that's yet to be seen."

"How so?"

"You're still calling Trevor an asshole. He has never done anything bad to you. Ever. Your dislike of him has nothing to do with him and everything to do with you and your jealousy. You used me as a way of hurting him for years, and took great pleasure in it, too, as far as I can tell."

He lowers his eyes, and darts his glance away before finally making eye contact again. "I did. I'm working on that now."

"And I'm glad to hear that. So long as you want to be in my life and in Hayzel's life, Trevor is going to be around. But that doesn't mean that I automatically have to take you back. Life doesn't work like that."

"True, you don't have to. You have to admit that it is still a possibility, though, despite the number of times you've said it isn't. I see the way you look at me. We share a lot of the same memories. You miss me in your mind, but also your heart."

"I have to go," I whisper as I hurry out of the kitchen, grabbing my phone on the way.

I rush to my bedroom and toss all my clean clothes into the laundry basket, not caring that all my folding is being undone in the process. Cal's followed me in here. He clears his throat. I look up to see him lean against the door frame, arms crossed.

"What's going on, Zee? Why the panic?"

"Things are hard right now, Cal. So many thoughts in my head."

"Like what?" But he's still smirking.

"You came back home and never once contacted me."

Now the smugness is gone. His expression drops. "This isn't home anymore."

I nod, understanding. "The Falls. You don't see Syracuse Falls as home anymore. You stopped seeing *me* as your home. That's what happened."

Cal shakes his head and lifts up from the frame. "I'm not doing this right now."

Instead of following him, I finish loading up the laundry basket, not so hastily this time. I even refold all the items that were messed up the first time I threw them in. When I'm done, I deposit the basket in the living room, finding Cal at the kitchen sink washing the dishes we used for dinner by hand.

There's this burning desire in me. The desire to ask all the things. To seek every single answer I need. I can't hold it back any longer. It might all come out at once, or it might come out in bits and pieces, here and there, but I have to let it free. I have to ask. I have to know. The time of holding it all in is over. "Where did you say your parents are?"

He looks at me, then back to the dish he's drying. "They've been moving around a lot. When Dad retired early, they decided to sell their house, buy some fancy RV, and travel whenever and wherever they want."

"You're kidding me, right?"

Cal laughs. "Yeah, my parents in an RV doesn't really make sense. Never thought they'd become vagabonds, but they love it."

Clearly, he doesn't understand what my question really meant. "Do you ever see them? I mean, they left the Falls to be close to you."

"Not much. Not anymore."

Now I huff.

Though he was about to put the serving spoon in the bottom drawer, he straightens and looks at me again. "What's wrong with that?"

"You are their only child. Hayzel is their only granddaughter. Where the hell have they been? You all professed to absolutely adoring me and her. You have no right to bitch about the Bernhardts."

"Hey. How did we switch into this part of the conversation?"

"Because you think it's odd that Hayzel has found a family in them and you're pissed about it, when your parents—her blood family—can't be bothered to visit us or call us. Ever. The last time they saw her was before the last time you did when she was still a baby."

"I don't care about the Bernhardts. They can spoil Hayzel all they want. She's a really good kid. She deserves it. It's *him*."

Oh. "What could you possibly have against Trevor?"

Cal doesn't answer.

I push harder. "Why were you such an ass to him? Where did all that hate come from?"

"He's just trying to poison you against me."

"Actually," I begin in a sharp tone I've rarely ever used with Cal, "he's been protecting all of us, I guess—you included. In all the years Trevor and I have been friends, he never went into much detail about what you did to him. I never knew specifics back then, so I hadn't realized how bad it was. I know them now, not because he wants to poison my thoughts of you, but because I was finally ready to hear the truth."

The truth.

Then it hits me, so hard I falter. I have to steady myself on the door frame. "It was me, wasn't it?"

Once again, Cal doesn't reply. He's done with the dishes now. After drying his hands, he turns and leans back against the counter.

For the first time in my life, I'm finally adding it all up. Trevor mentioned Cal torturing him with thoughts of us together, but I hadn't realized why. Not then. I see it now. "He started liking me when we were twelve. You and I first dated as teenagers. You knew Trevor liked me when you asked me out, didn't you?"

"It's not your fault, Zee."

I immediately shake my head. "Never said it was. All of that was on you, Cal. You did that."

"He deserved it."

"How can you say such a disgusting thing like that? *You* caused all that pain. Because you hated Trevor and his feelings for me."

Finally, he nods. "Yeah. I hated his guts for it."

"Why? Because you thought I'd choose him over you?"

"Of course not."

Except he doesn't really mean it. Not completely. I see it now. Cal was jealous back then but doesn't want to admit it. Does that mean he's still jealous now? Is that why he's still an ass when it comes to Trevor?

I'm not sure I want an answer. I push ahead anyway. "If I ask our friends from back then? *Your* friends? What would they say? Would they know why you felt the need to turn sweet Trevor into your personal punching bag?"

Cal shoves himself away from the counter. "He never shut up about you! It was Kenzie this and Kenzie that. 'She's so smart.' 'She's so good at everything.' 'She'll never be into you, Cal.' From the time we were twelve, that's all I heard from that little shit. I was over it. You and I belonged together. So yeah, he deserved it."

My stomach churns. Cal used me as an excuse to bully and beat Trevor. How can I ever make up for that? How has Trevor forgiven me? No wonder he never talked to me until Cal took off.

"I have to go," I whisper again.

He doesn't stop me this time. Grabbing the basket, I hike it up onto my hip and head for the emotional safety of Bernhardt Farms.

Chapter 33

Kenzie

Hey what do you think about stopping over for a little while? You and Hayzel. Just come hang out. We can make dinner or go out to eat.

THOUGH WE'VE SEEN CAL since our blowup, and though he's apologized for being an ass to me, he still hasn't really apologized for his words about Trevor. I don't know what to do with this, but I also don't want to keep Cal's daughter from him in the meantime.

Sure. I'm almost off shift, so after I pick up Hayzel from Lucy's, we'll be over. Do you have anything to cook?

I kind of hate having to ask if there's any food in my own fridge, but I also have to keep reminding myself that it's temporarily not mine.

Tacos good?

Yep. See you soon

Lucy meets me at the door before Hayzel does.

"She's a little down today. I think something might have happened at school. She already cried about me not having been her third-grade teacher, and that if I was her teacher now, I could make school so much better for her."

"Uh-oh," I say softly.

"Yep." Lucy closes the door behind us.

We're immediately bathed in the light reflecting off her yellow walls. It's a pretty yellow, not a school-bus color, but still, it's . . . a lot. My sister believes that everyone should live in their favorite color, and she's definitely done so here. But it fits her. It's cheerful and bright. Often exactly what she needs to feel refreshed. I know things are bad with her when she stops wearing yellow. Today, she's in a long, fitted lemon-hued top and gray leggings.

"Okay. Thanks for letting me know. I'll talk to her."

I find my daughter on Lucy's back porch, on one of her Adirondack chairs.

"Hey." My voice is soft. I wait for a reaction, hoping that a bad day hasn't made her short-tempered.

She doesn't look up or reply.

I step a little closer and motion to the chair next to her. "Mind if I join you?"

Before I can sit down, she quickly gets to her feet. "Can we just go home?"

"Yeah. Of course." I give her a warm smile, but she doesn't look at me.

Oh wait.

Cal's text.

First, I need to know which home my sullen tween wants to go to.

"So, sweetie, is that home as in Trevor's or home as in our apartment?"

Hayzel finally glances up at me with tears filling her eyes. "I want my own room for a while."

"Okay." I give her a nod, letting her know we can do that. "Would you like Cal to be there or not be there?"

"He can be there. I don't care. I just want to go home!" Her voice rises at the end, and she storms into the house.

Lucy steps out.

"Tweens are rough," I tell her with a sigh.

"I know, but I also know you're a good mom. She'll tell you about it when she's ready."

Hayzel's quiet during our short drive to the apartment. I already texted Cal to warn him she's in a mood and to tread lightly. He greets us at the door with a grin, the delicious smells of tacos wafting out from the kitchen.

"Hey, kiddo," he says to our daughter in a happy tone.

She silently glares at him.

He takes this in stride, and greets me with the same warm smile he gave her. "Hey, Zee."

I smile and am about to ask if he needs any help with dinner when Hayzel asks harshly, "Why do you call her that? No one else does. Why do you?"

Yet again, Cal doesn't flinch. His smile loosens but doesn't completely go away. "I call her that *because* no one else does. It's a special thing between the two of us."

"Whatever." Hayzel rolls her eyes.

Cal scrunches his eyebrows ever so slightly, then looks at me as if to ask, *Are you sure she didn't become a moody teenager overnight?* "Are you hungry?" He shifts his focus back and forth between us, patiently waiting for an answer.

Hayzel only shrugs.

"Very," I reply. "Do you need help with any of it?"

His grin grows wide. "Nope, but thanks. I wanted it ready when you two got home."

"Thank you." I choose to overlook the mess of him calling this *our* home while he's staying here, even though it technically is. "Want to eat?" I ask Hayzel.

She does a shrugging, eye-rolling combination.

Cal leads us to the kitchen, where we stuff ourselves on tacos with all the fixings. Then Cal risks a question about Hayzel's day. Unsurprisingly, she ignores this. I decide to tell a funny story about a couple of older men who came in today and the mess-up with their coffee orders, but the further I get, the more I realize the story was only funny in the moment, and not so much now.

I don't want to push Hayzel in asking about her day, but I hope she had some good things happen, too. Based on his expression, I think Cal wishes he could ask more, too.

Instead, he cautiously watches her for a few more seconds before turning to me. "You off this weekend? I thought we could have some family fun time again."

That really does sound nice, but I can't help but wonder how much sadness he's holding back sometimes. He obviously doesn't ask to take care of Hayzel himself because she doesn't know him well and it wouldn't feel right to either of them. It bothers him that Trevor can easily watch her himself whenever I need him to, but I think Cal understands the situation.

I pull out my phone to check my schedule for sure since a couple other servers asked me to switch shifts in a complicated trade-off.

"That boy called me Haybales again today," Hayzel says suddenly, looking down at her nearly empty plate.

I don't have a chance to respond before Cal says, "So hit him next time."

Hayzel and I both give our horrified replies in near unison.

"I can't do that!"

"She can't do that!"

"They'll kick me out of school," Hayzel cries as her eyes grow wide.

This seems to have no effect on Cal. "Maybe he likes you. Guys can be jerks to the girls they love." He gives me a smile, like that's supposed to make the past or this conversation all better.

Honestly, I want to scream. "Don't you dare teach our daughter it's okay for a boy to be mean to her just because he might like her."

"Why not?"

"You're not seriously asking that question, are you?"

"Kenzie—" he starts, but I interrupt.

"That's not the kind of lesson we use in this house."

"Well, I'm here now, too, so I get to have my own rules for the house." He looks at Hayzel again. "I say the next time that little prick makes fun of you, either kiss him or pop him one."

It's taking a lot of effort at restraint to not scream right now. As it is, I dig my nails into my palms, under the table where our daughter can't see. "Hayzel, why don't you go start your homework in your room?"

"I finished it all at Aunt Lucy's," she says, her tone back to temperamental teenager.

"Okay. Then why don't you go listen to Tay Tay for a little while?" I pull up the right playlist, knowing my parental controls are already set, and hand her my phone.

"Sure, Mom." But first, she gives Cal a dark stare before slowly walking off toward her room.

"Are you insane?" I practically hiss at him when our daughter is out of earshot.

"What? If he likes her, she gets a boyfriend."

"She's too young for a boyfriend, Cal, in case you haven't noticed."

"Come on, Zee. And if he's a jerk for the sake of being a jerk, so what? Kids today are too soft. It would do both of them some good for her to get a good punch or two in."

"Like the good it did Trevor when you popped him one every damn time you felt like it when we were in school? More than once a day. Sometimes more than three times a day, from what Trevor told me."

"It never bothered you then."

"I didn't know it was like that! I never saw that side of you, so I didn't believe you'd hurt him or anyone."

"It wasn't that bad. I mean, that asshole deserved way more than I gave him. Anyway, he needed to learn how to shut up, like this little jerk who's bothering Hayzel does."

"Is that what you told yourself when your fists met Trevor's face? Or his stomach? Or his ribs? Huh?"

He takes in a deep breath, forcing it out almost all at once. Several seconds pass. So many, in fact, that it feels like hours. "I can't help who I was then."

"Maybe you can't help who you are now either. Old habits and all that, right?"

Cal sighs, but it doesn't sound as violent as his last breath did. "I will talk to him. I swear, I'm working on me. I'm not that guy I was anymore. But I don't like talking about Bernhardt. I don't like you being friends with him."

"I'm more than friends with him, Cal. I'm in a relationship with him, and you know it. How many times do I have to say that to you?"

"Say it all you want. I know you still love me."

It sucks that he's forcing this out of me. This is so not the way I ever envisioned telling Cal that I've loved him all these years. Not in a fight. Not when I kind of wish he would leave. "Of course I do, but that's not the point."

"Isn't it? You're mad at me. And I get it. I hurt you and Hayzel. I hurt Trevor. Hurt a lot of people. You are the one that matters the most. You are the person I want, and the person I love. I'm not leaving just because Bernhardt finally got ahold of you after all these years. It won't last. I can promise you that. He can't love you the way I do."

"You need to stop saying that to me," I practically whimper.

He gives the slightest shake of his head. "No. I don't. I need to say it to you every day, but you won't let me. You won't listen."

"For. A. Reason."

I take a breath in and let it out. This conversation is going nowhere. Hayzel wanted to spend some time in her room first before going back to Trevor's, so it's probably not a good idea for us to leave.

"Maybe you should take off for a little while," I tell Cal.

When he immediately opens his mouth to speak, I cut him off. "Not out of town. Just for a little while. Give us some space to be home alone in our apartment without you or anyone else here. Let us feel normal for a bit."

"Yeah, I can do that," he says after a few seconds. "Just let me clean up from dinner, and I'll go."

I wave him off. "It's all right. I'll get the mess."

"If I knew how to make everything better, I would."

I nod. We can't do anything about that anyway. Time travel machines don't exist for a reason. "What I need you to do now is just give me what I ask for."

"Okay. I'll text you later."

Once he's shut the door behind him, I text Edin with an update on our miserable evening. She calls in return.

"I realize I'm not a parent, but even I know not to give advice like that."

I give a kind of bewildered laugh, then reply quietly, "You'd think he'd know better after his history."

"I mean, he seems like a better guy now, but telling your daughter to hit some kid is disturbing. Not at all what Trevor would say."

"I know."

Edin's silent for a few moments. "Clearly, I'm not the person to give you advice on letting go of exes."

I'm not sure if she means this more about Rhett, Cal, or both.

"But I will say this: Holding on has to be worth it. What's the point if it just hurts all the time?"

Chapter 34

Trevor

HAYZEL'S HANGING OUT WITH me and Mom in the orchards today while Kenzie's at work. Several of the farm's employees are here, too, since we have a lot of apples to pick. Many of them are walking around with padded extendable fruit pickers with baskets to hold on to the apples. Hayzel likes to help sort the good apples from the not so good ones, putting each into their designated bins.

"We got lucky this year," Mom says with a smile as she finishes sorting another bin full of freshly picked apples.

Well, I say picked, but they're more like gently twisted off instead of pulled or yanked.

"Yep. With BFO, for sure. Not so much for the community garden."

"Oh, I know." Mom sighs. "I think poor Lourdes is taking that harder than anyone. At least this month's dinner should happen as scheduled."

"Hopefully."

With as much stress as Lourdes has been under due to her grandma moving into an assisted living facility and everything she and Spence have been through and have also been reliving this summer, Lourdes more than deserves a day to be happy.

"How's the Apple Fest coming along?" Mom asks, following me to the next tree. "I know everything's finalized, but unexpected issues inevitably come up, especially the week of."

"Everything's going really well," Hayzel answers for me. She also walked over to this tree with us. "Mom says Trevor's the best person to run the fest, even if it does make him tired because he has to work more."

"Your mom's right." My mother smiles at Hayzel, who begins sorting another basket brought over by one of the workers.

As we move along, Hayzel and I end up on our own farther down in the orchard. She's been quiet the last several minutes. When I asked her if she was okay, she only nodded. She also said she didn't have anything on her mind, but I think she might be afraid to talk about whatever it is.

Suddenly, she says, "My dad was mean to you in school, wasn't he?"

Wow. Okay. I was definitely not expecting this. I'll have to work through this delicately. I don't want to give Hayzel images in her head of what Cal was capable of. She never ever needs to know the depth of her dad's brutality against me.

"What makes you say that?" I ask.

"The way you act around him."

Damn. I've always known how perceptive Hayzel is, but I hate that she's figured out what an asshole her dad has been.

Then she adds, "You aren't scared of him anymore."

"No, I'm not."

"Do you think he's changed?"

I don't answer right away, choosing to focus on a stubborn apple that doesn't want to leave the tree. "That's not for me to say."

"I'm supposed to be happy he's here. That's what everyone tells me. They all think he's better now. Mom. Aunt Lucy. Even Uncle Dom. And it isn't like I don't like him. I do. He's nice to me and to

Mom. Having my mom and dad together is supposed to be a dream come true for me. But what if it isn't?"

This I also hadn't expected. "Only you can decide that."

"Do you think she should remarry him?"

This question tightens my chest. "Your mom needs to do what's best for her and for you, not anyone else."

She's quiet a moment. "Did you love her back then, too?"

"I didn't know her well enough back then." This is a lie, and I think Hayzel knows it based on the way she narrows her eyes at me.

I hate lying to this sweet little girl, but I also can't tell her that I pretty much fell in love with her mom in seventh grade, when Cal's bullying started.

I amend my answer. "Your mom and I only became friends once he left town."

Two days later, in fact, when Kenzie sobbed in my arms, hoping I understood what a selfish jackass and all-around pitiful excuse for a human Cal was. How does she not know he still is? And why the hell can't I bring myself to the point of asking her?

"You knew my dad well enough to know he didn't deserve her."

I don't have a reply.

Hayzel nods. "That's all I needed. Thanks, Trevor." Then she adds, "For what it's worth, I don't think she should remarry him."

"Why not?"

"I think she should marry you."

"Thanks, Hayze." I give her a smile.

She shakes her head. "You two are already dating. Why would anyone want you to break up just so she could marry him?"

"I don't know, kiddo. I wish I knew."

Chapter 35

MY APARTMENT IS NOT my own anymore, temporarily, but I'm still obviously getting mail here, so I check it every day or two. Cal gets his mail sent here, too, apparently. I don't mind. He doesn't have a permanent address, though he did end up asking Gwenn for help in finding a house.

However, this is the first piece of mail that's been forwarded here. I look at his previous address, unable to control my curiosity.

Albany, New York.

That can't be right.

No calls. No visits. I'd assumed he lived thousands of miles away, which was why he came back to the Falls so rarely. Out of sight, out of mind.

But freaking *Albany*?

Immediately, I pull out my phone and text Charisma, hoping she's on lunch already. While she works at the school with Lucy, they teach different grades, so their break times aren't the same. Charisma calls a minute or so later when I'm floundering in the stairway, debating going up to my apartment or not. Cal's home. Well, Cal's in *my* home, and right now, I'm not sure I can see that.

"What's the matter?" my bestie asks.

"He lived in Albany."

"What do you mean? Who did? Cal?"

"Yes." I pace the staircase, up and down then back, as I talk. "He lived in *Albany*, Char. So close. How could he have been less than three hours away? And how did I not know this before?"

"Does it matter? He came back to town and couldn't be bothered to visit you. Why do you care where he was?"

"Because I wanted him. That's why it matters. I thought he moved thousands of miles away to be rid of us, and we could have driven to him in the time between breakfast and lunch."

Charisma sighs. "Kenz, you're never going to be happy with the past. He broke you when he left. I think he's trying to be a better guy now, but that doesn't necessarily mean he's made amends with you. Only you can decide that. If knowing where he's been living all this time is this painful, clearly he still has more work to do."

Someone's on the stairs with me now as I head down. I can hear their footsteps. When I make it to the bottom and turn, Cal's smiling at me.

"Gotta go, Char. Call you later."

"Hey," he says once I've ended the call with Charisma.

I try to smile, only it doesn't work.

His eyebrows scrunch together. "Take a ride with me? Just real quick."

I'm too emotional to speak at the moment, and if I try to run away, he's just going to ask me what's wrong or follow me. So I nod. I don't even think to ask where we're going. I simply follow him to his SUV and climb in, buckling quickly so I can get comfortable.

"Do you have plans today?" he asks, a glimmer of something in his expression.

When I shake my head, he gives a little laugh. "No words today, Zee?"

"Sorry. I just . . ." I can't bring myself to say it. I can't ask him about it. I don't think it'll do any good.

"It's okay. You don't have to explain."

He takes the road that leads to Quill Bridge.

"In the mood for some nature?" I ask.

"You look like you could use a little peace in your life."

If only he knew why. But he's right. I need to relax. I've cried more since he's been back than I have in years. That's not good. Not for my emotional well-being. Not for my physical health either, since I've felt so drained lately.

We're lucky there isn't anyone else at Quill Bridge when we arrive. Though Cal doesn't take my hand, he stays next to me as we walk up to the bridge, which overlooks the waterfall our village is named after. The only sounds I hear are the rushing water, birds, and maybe a few woodland creatures. No traffic. No tractors. No people. No chaos.

I lean against the railing and look out one of the built-in windows of this practically ancient wooden covered bridge. Our summer was pretty dry, but we've been lucky enough to have normal amounts of rain these last few weeks.

Cal leans against the railing next to me. We aren't touching, but he's still close. I'm not sure how long we stand here in the quiet. If this were ten years ago, we'd be sitting on the bridge, his arms wrapped around me. As it is, I'm grateful there's no physical contact. Every time he's hugged me or kissed my cheek or even just smiled at me, I've longed for more. That isn't fair to Trevor, or me, or anyone, not even Cal.

He forced me into this mess in the beginning, but I let him. I allowed him to remove the covers from all the memories and the pain I put into storage, unable to deal with it in any other way. Dust is flying now like shrapnel, and I can't see a safe way out. Will we have to take those hits to try and make it out alive? Isn't there a better way?

Eventually, Cal turns to me, breaking our silence. "Better?"

I mull over his question. In some ways, no.

I don't have answers that I want. I'm still in shock that he lived so close without so much as a hello for ten years.

But in other ways, definitely yes.

Even with the silence, this has been one of the best moments he and I have shared since he came back to town.

I think we needed this. I know I did.

"Better. Thank you."

He reciprocates my smile. "Ready to go home?"

"Yeah. Let's go home."

I don't think I need to tell him I mean separate homes. Pretty sure he means that, too. He's not pressuring me this time. This is the gentle Cal from our early days. This is the Cal I missed all those years. The one I'm so glad to see. He's faded in and out over this past month, but I'm glad it's this Cal with me now. He could have chosen to pick a fight at my silence or my sour mood. The fact that he didn't—that he often doesn't now—tells me he really is working on being a better man, and I love him for it.

Chapter 36

Kenzie

Trevor's right.

Cal is an ass.

Correction: an ass who clearly ate something messier than iced jelly doughnuts and got it all over my carpet by the sofa. Then he clearly "tried" to clean it up, because it's smeared everywhere, deep into the carpet in some places. It's probably a worse mess now than when he first spilled whatever it was.

Hey, do you have a carpet cleaner?

Lucy

Sorry, no. Mom probably does if you want to ask her.

I kind of don't, though. One, I don't want to bother her with it. Two, she might become indignant on my behalf, which I also don't want.

Do you know anyone else who might have a machine?

I can't tell Joanna, the property manager here at Oak Avenue Apartments. She'll be pissed, and if it doesn't come out, I don't have the money to pay for carpet replacement. Besides, Cal is practically subletting at this point since Hayzel and I aren't staying here, and he even gave me rent money—six months' worth, which I tried and failed to refuse because he wouldn't let me—though nothing has been made official. I'd hate to make waves and give Joanna a reason not to like any of us.

Lucy

> Honestly, I'd go with Mom.

> What happened anyway? Aren't you staying with Trevor? Make Cal pay for renting one.

I should. I know I should, but I probably won't.

While I'm digging through the various detergents in my laundry slash cleaning slash linen closet, I hear the door open and close.

"Hey," Cal says, behind me sooner than I expected him to be. "Didn't know you'd be home, but I'm glad you are. Where's Hayzel?"

"With Deb," I reply, trying to control my frustration, which was already near a boiling point before he arrived.

"Oh. Well, I hope they're having fun."

"I'm sure they are."

Can he hear the annoyance in my voice?

I'm not sure, but I do know that I'm not nearly done with him yet.

Turning around to face him, I ask, "What did you do, Cal?"

His expression dulls and his shoulders slump. "What is it now?"

"The floor."

"It's just a stain. I'll take care of it. What I'm more concerned about is why the hell you live here in the first place."

"I don't, actually. Not since you barged in here and stole my apartment." I push past him and head to the kitchen in search of some baking soda. Maybe letting that sit or soak or something will help.

Cal follows me. "Why do I keep hearing everyone around town talk about hiring you for parties? What is that?"

"If you heard why they want to hire me, then you should know what that means," I say, not bothering to look at him. The baking soda is easily found, but then I think I might need water or vinegar or some other kind of liquid. I'm sure I know all of this already, but my brain just can't focus right now.

I pull out my phone to search for homemade carpet-cleaning solutions.

"A party planner? Seriously, Kenzie?"

Now I glance up from the screen. "Why do you say it with such derision? And if you want to be correct, it's *event* planner, Cal."

"Same thing. What do you plan? Little Johnny's third birthday party? So, which do you pick, the clown or the bouncy house?" He scoffs as tears prick my eyes. "Come on. That's a job for a teenager, not the mother of my child."

I don't bother telling him I've planned weddings, engagement parties, even festivals and also large corporate gatherings at BFO. He clearly doesn't want to hear that. He's most likely heard all of that already. "You didn't care about us or what we were doing before. Why now? Just because you're here? Who do you think you are?"

"You're real high and mighty for someone who couldn't keep the palace I provided you."

"What are you talking about?"

"Why didn't you keep that house? It was a thousand times better than here. Practically a mansion."

I tell myself I won't cry even though I know better. I'm just so damn tired of crying because of this man. Because of all the emotions he makes me feel and the way he sometimes still drags me down and the way I now drag him down. It's exhausting. "I couldn't afford the house anymore. You moved away when we had a brand-new baby at home, and your parents went with you. You all just up and *left*. Not once in all those times you came back to visit the Falls did you ever call us or come see us or ask us to meet with you."

"Why does it keep coming back to that?"

My hands shake now. So much so that trying to type in what I need to look up in the search bar just isn't feasible. "Are you serious?"

"Why don't you live in our home anymore?" Like that's a perfectly reasonable, logical answer.

"Our home was too hard to keep. You promised to take care of us, then suddenly I was a single mom raising a baby on my own with debt leftover from *you*. We had to live with my parents for a long time."

"Then you got the waitressing gig. You've done well on that. So why screw with that? Why chase some dumb pipe dream now?"

"Because you are the expert at making the right decisions?" I lift my eyebrows at him. "What? You think I should write a pro-con list for becoming an event planner?"

"I think you should stop giving fancy names to a crap job."

"Tell me," I say, ignoring that for now. "What did your pro-con list for abandoning us look like? How did you make that choice? I mean, it was the right choice in the end, since you apparently never make bad decisions."

"My only bad decision was hooking up with you."

I'm so taken aback by this that I literally step away from him.

He puts a hand up and tries to follow me, but I shake my head at him.

"I didn't mean that, Zee."

"Yes, you did. That's the difference between us. I will never regret our relationship because it's what led to us having Hayzel. I do, however, regret even considering giving you a second chance. One you sure as hell have never deserved."

"I'm trying my best." His voice strains as he emphasizes every word.

Since I'm so damn tired of hearing this, I ignore it. "I guess I needed to know for certain that she and I will always be better off and have always been better off without you in our lives. I waited and waited and *waited* for you. You were all I wanted. And now all I want . . . is your departure." My tears fall harder.

"You waited for me, but now you want me gone? That doesn't make any sense."

"Yes, it does," I cry. I leave the baking soda and my phone on the counter so I can pull a paper towel off the roll and dry my cheeks, then head out of the kitchen. Problem is, once I reach the living room, I end up staring at the damn carpet stain again, all red and splotchy and mocking me.

Once again, Cal follows me. "I told you, Zee. I'm not going anywhere."

"Fine."

So I storm out, which is stupid because it's my apartment.

It's also stupid because I just realized I didn't grab my phone on the way out.

Damn it. Now I have to go back in.

I don't make eye contact with Cal when I'm inside the apartment—not that the moisture in my eyes would allow me to do that anyway. I don't even look in his direction. I simply head for the kitchen. Only my face is hot and sore now. I'd really like to press a cool, damp washcloth on it to help soothe it.

Cal stands across the room, staring at me. "You okay?"

"You seriously think I could be right now?"

"Okay, Zee. Have it your way." He returns to the living room, plopping onto the sofa and grabbing the TV remote.

I head to my bathroom to cool my face a little, only I don't make it there. When I'm on my way down the hall, the front door opens.

From behind me, I hear Cal say, "Why do you have a key? Why are you even here?"

The only other person who has a key is Trevor. Trevor being in a room alone with Cal is probably not a good idea. I rush back into the living room, still crying.

Immediately, Trevor's worried, which was exactly what I didn't want. "What did you do to her?" he snaps at Cal, who puts his hands up.

"I swear, I didn't do anything. We were just discussing things that have nothing to do with you."

Trevor's definitely not going to leave now. Not unless I go with him.

"I'll take care of the mess," Cal promises me before I step through the entryway, phone now in hand.

I nod, but I don't actually believe him.

·❤·❤·❤·❤·❤·

It's super early in the morning, but I have to at least try to get rid of the stain before heading into work. I'm not sure if Cal is up this early or if he's even here. If he is here, I hope I don't wake him up.

The stain is the first thing I see when I open the door. That is, the lack of a stain. It's completely gone. If I didn't know any better, I wouldn't be able to tell where it was. All the carpet I see looks brighter, like it's all been freshened up.

The carpet isn't the only thing he cleaned either.

Everything sparkles or shines. All the shelves, décor, electronics, pictures, you name it. The tile floors look mopped. The kitchen is spotless once again.

Slowly, I spin around, taking it all in. Before Cal moved in, my apartment hadn't been this perfectly spotless in a long time. I just don't have the time or energy to put into it. He must have been up late into the night getting it all done for me. Honestly, I'm almost misty-eyed at how sweet this is. Cal never put this kind of effort in after Hayzel came along, but he did at times before her, earlier in our relationship.

He was good with words. He was good with actions, too. That's how I fell for him all those years ago. High school Cal and thirty-something Cal still have a lot in common, but that's a double-edged sword.

Cal steps out from the inner hallway in only a pair of carpenter-style khaki shorts. He has a blue T-shirt in hand, but makes no move to put it on.

"Thank you for doing this," I whisper.

I don't mean for my voice to be so soft. I don't want him to make me feel weak.

But all of this reminds me of the first time we moved into our new house when we were married. It was a new construction but still needed cleaned up a little, which Cal helped with. I ask if he remembers that.

"I'm sorry, Zee," he says with a slow head shake.

"Oh." I can't hide the surprise in my voice. Then I try to shake myself out of it. "Well, anyway, that story makes me think of when we helped your aunt and uncle clean out that apartment over their garage they built to rent out. We were the only ones there."

"We must have had some fun." He says this with a small smile, but it's enough to reinforce the fact that he doesn't remember this either. He hasn't recalled a lot of memories lately. Like they're all gone for him.

I believe we conceived Hayzel that day at his aunt and uncle's, but there's no way I can say it out loud. If he doesn't remember those other things, he probably won't remember that part of the story either, which would be far too much to bear.

"I'll see you later," I whisper, then head out, on my way to the diner.

I can't cry now. I really, truly can't. Be emotionally strong. That's what I need to do. No crying. Customers don't care what kind of day you're having so long as their eggs and hash browns and burgers and fries all arrive in a reasonable amount of time, cooked to their liking, and still warm.

This is one of those many moments where I have to stay emotionally strong. No falling apart at work. No falling apart at all.

Chapter 37

Trevor

"You're not making a mess of your life."

"How can you possibly say that?" Kenzie responds, her words wobbling.

The apple orchard around us still holds several full trees, as part of our U-pick area for customers. It's late, though. Dark enough that Kenz and I need battery-operated lanterns and candles to give us light. We have jackets and blankets to keep us warm. I would normally snuggle with her, too, but she's not in the right mood to want me to hold her.

"You're not making a mess of your life," I repeat with a firm voice. I need her to listen to me. I need her to understand.

She just shakes her head at me and doesn't say a word.

"You're allowed to have goals. It's good to have goals. Just think of it as exploring uncharted avenues."

"You think?" She's doubtful, and I hate the reason for this. *Him.* Cal. He did this to her. He always does this to her.

I nod. "Absolutely. It's like here in the orchard. There are places completely covered in vegetation that seem obvious for pathways. They just haven't been mapped out yet. Doesn't mean the potential isn't there. Doesn't mean it won't happen," I add with emphasis. "What if I never added that avenue down by the creek?"

"I love that one," she says with a wistful smile.

This sets my heart racing, per usual. I'm a sucker for Kenzie's smiles. "I know. If I hadn't worked at it, I'd never get to see that big grin on your beautiful face when you walk it. I would have lost out on those moments with you."

Now her smile upturns even more. "We can't have that." Only it starts to fall again.

I hate that freaking asshole.

"If you want to leave the diner, that's okay. Aunt Dottie and Francie will be sad, but you know they'll let you go if it's what you really want."

Kenzie doesn't reply.

"Listen to me, Sweet Cake." I crawl over to her and gently take her face in my hands, making sure she looks in my eyes. "You've designed amazing things. You have the skills and talents and creativity necessary to be successful at this. I know you do. I've seen it. Look at all the events you've done so far. Not just birthday parties. You've done weddings, engagement parties. You helped Edin with the launch party for her new bakery. You helped launch other businesses around town, too. You did that, Kenz. Don't give up on that just because someone says it's a bad idea." I don't say who the *someone* is, but we both know. And I can't let it go. "Who gives a shit what he thinks?" I add, to drive the point home.

When she starts to pull back, I make sure she sees in my eyes that I'm not done yet. She stills, telling me she's going to let me finish. "I understand that you care about him, but come on. His opinions shouldn't rule your thoughts. He lost the right to have so much sway with you when he walked out years ago. Why are you trying to give that back to him?"

She starts to bristle, but then relaxes. "I guess I hadn't thought about it that way."

"Really? Every time Charisma or Edin or I have pointed this out before?"

"It's hard, Trev. For you. For me. For all of us. I get that. Okay? I get it. But I've—" She stops.

I know what she doesn't want to say.

She's loved him.

She's missed him.

She's over the moon about him having come back to town.

This puts me on edge. But I know I have to tread lightly. I *hate* that I have to tread lightly. His mistakes aren't only in the past, though. I don't give a shit that the guy is "working on himself." He's hurt Kenzie too much. I know something that will cheer her up. Something that's been in the works for a while, at least in my mind. Renovating the barn for an event venue was only part of my plan.

"Sweet Cake, I have an idea."

"What's that?" she asks, still in a serious mood.

"Why don't you set up a business?"

Kenz scoffs. "Seriously? How do you think I'd do that? And with what capital? I'd never be able to launch a business. Where would I even work?"

"My office."

Now she laughs. At least she isn't scowling anymore.

"Hey, listen. You are so good at what you do. You've helped countless friends with their engagements and weddings. Why not take the next step and become an official event coordinator? You don't want to stay at the diner forever. You're not Aunt Dottie. This is a good step for you."

"Why doesn't it feel like that?"

"I've been told excitement and anxiety can feel the same. You aren't getting encouragement from someone you hoped would support this decision. Those two reasons right there are enough to make this seem like it's the wrong thing for you, but that's not true."

"I can't just quit my job right now. I need money, and there's no guarantee I'd make any as a planner."

"Sweet Cake, I promise you, as soon as you put the word out that you're available to coordinate parties and events full-time, you're schedule's going to book up faster than you can blink. Look how much you helped with the corn roast and Apple Fest."

"If you say so." But still, she doubts.

This is probably the best answer I'm going to get from her right now, so I'll take it.

"Hey, remember that little hole-in-the-wall restaurant we went to after taking Lucy back to college winter of her freshman year?"

Kenzie looks up at me with wide eyes. "Yeah. You remember that, too?"

I nod. "Of course. I actually found a place in Bayberry that's almost just like it. Want to go check it out soon?"

Though she perks up, there's still plenty of lingering sadness coursing through her. "I'd love to, Trevor."

When she kisses me, I get the feeling that she's still holding back, but this definitely feels like a step in the right direction.

Chapter 38

Kenzie

SYRACUSE FALLS HAS NEVER looked better.

Well, I'm sure it has, but Apple Fest just gives it something extra.

When the townspeople first mentioned bringing Apple Fest back after decades of not celebrating it, no one seemed to know what to do with it. Then Trevor took over BFO, and suddenly, everyone looked to him for ideas. He turned to me with lost puppy-dog eyes. Most of the plans he helped put into place were because of me, but honestly, I just suggested things that a lot of people who attend fairs and festivals seem to like, like a parade, an art and photography show, an apple-pancake breakfast, and a hand-pie eating contest.

While Trevor is point man for the festival and has been since that first year, I still help when I can and when he asks me to, which is basically an annual thing. Events happen all over town, from Main Street to the little square, over to the park. Everything is within walking distance, though this is the third year we've offered free shuttles for those who might need them.

The pancake breakfast was early this morning, as was the Apple Parade featuring the Apple Princess. Hayzel got to ride on one of BFO's floats. I rode with Trevor in his truck. Now Cal's here. I think he's been feeling left out lately. It's hard for me with him around, so I've avoided him. Maybe a little too often, because Hayzel commented this morning that she hasn't seen her dad very much.

So it's Hoffman family fun time today. As much as Trevor hates it, he knows this is important for my daughter. It's important for Cal, too.

Lucy and Pete are here somewhere, as are my parents, my brother and Charisma, Edin—whose staff is running the bakery for her for a little while so she can judge the pie eating contest—and probably just about everyone else we know.

"What's next, Hayze?" Cal asks once we've stuffed ourselves with roasted-apple pork chops, loaded curly fries, and caramel apples.

"Can we go look at the paintings? Our art teacher said some of ours were going to be in the show."

"Of course." He gives her a big smile.

She grins back.

Unfortunately for Cal, she and I are pretty much the only two people from this town who have smiled at him, apart from my family and the few friends of his who came today.

As Hayzel walks a bit ahead of us, I carefully tug on his arm, wanting him to hang back a little.

"What's up?" he asks, his eyes roving over my face. I ignore the fact that he's now focused on my glossy lips.

Yet another person I know has just scowled at him like he's the scum of the earth.

I mean, I completely understand where that's coming from. I'm the one he abandoned, along with our daughter. But the way they've acted? It's like he murdered us instead. And while they've been civil, or even borderline friendly, the moment he glances away, they seem to wish he'd disappear into a smoke cloud.

"Is it always like this when you come back? Everyone treating you like dirt?"

Cal turns his gaze away from me. "Yeah, I don't know. I guess I don't pay attention to it." Then he clears his throat.

I hate how sad he's made me and Hayzel, but I also hate how sad everyone has made him feel. He can pretend it doesn't bother him all he wants. I know better. I know him. He has stuck around for more than a month. That should count for something.

"Hey." He gently shakes my arm, pulling me out of my overthinking stupor. "Don't worry about it. Let's go enjoy the rest of this thing with our daughter, okay?"

I nod, giving him another smile.

Hayzel's painting isn't in the show this year, but she's really happy that both Violet and Wyatt have pictures on display. After we've looked at as much art as Hayze can handle, we head over to the rides, where she convinces Cal to join us on the Ferris wheel.

"I haven't been on one of these things since I was nineteen," he says with a laugh as we slowly rotate up toward the sky.

"I remember," I reply.

We made out near the top of one of these when it got stuck for about half an hour one night. It was the type of Ferris wheel with larger gondolas instead of two-person bucket seats. Cal pulled me down to the "floor" of it with his sexy smirk, his body encouraging me to straddle him, and I was never going to say no to that.

"Why are your cheeks red, Mom? Are you warm?"

They burn even hotter from embarrassment now.

"Yeah. Why are your cheeks red, Zee?" Except Cal's expression tells me he knows exactly why. Maybe that ride is one thing he does remember.

"Who wants some caramel apple cider when we're done?" I ask, hoping they'll let me change the subject.

Hayzel replies with a quick "sure" and a shrug.

Cal chuckles. "Whatever you want, Zee."

After the Ferris wheel—which we ride twice—the three of us get apple cider and also caramel-apple soft pretzels and apple-pie elephant ears to share. I'm at one of the picnic tables Trevor and the town "rented" from BFO while Hayzel and Cal go get us Knox's apple-and-bacon fried cheese curds from the Button's Diner tent when Trevor's voice is suddenly in my ear.

"Having fun, Sweet Cake?"

I turn to my boyfriend with a wide smile. "So much. But I've missed you."

We lean in and share a quick kiss.

"How are things going?" I ask.

"Pretty good. Not too many catastrophes. How about you? How many times have you wanted to throttle him or cry in your car?"

"None, actually."

He gives a grin, but there's something sad about it. "That's good. Different than usual."

"Yeah." I nod, glancing over at Cal and Hayzel, who are almost within earshot. "I think today has been good for both of them."

"I'd say all three of you." Trevor looks like he wants to add something to this, but we're no longer alone.

"Hi, Trevor! I got my dad to go on the Ferris wheel, and he hadn't been on one since he and Mom were nineteen. Isn't that funny?"

Doesn't look so funny to Trevor, but he won't let Hayzel know this. "Sure is, kiddo."

"Hey, man," Cal greets him.

"Hey," Trevor reciprocates. He gives me another kiss on the lips, just a bit longer this time—I'm sure for Cal's benefit—then says he has to get back because Polly's waiting at the BFO tent.

"You all right?" Cal asks once Trevor's gone. "If you guys want to go hang out with Bernhardt, it's okay."

I shake my head at him. "Don't worry about it. This is our time, just the three of us."

Cal smiles. "I'm glad to hear it."

Hours later, when it's finally time to go home and Hayzel's enjoyed everything this festival has to offer, Cal pulls me closer for a moment. "I appreciate you spending today with me," he whispers in my ear. "Thank you, Zee."

And that right there is the cherry on top of my wonderful day.

Chapter 39

Kenzie

I hate today.

I always hate today.

Normally, I take the day off, spend hours in the gym pushing through all my heavy emotions, then get completely hammered with Charisma and watch stupid movies we can laugh at and not feel any sappy feelings about.

It's different this time, though.

Cal's here.

He's never been in town on what used to be our wedding anniversary. We only ever got to celebrate for two years. We were only married for two years, though we lived together longer than that.

I can't avoid this. I can't avoid him. It's like I'm the freaking cliché of a moth to a flame. I'm a wife scorned, desperate to see the guilt and shame on his face and in his eyes. I skip the gym. After calling Mom to check in on Hayzel, I head straight for my apartment. Doesn't matter that it's only eight in the morning on a Sunday.

"Hey." Cal greets me with a grin. He's lounging on the sofa, shirtless, TV remote in hand, flipping through what looks like one of the sports apps he downloaded. Then he clicks out of that into a different app.

Logically, I know I should begin with a kind—or at least civil—greeting. Catching more flies with honey and all that, or whatever. I try. "Hi." Except I feel that my smile is only sort of spread out. It must look as ridiculous as it feels, because Cal looks at me strangely.

"Everything all right?"

"Yep. Yep. Sure thing."

"Okay." His grin falters, and he's still eyeing me like I'm an alien. "Care to join me? We don't have to watch this game. We can watch anything you like. I'm sure you've got plenty of Henry Cavill or Keira Knightley movies saved."

I walk over to sit next to him. "Not really in the mood for a movie I like. A game is fine."

"Okay."

Cal doesn't press the issue. He selects a football game that was played yesterday, then sets the remote on the end table beside him. Seeing him stretched out in this space brings to mind us in our house, me watching him do this same thing. Of course, back then, usually all his friends were over, too.

We are sitting on my sofa together on what would have been our anniversary, ten years after he left me. This is more than surreal. Does it feel odd to him, too? Does he remember?

Oof.

That's a hard one.

What if he has no clue what today is? Not the date, but the significance of this day.

I should go at this in a careful, deliberate way. This is a delicate topic for me, even if it isn't one for him. But I have to stop assuming he doesn't know just because he hasn't mentioned it. Right?

"What are you doing today?" I ask.

"Nothing much. It's nice being off for the weekend. Back to the grind early Monday." He gives me a sad-looking grin that tells me while he likes his new job, he definitely doesn't like having to work so many hours. He never did. "What about you?"

"I'll probably work out later."

"You always were a fitness freak." But he gives a sweet laugh as he says it.

"It's always kept me healthy and energized, even when Hayzel was little." Then I realize what I said. I dart my eyes to his face.

"What? Why'd you stop?"

"Nothing. I just . . . you don't ask a lot of questions about Hayzel's early childhood. I didn't think you'd want to hear any stories."

Cal mutes the TV and turns his whole body toward me. "Zee, I don't ask because I don't feel like I have a right to."

"It feels like it doesn't matter to you."

He cocks his head. "Seriously? You're just going to tell me what I think now? Not even bother asking?"

I don't respond. To be honest, I hadn't realized I was doing that.

"I'd rather live in the present," he continues. "Enjoy the time that I have with her and with you now, not the time I lost."

"Do you know what today is?" I blurt out.

"September twenty-fourth." He looks at me like I'm a little crazy. "What does that matter?"

"Think about it."

Instead, Cal throws his hands up and stands. "I'm not doing this with you. I don't even know what this is." He shoves a T-shirt over his head then stalks off into the other room.

I follow him to the kitchen, hot tears burning, cheeks burning, lungs burning. Why does every freaking thing have to hurt so damn much? Physically. Emotionally. Doesn't matter. It all sucks.

We end up at the table together, me sitting across from him. He lets out an annoyed groan-sigh that I was definitely supposed to hear. "Why is it all we do is fight?"

"I thought we had a nice time yesterday. You wanted a fun family event with us. You got that. Was it not good enough?" I can't hide the hurt in my voice.

"But still. We just fight all the time, apart from that. One good day doesn't fix the rest. Ever since I came back, arguing seems like the only thing you want me for. Don't you have a boyfriend you can bitch at?"

"I'm not bitching at you." My stupid tears refuse to stay in my eyes. My stupid lungs refuse to breathe normally.

"Then what do you call it? Why do you constantly fight with me? I feel like I have to jump through flaming hoops, and I'm tired of getting burned. Why can't you see that I want to spend time with you? *Quality* time, not whatever this shit is."

"It's not. On purpose. The fighting." This comes out stilted from my heavy crying. "I . . . need . . . answers." I sob in between each word.

"Well, I don't have them." He stands up and goes over to the fridge. After yanking the door open, he takes a deep breath. Then I watch him lean over. When he's upright, I realize he reached in for a bottle of water. Then he turns and takes in my face.

I angrily swipe at hot tears, looking away from him.

Hearing his footsteps, I glance back and see that he's standing in front of me. He sits across from me again.

"I can't promise I'll have an answer for everything. But fine. Ask away."

"Where were you all that time, Cal? Why'd you never come see us?" I don't think he's aware that I know he was living in Albany. Neither of us have mentioned it. I guess I'm testing him right now, hoping that he'll actually tell me.

Already, he's shaking his head. "I'm here now. Who cares about the rest?"

"I care. You know, you used to say that all the time. You'd disappear for hours when we were a couple, especially when we were married. Then you'd come back and say, 'I'm home now.' Like I was supposed to forgive, forget, and immediately drop my panties for you."

"Which you were more than happy to do." He grins.

I'd like to smack that smirk off his handsome face. Charm can't get him out of this. His smile fades when he seems to realize that I'm not interested in the flirting.

"What were you doing?" I push again.

"You want me to account for every second I've been away from you? Nah, I'm not doing that. Stop listening to the small-minded people in this town. You either trust me or you don't."

He's kidding with this, right? Why did he even bother sitting back down if he's not interested in trying? "You didn't earn my trust before, even though you had it. You certainly have not earned it now, and I'm not giving it to you."

Cal scoffs, but I ignore that. "How did it happen, Cal?" I sniffle. "How were you just . . . gone?"

Please say it, I think. *Be honest. Man up. Tell me the truth.*

"I had better things to do than change diapers and clean up baby vomit all day."

"Well, damn." There's no conceivable way to hold in my shock. I suck in a breath and let it out, as if I've been hit. Sure as hell feels like I have. "I wanted honesty, and you certainly gave me that." I take a moment to breathe.

He doesn't speak.

"Better things to do?" Each word is enunciated with scorn. "Are you kidding me? She is our *daughter*. You were supposed to be here to care for and to love her. You ditched her before she was three months old."

"I made vows to you, not her." He doesn't even flinch at the mention of our vows, or what's left unsaid about him breaking them.

"Helping to create her is binding enough, jackass." Now I'm talking through clenched teeth. My jaw is tight, and it's starting to hurt my muscles. "Go away."

"What?" he asks. Stunned into stillness. He was holding his water bottle, but now his fingers have let go. It slips down to the table and spills some of its contents. Cal grabs a nearby towel and wipes up the liquid.

"You've done it before. Do it again. Wherever it is you go when you're not here. Do *not* come back drunk or drugged out. But go. I need some time away from you."

"Are you kicking me out?"

"I sure as hell should, but no. Despite your obvious dislike of parenthood, I can't deny my daughter the chance to get to know her dad. She seems happy that you're here. But that doesn't mean I have to talk to you or see you when she isn't around or when I'm pissed at you."

"But I'm staying here."

"Not for at least the next hour. I'm staying here, so you need to leave."

"Zee, it's Sunday morning in the *Falls*. Where do you think I'm going to go? There's the diner, where I'm not allowed. The market. The gas station. Nothing else to do here."

"Then drive into town. Head out to Marcellus. Go hike in the Catskills. I don't care where. Just. Go. Away."

He scoffs, grabs his phone off the table, and leaves. I look around, still pissed at myself for letting him take over my apartment. And hating this damn table. It seems like I can't sit here without ending up in tears, angry at my ex-husband.

Chapter 40

Trevor

THERE'S NOTHING SHORT OF a celebration going on at Blooming Cascade this bright Sunday morning. Everyone's all smiles and laughter, I notice as I walk in, my arms full of flower boxes. I settle those on the far right table and head over to the large group that spills into the workroom from the showroom through the wide open doorway. I smile, too, and ask Carlie—one of the workers—what the occasion is.

"Marcy and her boyfriend just got engaged yesterday," she says, then everyone cheers.

"Hey, congratulations," I say to Marcy—another Blooming Cascade employee—when she looks over with a grin.

"Thank you," she gushes.

"I'm happy for you. Kenzie will be, too. If you go to the diner, I'm sure she'll give you free pie."

Marcy thanks me again.

I pause, thinking, doubting, questioning. In the end, I know it's right. I know it's what Kenzie deserves. "If you need any help planning the wedding, Kenzie can do that, too."

"She's really good at it," Carlie adds. "She helped my sister with hers in the spring."

Marcy smiles. "Thanks. I'll ask her."

Since I have more boxes to bring in, I return to my van. Lourdes joins me.

"To what do I owe the honor? You usually send Kerensky on Sundays."

"Need to stay busy."

She looks at me with slightly narrowed eyes. "You and I both know you have enough to do. Is it Cal?"

"How do you do that?"

"Do what?"

"How do you just know?"

"Trev, I didn't get a degree in psychology just for the hell of it."

She's right. She's also really good at this. "What I just did in there, recommending Kenzie as an event planner for Marcy? Cal won't do that. I see it in him. He hates that she has this incredible goal. Not a dream—more than a dream, because she's been doing it. She has the skills. He wants her stuck at the diner. And if he gets her to push me away, too . . ." I drift off, unable to say the rest.

"He thinks he'll get her back for good."

I nod.

"Trev, you can't let that happen."

"I don't control Kenzie."

"No, but you do control your actions and words. You control your behavior. She can only run you off or scare you off or push you away if you let her. Don't let her. He's toxic. She needs a clear head to be able to see that. You know you're one of the only people who can help her reach that point."

I used to know that, but now . . . "Lately, I think I just make her feel muddled. I can't keep doing that to her."

Lourdes narrows her blue-green eyes at me. "Don't you dare walk away from her."

"You know from experience that it's possible to get someone back after a separation, even a decade later."

"I don't know if you're actually talking about Kenzie and Cal or if this separation on your mind is about Kenzie and you, but I don't care. I wish with everything in me that Spence and I hadn't spent ten years apart. It nearly broke both of us. Learn from our mistakes. Talk. Listen. Don't give up. Also, just because they still love each other after ten years does not mean they belong together. I think Spence and I are an anomaly and not the norm."

"Yeah. Maybe."

She glares at me again, harder this time. "Trev, I told you this once already. You suck at relationships. Kenzie needs you. Do not abandon her."

Chapter 41

Kenzie

LATER, AT LUCY'S—WHERE HAYZEL plays with Ranger, who Lucy is dog-sitting—my sister and I discuss an upcoming surprise Spence has for Lourdes.

"It makes total sense for them, though," she adds with a grin after giving me all the details Spence made her promise not to tell anyone who might mention it to Lourdes ahead of time and ruin everything.

I nod. "So perfect, honestly. She's lucky to have a guy like Spence, even with all they've been through."

This brings to mind the argument I had with Cal this morning.

Obviously, I left before the hour was up, and even texted him that he could return to the apartment if he wanted to. He didn't respond to my apology text that followed, but I didn't expect him to. Can't say it didn't hurt, though.

Lucy's quiet a few moments. "You once asked me about what to do when the person you miss most isn't thinking of you." She pauses. "I think that might have been the wrong question to ask."

"How so?" I don't bother blinking back my tears that spring up. I remember this conversation vividly. We discussed Lourdes still being hung up on Spence, long before he came back. At the time, I was upset about Cal, having found out he'd returned to town yet again and never bothered to contact me.

I don't see how that could have been the wrong way to see it. I look at my sister with my brows scrunched up, wiping away the wetness from my cheeks.

"He was thinking of you. Cal. Just not the way you wanted him to. I think the better question is: What do you do when the person you miss most is not the person you want them to be?"

I don't have an answer. In just a few sentences, my sister has given me so much to think about.

"Oh wow," Lucy whispers.

"What?" I ask, though I'm still a little distracted.

"I can't believe I didn't see it before. You're Marianne. Trevor's Colonel Brandon. Cal is Willoughby."

She has my attention now. Definitely my curiosity. "Who?"

"Jane Austen. *Sense and Sensibility.* Ages are different, and circumstances are, too, but the sentiment is the same. Marianne couldn't get over Willoughby deserting her. Colonel Brandon loved her since he met her and was always there for her, even when he thought it would end in her marrying someone else."

Before I have a chance to reply, Lucy adds, "Willoughby loved her, but not enough to stay. He wasn't a 'better or worse, richer or poorer' kind of guy. Actually, he married another girl for her fortune."

"That's depressing. Was he at least happy?"

"Not sure you want that answer, but Marianne and Colonel Brandon end up very happy. She realized steady love was better than wild love."

"I want both."

"You have both." Lucy looks at me pointedly. "Trevor has loved you since forever. He kept it to himself so none of us really knew, but it was always there. He's also wild about you. He burns white hot for you and you only."

"What else happened with Marianne and Brandon?"

"He treated her like a queen, just as she deserved."

I smile.

Lucy sobers for a moment before speaking again. "Marianne almost died in her grief of losing Willoughby and all he'd done. Don't lose any more of yourself grieving Cal. You've sacrificed enough. Good guy or not, no man should have that kind of power over you or your thoughts."

Only, this kind of breaks me.

Well, there's no "kind of" about it.

The slow stream of tears turns into raging torrents. Lucy looks like she doesn't quite know what to do, and honestly, I can't say I blame her. I never fall apart in front of her. I'm the hard one. The predictable, steady, dependable one. I don't cry to my little sister because of a guy. I don't often cry to her about anything. Today is an anomaly. I just can't help it.

"He doesn't know what today is."

Lucy doesn't reply. She's immediately on her phone, her fingers quickly moving over the screen.

I, meanwhile, have run out of tissues in this box. Since we're at Lucy's, a new box could be in the linen closet where she's kept them for the last few months, or it could be in the bathroom closet where she kept them before that. It could even be under the kitchen sink with the paper towels and dish detergent. All three options make total sense to her.

"Where are the tissues?" I ask, trying to control the sobs, willing them to suppress themselves down into a quiet, dignified cry to no avail.

"Linen closet," she replies distractedly.

See? I was right the first time. I wander down the tiny hallway, past the partially closed door of Lucy's guest room, where my sweet daughter is attempting to teach Ranger to shake his paw, like shaking someone's hand. Doesn't sound like it's going well, but Hayzel's pretty good-natured about things like this. She loves a challenge as much as I do.

"No, silly boy, paw. Your paw." Hayzel giggles. Then I hear, "I didn't tell you to sit yet, but you can have the treat anyway."

This leaves a smile on my face as I reach the linen closet. What do you know? Luce actually has two unopened boxes of tissues instead of just one. Then Lucy's voice is nearby, talking to Hayzel. I turn to ask her why she told my daughter to find her jacket, but Lucy motions with her hand like I should stay put for the moment.

She comes over to me, pulling me into her bedroom. "I mean this in the nicest way possible, but you need to fix your face before your daughter sees you." Then she drags me a little farther, coming to a stop in front of her mirror. Mascara is running down my cheeks to the point that it almost looks like black candle wax was poured on me.

"Makeup wipes are in the top drawer of the bathroom vanity. My foundation should be the right color for a quick fix if you don't want to stay bare-faced. Hurry up before Hayzel leaves." Then Lucy's out of the room.

It takes me probably a full minute to realize Lucy said Hayzel is leaving. Where is she going and with who? No one asked me anything.

When I return to the living room in a normal state once again and not looking like a Halloween decoration, I see that Dom and Charisma are here. "What's going on?" I ask, my voice cheerful, but my eyes ready to throw daggers if need be.

"Uncle Dom's going to take me over to Gramma and Grampa's for a little bit," Hayzel tells me excitedly. "They even said I could take Ranger with me. Isn't that fun?" The huge grin on her face reaffirms to me that she can't wait.

"Sounds awesome, sweetheart."

She and I share a big hug. Dom hugs me, too, which means he knows I'm not okay right now. Then Dom and Hayzel leave with Ranger. As I'm about to close the door, Edin steps up.

"Hey," she says.

At this point, I don't bother asking why she's here. Lucy called her. Lucy did all of this.

We join Luce and Charisma in the living room.

"You okay?" Edin asks.

My tears flow freely again. I don't have any reason to hold them back now. "He doesn't remember," I say in between sobs.

"Hello?" Lourdes's voice asks.

We all look to see her and Gwenn come in Lucy's front entry, the door of which opens to the room we're in.

"What's going on?" Lourdes continues. "We thought we'd surprise Lucy with ladies' night, but you already had that idea." Then her gaze catches me. "Are you okay?"

"He doesn't remember," I repeat for Gwenn and Lourdes.

Their faces wrinkle in confusion.

"Who doesn't remember what?" Gwenn asks.

"Cal," Edin says softly.

Thankfully, Lucy adds the rest, because I can't. "He doesn't remember that today would have been their wedding anniversary."

Lourdes and Gwenn sit nearby. All six of us are kind of in a semicircle, their eyes on me.

"How much does it really matter, though?" Charisma asks.

This sounds callous. I know what Lourdes or Gwenn might think since they aren't as close to her as the rest of us are.

"So he doesn't remember," Char continues. "Holding grudges gets us nowhere. Look what I did. Look where I've been. It's awful."

I know what she's referencing, and I also know that she makes an excellent point.

"Can you let go and forgive him for something that maybe he can't even help? For something that might not exactly be his fault?" Charisma asks. "It's too easy to assume things, and we can't all remember every single detail of everything. He remembers enough of you. He remembers he loves you. Can you honestly tell me you remember every single detail of all the moments you had with him? Nothing is blurry? Nothing is missing? Really?"

By the end of Charisma's speech, I'm still crying, but less so. "No, I guess I can't."

"Everyone remembers things wrong at certain times. Maybe he deserves some grace," Gwenn adds.

Edin scoffs like she disagrees.

"What?" I ask, wanting my other bestie's opinion.

"Just that . . . give him grace? Fine. Forgive him? Sure. But also—more importantly—*let him go*. And I don't mean kicking him out of your life. Just don't hold on to him anymore. You deserve so much better than that. Trust me."

We all know she's been there with Rhett. None of us will say that now in front of both her and Gwenn, but it's clearly what we're all thinking. I love that they're friends now, but my heart still hurts for the pain Edin went through.

"It's easier said than done," Lucy adds.

We all know this is true, too. Every one of us has had some painful hang-up with a man that seemed impossible to get over. Some of them dealt with those issues with the men they're currently in relationships with.

"Let him go?" I ask.

They nod.

Let Cal go?

Tried that for ten years.

Didn't work.

Except it did, though, didn't it? I mean, I'm in love with Trevor now. I don't want Cal back. But I wish Cal wanted me when I still wanted him. I wish his memories of me were still intact. I wish I wasn't such a throwaway to him. That's all I feel like now. An unremarkable throwaway.

Chapter 42

Kenzie

I SIT WITH THESE questions for a little while. I'm sure Lourdes has a customer asking her for help since she obviously works on weddings, but there are so many aspects that a florist just can't do. If I'm going to put myself out there as an event coordinator, I'll need all the experience I can get on top of what I already have. Besides, I do love a good challenge like this one.

It's feasible, absolutely, but it'll take a lot of work when against the clock like that. But I also have connections with people who could supply a couple with what they might need on short notice, even with a small budget.

I'd be more than happy to meet with her if that would make things easier.

It takes Lourdes longer than I expect to reply.

You already know her.

I do?

I do? I can't think of anyone who just got engaged. That's usually something that spreads like wildfire in this town.

Oh wait. Marcy? I already told her I'd help with hers.

Not Marcy

Me

Wait, what? Lucy told me Spence's plans, but she never mentioned that he was proposing so soon. I figured it was a few weeks out, not a few days. And of course, I can't let Lourdes know that I was aware of his plans ahead of time.

You're getting married???

Lourdes thanks me, then we agree to meet for coffee sometime this weekend to iron out the details. Being a wedding florist, I'm sure she realizes there will be so, *so* many details. She's also not the kind of woman who gets overwhelmed by things like that so it should be pretty easy to plan with her.

I've just put a table's order in at the kitchen when Dottie walks over. "Go home," she tells me.

"What? My shift's not over yet." Even though I've been here since opening, I'm supposed to be here the rest of the evening, too. It's only four-thirty.

But then she smiles. "Go home, Kenzie. Trust me."

"Okay, I'll go clock out."

Dottie waves me off. "I'll take care of that. Go home."

When I get back to the house, I see Trevor's here. He's not actually in the house, though. His truck is home, but he isn't. My phone dings.

Trev

> Hey, Sweet Cake. Go take some time for yourself and relax. Take a shower or a bubble bath. Take a nap. Whatever you want. Hayzel's with Lucy. I'm around. Call or text me when you're ready.

> Ready for what?

He sends me a winking kiss-face emoji.

A nap and a bubble bath both sound nice, but I'm too excited for either of those. They take too long. I decide on a quick shower, stripping out of my work "uniform" of a stretchy cotton top and leggings before I even reach the bathroom doorway. When I'm done, I put on one of my flowy blue dresses, swipe on just enough makeup to cover any flaws and add a bit of sheen, and add a little mousse to my hair, leaving it down instead of in the ponytail I've had all day.

"I'm ready. What are we doing?" I ask as soon as Trev answers.

He laughs. "That didn't take long. You don't want to pamper yourself?"

"Oh, I already did. I'm more interested in what you have planned than I am in spending any time alone."

"Be there in five minutes."

He's true to his word.

Fifteen minutes—plus some hair, dress, panty, and lipstick fixing—later, we're on our way to dinner in Syracuse. It's a cute little spot we haven't been to in a couple years. Inside, I realize the seating, the lighting, the entire ambiance is all very intimate.

"Last time we were here, did you want that to be a date with me?" I ask as we snuggle in the tiny booth. We didn't cuddle together before, but we might as well have considering we sat so close to each other.

Trevor nods. "Yeah."

"But you told me you were supposed to have a date here and she bailed. That's why you asked me."

Now he laughs.

"That wasn't why you asked me, was it?"

"I couldn't summon enough courage to ask you as a real date."

I think about this our whole dinner and all the way back to the Falls. Once we're at BFO, Trevor parks the truck at the house and grabs a large covered basket of stuff from the mudroom. We walk down to my favorite garden, the sun just setting beyond the trees in the distance.

Trev has a portable firepit set up here with a pile of blankets, which I'm grateful for. It's chillier than I expected, and since we were more than a little distracted on our way out of the house, I didn't think to grab a sweater.

We sit on the blanket spread over the grass. Once he's started the fire, Trevor digs inside the basket.

"Need any help?"

"I got it. Thanks." He smiles at me the same way he did when he greeted me at the door, wolfish and hungry for me. Then he pulls out a bottle of wine I've never tried before and a small cake box I recognize immediately as Edin's.

"Have help with this, did you?"

He gives a small laugh. "No one wants to know that you're planning a romantic night alone with your girlfriend so you can seduce her, but yeah, I had to ask for help."

"You promised me dessert, but you didn't say anything about pre-dessert activities," I tease, pretending to ignore how warm it's getting between us already.

That wolfish smile is back. "Before dessert. After dessert. During dessert. Take your pick."

"Let's see how it goes," I tell him with a wink.

I know exactly what's going to happen, and it'll definitely be all three. Letting him work for it is fun, though.

"There's more in here," Trevor says, genuinely surprised. He pulls out another box from The Sprinkle Scene and opens it. Inside, we find handmade chocolates that Edin only ever makes small batches of, a few of her pink champagne cookies, and a few other cookies that are chocolate but smell a little like wine. There's also a note taped to the side of the box, I see.

I pull it off while Trevor closes the box, sets it aside, and takes two travel-safe wineglasses from the basket, as well as a wine opener.

"'Dearest Dears,'" I read from Edin's note. "She even added a laughing face drawing."

Trev smiles at that.

I continue. "'Love sucks, but not yours. The best way to make a romantic date special? Chocolate, of course. You have dark chocolate coffee truffles, pink champagne cookies with white chocolate drizzle, and milk chocolate cookies with the merlot I suggested Trevor buy.'"

He dutifully holds up the bottle, which makes me smile.

"She goes on about having fun, not giving her any details, and calling her tomorrow."

"All for you, not me," Trevor says with a grin.

"The dessert's here for you. I'm here for you, too," I add in a lower voice, my smile just as lustful as his earlier one.

"Oh yeah?"

Mm. The flirty tone is back.

Instead of answering, I look at the basket's contents on the blanket. There's one more item I haven't said out loud that Edin added, which Trevor hasn't dug out yet. She packed it all in a small blanket inside the basket so nothing would break. It must be hidden from his view.

"You're missing something."

He gives a half smile, tilting his head at me. "I don't think so. I've got everything I need."

I tip my head toward the basket, controlling myself enough to not rip my dress off this minute. "Check it again."

Leaning forward, Trevor looks in, digs his hand around a little, then pulls out a small jar full of a thick, dark substance. He darts his eyes up at me, the spreading smile on his face telling me he knows I know what this is.

"Merlot chocolate sauce."

"Yeah?" Trev raises his eyebrows at me. "And what should we do with this, Sweet Cake?"

My dress is now up over my head. I toss it to the side, not caring if it lands on the blanket or in the grass. I also don't care how chilly it is out here. I know I'm about to be hot and sweaty.

Trevor eyes me in my lacy undergarments, the ones he felt over and under earlier, ones he moved but didn't remove.

"How do you feel about dessert all night long? Or until we drop?"

My boyfriend's only in his pants now, having taken off his shirt and shoes while I spoke. He's on his knees crawling over to me as I slip one arm then the other out of my bra straps. The chocolate sauce is in one of his hands. "Sweet Cake, I promise when we're ready to be done, it'll be well after sunrise."

Chapter 43

Kenzie

IT'S BEEN SUCH A long day. Two-hour workout starting at four since I've been slacking on my exercise. Shift starting at six-thirty, forcing me to rely on Trevor to take Hayzel to school once again, even though he had his own work to do. Ten hours at the diner. Then realizing the dress I want for my date with Trevor tomorrow night is at my apartment.

Obviously, it's a good reason to be here.

Only I don't want to be.

I don't know how to get along with Cal anymore. I don't know how to not ask him all the questions and not throw all my fears and abandoned hopes and thoughts from the past ten years at him like tennis volleys. I want to know everything. Every teeny, tiny detail. Maybe as a way to see where we went wrong. Maybe as a way to see when I could have fixed things. Or perhaps as a way to see when I lost him for good.

The door to the public hallway opens. Cal gives a startled laugh.

"What are you doing out here, Zee?"

"Staring at the door."

"You okay?"

"No," I reply, not bothering to sugarcoat anything. "No, I'm not."

He gently takes hold of my hand. "Come in here. Let me help."

I allow him to lead me inside, never pulling my hand away or even wanting to. Cal shuts the door behind us and gently guides me to the sofa. After urging me to sit down, he joins me. His eyes peruse my face.

"You want to tell me what happened?"

"All we do is fight."

Cal still holds my hand. He gives it a squeeze. "I know I said that before, but it isn't exactly true. We've had a lot of good times over this past month or so."

"Seven weeks. You've lived here for seven weeks."

"That's not a lot of time. Yet it's also felt like forever."

Moments pass. It feels like Cal is trying to silently make sense of what's going on with me. "Are either of those things good or bad in your eyes?"

"Yes." I nod to reaffirm my answer.

"Which one?"

"Both." I hadn't expected this answer to choke me up.

He doesn't say anything, but I can see it in his eyes. *Why are you crying again?* It was a constant question toward the end of our marriage. Everything made me cry. Every time I cried, Cal got pissed or annoyed, to the point that he stopped asking if I was okay or if he could make it better. He stopped caring.

A wave of the pain from this washes over me. It feels fresh, though it's more than stale. The man is holding my hand right now, offering me comforting words, and I'm still stuck in the past, probably about to start weeping over things he's long moved on from.

"I don't think I'm okay with you here."

"Me living here? Or you being alone with me? Because you know I'll never hurt you. Bernhardt needs to learn that, too. I swear you're safe with me, Zee."

"Except I'm not. My heart isn't."

He lets my hand go to rub his face for a few seconds. "Back on this? Really?" I don't miss the bitterness and acidity that accompany these words.

"No matter what you do or where you go, I'm always the one with a broken heart. Always have been."

Cal doesn't reply. He only stands, looking like he's about to walk away.

"See? That's what I mean. You can't even give me anything in return. You don't care."

"Of course I fucking care, Zee!" he shouts in a rare outburst. His jaw is clenched, his face tight. "Of course I care." Cal emphasizes every word. "I loved you. I always loved you."

I shake my head. "No, you always *wanted* me, from the very beginning. There's a difference."

"Yes. Wanting you and loving you are two different things, but I felt both. I still do."

"But it isn't enough, is it?"

"Why the hell not? You loved me for all these years. I'm standing here telling you I love you, too. Why is it not enough?"

I force myself up to my feet. "Because you don't fucking get it!"

Cal and I both are in rare form tonight. Never have I yelled at him this way before. Neither of us ever shouted at the other. We held a lot in back then. Guess it was time for a change.

My hands won't stop trembling, but I won't let that keep me from saying what I need to say. "Did you not hear what you said to me?"

He silently stares at me for a beat or two. "No. What did I say?"

"I have to remind you? 'You always know how to make me feel good about myself.'"

"Yeah? And? You encourage me. You lift my spirits. How is that bad?" he says with a slight tilt of his head.

"How do you make me feel about myself, Callum?"

"Is this a trick question? Am I supposed to hazard an answer, only for you to bitch me out either way?"

"Not a trick."

He's quiet for a few beats. "I hope that this is mutually beneficial."

"Mutually beneficial? Are you kidding me right now?"

"Enough, Zee. Just tell me what it is you want me to understand."

"Event planner."

He huffs. "Are we seriously on this again? Why would you give up a stable job for a crapshoot?"

"No one said I have to quit my job. You just assume I'm going to do things wrong. You assume I'm going to screw up."

"No, I don't."

"And yet here you are, doing just that."

"You know what? I'm done with this right now." He turns and walks away, grabbing his keys off the living room side table on the way.

I swipe roughly at my eyes and cry harder. "Of course. Here we go again."

"What does that mean?" he snaps, barely shifting his body enough to look over at me.

"This is what you do. You leave."

"That isn't fair. My walking away now has nothing to do with the past and everything to do with the fact that I don't want to fight with you."

I ignore this. "You don't get it. That's the problem. You broke my heart too many times. Every time you left, or came back and left again without a word. Whether you wanted to stay gone or not doesn't matter. Whether you were doing wrong or not doesn't matter. The intention is still worthless. You chose to stay away. I can't keep forgiving you for that. You want to leave again, so go."

He doesn't even try to protest. Just stalks out the door, shutting but not slamming it behind him.

I hold myself together until I make it to the tiny kitchen table, crumbling onto one of the chairs. I never thought I'd cry as hard as I did when he walked out the first time, yet here I am.

How the hell can this man still have such a hold over me?

I'm in love with Trevor. So, *so* in love.

And yet.

The past is a pretty damn powerful thing. Memories. Hopes never given up on. Desires coming back to light.

The door opens. Within a few moments, Cal's in the kitchen with me, sitting across from me on the other chair. "I don't want to leave you. I don't want to fight with you. The argument we just had? That really sucked." The second he's finished speaking, he's on his feet, almost immediately crouched down in front of me.

"Maybe we need to fight," I tell him, wiping my eyes with my hands, then wiping my tears onto my jeans. "We never fought back then. Maybe that was part of our problem. You just walked out. Never gave me a chance to ask you to stay."

"Why won't you ask me to stay now? Why aren't you happy when I tell you I'm in the Falls for good?"

"You wanted out long before you actually left."

He doesn't reply. We both know he can't. The guilty expression on his face tells me he also knows we're both aware of this.

"Staying with me when you didn't want me made you cold and distant. And we weren't even that close anyway," I add in a burst.

"How can you say that?"

"Easy." Though this isn't actually easy. It's like being stabbed in the heart. "You were never my best friend," I croak.

His eyebrows immediately scrunch together. "What?"

"Charisma was always my best friend, then Trevor, too, when you were gone. But it was never you." I take a moment for some deep breaths to calm the hitching that's starting to overwhelm me. "I never had that moment where I thought, 'I'm married to my best friend.' It was never you. It was never supposed to be us."

"Don't say that," he tells me, his hands on the sides of the chair I sit in, his arms caging me in. "I wanted you. Always, *always* have." He shifts his body, placing his warm hands on my bare arms. "It was supposed to be us."

"Back then, maybe. But you left too soon."

"How many times do you want me to apologize for that? I'll tell you I'm sorry every day if that's what you need."

I push him off me and stand. There's no way I can feel his touch on me anymore. I can't handle it. I don't want his comfort or his pity. I want his truth. "Why care about what I need now? Why not then? You forgot about me! You left, and you forgot about me." My voice is ragged. I let the sobs out as they come.

"I didn't forget you." His voice isn't wobbly like mine, but it also isn't steady.

"You didn't think about me either."

"Zee, I swear—"

I put a hand up to stop him. "Don't say things you don't mean. Don't make promises to me that aren't true. Do not lie to me to spare my feelings."

He heaves out a breath and scrubs his hands roughly through his hair for a moment or two. "It had been so long . . . I don't know. I didn't intentionally forget you. I just . . . I guess I just—"

"You forgot to think about me." I finish his sentence for him, knowing it really is exactly what he's trying not to say. I back away, my bottom running into the cabinets in only a matter of seconds.

Cal nods, slowly, quickly, one bob down and up and he's done. One microsecond of acknowledgement, and though it burns my insides, it's precisely the kind of honesty I need.

When I finally find the strength to speak again, my words are whisper-soft. "You'll forget about me again."

"Zee, no. Never."

I shake my head at him, knowing I'm not wrong. "You will. You've done it before. Maybe it was easy, maybe not. Either way, I am forgettable."

"Kenzie—"

But I can't let him finish. "Don't say that I'm not. You can't. You know it's true. I'm forgettable. At least to you."

"You're not. Of course you're not. No one could ever call you forgettable."

I rush to reply, desperately needing to get these words out. "Cal, you don't get it. You forgot about me. *You* did that. The once love of my life *forgot about me*." I emphasize those last words, and then let them linger.

He starts shaking his head, his hands reaching out to me again. I try to step back, but the counter's behind me, leaving me nowhere to go. All I can do is lean away. He lets his hands drop back to his sides. "Why won't you let me touch you?" he asks.

"Because you *will* forget about me again. Intentionally, unintentionally. It doesn't matter. I know it's going to happen. I won't always be Zee to you. I'll be some girl you were married to for a while. Maybe the girl you were temporarily happy with. Then I'll be some girl you kind of remember having a little bit of fun with. Then I won't be anything to you at all." My words catch, barely leaving my mouth. "Those thoughts hurt like hell. Like *hell*, Cal. Do you even understand that?"

"Of course I do."

"And yet you'll forget me anyway, because it isn't in your nature to hold on."

He doesn't reply. He just stands there, his hands at his sides, his eyes on mine, his chest rising and falling as fast as mine.

I push a little more, hating us both the whole time. "If you were the type of guy to hold on, you would have stayed."

"Zee—" he starts. His voice is soft, but there's a resignation in it I recognize. "If we're not together, then yeah, I'll get over it. I won't let myself think about you anymore, until eventually, I just won't."

"How soon?" This comes out in a haggard rush.

"I don't know. Do you really want me to answer that?"

"How many times in the past did you automatically lie to me just to spare my feelings?"

He doesn't speak. Not right away. His silence is my answer. I know the truth now.

Then he says softly, "What makes you think that my absence was worse than my presence?"

"Are you serious right now?" I can't help but scoff. He's kidding with this shit, right? But it doesn't look like a joke to him. "How can you say we were better off without you around?"

"I wasn't happy, Zee. No matter what you said or did, I wasn't happy. It wasn't because of you."

"No, it was because of Hayzel," I snap.

He gives me a moment to breathe—and to regret this remark—before continuing. "No, it was because I wasn't ready. Hayzel came out of nowhere, and—"

"You can't say you're one hundred percent ready, tell me you want to be a dad, skip birth control of every kind, then say a pregnancy comes out of nowhere. We were married. Financially stable. We knew what we were doing. You said you wanted to be a family. 'You, me, and our baby. It'll be perfect.' Your words, Cal. Don't tell me she was unexpected. We'd already had many, many discussions about having kids. You knew how badly I wanted to be a mom. She was not a surprise or a shock. She was a gift."

He nods. "She was. I know this now, I swear I do. But I didn't know that then. I wish I had. I wish I'd known how magical and special and incredible she was and is. I wish I'd actually put some effort into being a dad." He pauses to take a breath. "But all I saw was crying and disgusting bodily fluids all over her crib and the blankets and the carpet and you. It was too much."

"That's not reason enough to leave."

"It is when the guy you would have been stuck with would have been no help at all. If I'd stayed, you would have just resented me more and more. You would have hated me more and more."

"No," I whisper. "No. I didn't hate you. I loved you. I never would have hated you. Still haven't managed to."

Somehow, he chuckles for a moment before sobering. "Trust me. I just needed a little more time to make you hate me. It was inevitable."

"I don't think so."

"How's that?"

I need to phrase this just right, but this is also no time to mince words. "Being abandoned by you, whether physically or emotionally, isn't enough for me to hate you." I pause for a second. "Maybe it should be, but it isn't."

"You really loved me that much?"

"You really didn't love me that much?" I counter, breathless, desperate for his answer.

I've been avoiding eye contact, but I catch and hold his gaze now. His eyes are watery.

"Not as much as I should have. Not as much as you deserved."

It's taking all I have not to crumple into a sobbing mess on the floor. All I can do is put my hands behind me and hold on to the countertop for support. I close my eyes, wishing I could retract the tears that escape in the process. "I'm just going to be 'some girl' to you one day. Then I'll be nothing to you at all," I repeat. Eyes still closed, I shake my head, wishing this would rid my brain of this knowledge. "I always knew I loved you more." My voice cracks at the end.

"Zee."

His voice is suddenly much closer. I sense that only a few inches separate us now.

"Don't for one second think I didn't love you as much as I was capable of doing. I loved you with everything that I had. I just didn't have what I needed to be worthy of your love. To love you in the way that made you feel like the single-best, most amazing, incredible woman that you are. I made you feel like shit. That's on me. That will forever be on me."

This time, when he tentatively puts a hand on my waist, I don't jerk away. I let him slide both his hands around to my back and pull me to him in a hug that's ten years in the making. All the times he held me before this—even once he returned to town or after he moved in—just didn't mean the same as this moment.

I keep my eyes shut as Cal and I hold each other, our breathing syncing up.

I take in a long breath, letting him steady me, before slowly letting it back out. "I will always love you. I'm just not in love with you anymore. I thought I was. I thought you'd come home and we'd be a family again. The thing I forgot is that we will always be a family. We just have a different version of us now than the one I'm letting go of."

"I love you, Zee."

I nod, my head accidentally rubbing against his neck as we continue to hold each other. "It's a good thing, Cal. It's good for us to still love each other. In this new way, not the old way. That was toxic. Even if neither of us was entirely aware of it, it was still toxic. We can love each other better this way now."

Then I shift so my head nestles between his neck and shoulder. "It's okay, Cal. I forgive you."

"What?" he asks into my hair. His voice is so soft, it's almost less than a whisper.

"I forgive you," I whisper back. "I don't hate you. I'll never hate you. Ever. It's okay."

He breathes out, tightening his grip on me. Though he doesn't say anything, he does clear his throat, a sure sign this is too emotional for him. But now is not the time to casually change the subject like I normally would. I think he needs to hear this.

I snuggle closer, cradling him, my hands gently caressing his back. "I won't hold it against you anymore. My pain. My hurt. I don't blame you anymore. I won't. I promise."

"Aw, Zee." Cal squeezes me for a moment or two. He doesn't say more, but he doesn't have to. We both understand.

Then he pulls back so we can look into each other's eyes. His look as wet and red as I'm sure mine are. "What do you need me to do?"

I slide my hands to his shoulders, on my way to letting go completely.

Deep breath in.

Deep breath out.

Repeat.

This is the moment I've been so terrified of.

While it hurts as much as I imagined, it isn't as scary as I used to think it would be.

I can do this. I *have* to. "You need to live somewhere else. It's time."

Cal nods slowly. "Thank you for everything."

"Thank you, too."

He moves his head back—eyebrows pushed inward—but keeps us in each other's arms. "What could you possibly have to thank me for?"

"I needed this. I needed you here." Another deep breath in and out. "I needed you to say you were sorry. So, *so* much. I've never known for sure how much you cared or how much it affected you, if at all. Now I know."

"Zee, I'm so—"

"Don't. Please," I interrupt him. "You don't owe me any more apologies."

He nods again.

"We're okay now, Cal. It's okay."

When he leans closer, I know I can trust him not to do something he shouldn't. He proves me right when he kisses my wet cheek, then the side of my head. "I'll talk to Perry. I'm sure he'll let me stay for a little while. I think I'm about to close on that house your friend Gwenn found for me. The one I hoped I'd be able to convince you to move into with me."

I smile, letting that last part slide. "I told you she's the best."

"No." He holds my gaze. "No, you're the best, Zee. Always have been. Always will be. I love you."

Slowly, I lean and kiss his cheek as well. "I love you, too."

"I'll start packing," he whispers, stepping away from me.

I let him go.

<h1 style="text-align:center">Chapter 44</h1>

Trevor

Pollywog

Got a question. Call me back

Len

How's it going, bro? Things good there?

Jade

Hey, Trev. You been busy at the farm today?
Have you gone into town yet?

Len

Busy day?

Jade

Call me soon?

Dawse

Stuck at BFO? Big crowd today? Get stopped
by any babbling old ladies yet?

WHAT ON EARTH ARE my siblings talking about? And why are they texting me at the same time?

Then my phone rings.

"Couldn't wait for me to text you back?" I ask Lennox by way of greeting.

"Hey, man," he replies. Just those words.

"That's all I get?"

"What do you mean?"

"Well, with the way everyone's messaging me, you'd think the farm was on fire or something," I say.

Len clears his throat. "Look, I . . . Hey, want to watch the game tonight? I can go there, or you can come here. I'm sure my horses would love for you to bring some snacks for them."

Sometimes I really hate feeling like I'm the most sensible of us five. "What's the thing you need to tell me but won't?"

"Seriously, game tonight. Or hey, better yet, I can get out of here a little early I think. My last two appointments are off the calendar now. One canceled, the other rescheduled. I can probably be at the farm in twenty minutes."

"What's the rush?" I ask, knowing something's definitely up. Lennox never offers to come here during a weekday, lest he be put to work somewhere around the farm.

"Nothing. Nothing's going on."

I pinch the bridge of my nose and let out a hard exhale. "Len."

"Okay, look. I didn't want to tell you over the phone. We've just been trying to gauge what you might have heard or what you might know."

"About what?"

Several moments pass before I hear my brother's voice again. "Kenzie getting back together with Cal. Technically, remarrying Cal."

Has the ground completely crumbled beneath my feet? Has the Earth's gravity pulled it inside out? Does anything else actually exist right now? No freaking idea. All I know is that what my brother just said to me damn near knocked the wind out of me.

"Say that again," I demand, my voice hoarse.

"I'm sure there's nothing to it," he says instead. "Stupid small-town gossip. You know how it goes. But we just wanted to make sure you were okay, on the minuscule chance it really was true."

Though I'm alone at the moment on my family's farm, I'm still officially at work. Any one of my crew or relatives or customers could find me. I can't exactly throw things and yell my frustration out.

"Is it possible there's some truth to the rumors?" Len asks.

I know Kenzie, better than anyone else does. Certainly Cal. But I could have missed the signs. Did I miss the signs?

I think back on the seven weeks Cal's been in the Falls. He and Kenz fight a lot. She's had a really rough time with all the emotions that keep pouring out of her. Of course, it isn't like that's a definite deterrent. I'm supposed to be the deterrent. Her love for me is supposed to stop any of that from happening.

"If she's going to remarry the guy, the least she could do is break up with me first," I snap before ending the call.

Len texts me immediately, but I'm already trying to find Kenzie. She doesn't answer my calls or texts, so I take the UTV I drove to this part of the orchard and speed over to my house. She isn't here. If I call too many people looking for her, they'll start to worry. Even more rumors would spread. I need to keep this as contained as possible.

Hey, you heard from Kenzie today?

Jade

Shit. The rumors are true, then?

Then I text Aunt Dottie, even though Kenzie wasn't scheduled for today.

A nap is good for her. A nap with that asshole there is a recipe for disaster. If she's considering—

I can't even bear to complete the rest of that thought.

Because with the way he looks at her, the way he talks to her, the way she looks at him . . .

I *have* to find her.

I have to stop my girlfriend from leaving me for her ex-husband.

Though I haven't finished all my tasks for today, I hop into my pickup truck and head over to Kenzie's apartment.

That's weird.

She isn't here either.

Where the hell could she be?

I don't expect an immediate answer for my messages to her, but this is the moment I need her impeccable punctuality the most.

Without really wanting to, I text Lucy, casually asking her if she's with Kenzie. I lie and tell her I'm off for the rest of the day. Depending on how all this goes, however, it might not end up being a lie.

Lucy

> I'm not, but she mentioned wanting to visit you at the farm. She's probably still around there somewhere. Just text her, and she'll tell you which barn or garden she wandered off to.

Well, that's a start, I guess. At least I know she's around the farm somewhere. Problem is, I'm still at her apartment. I run back down the stairs, getting a scolding from Mrs. Faber on the way, and jog out to my truck. Within minutes, I'm back at BFO. Where would Kenzie go? Well, that depends on her mood. She has special places all over this farm for when she's happy, sad, angry, depressed, frustrated.

Then it's like a switch is flipped in me. I know where to go.

Chapter 45

Trevor

THIS ISN'T HER FAVORITE garden, but it's exactly the right place for her to be. Lourdes, Lucy, and our moms all worked together on this elaborate, flower-covered arbor and its nearby flower neighbors. They actually used this as practice for one they wanted to use in the community garden, only it didn't take long for them to realize doing another would require too much work, as would the upkeep.

Kenzie's eyes are closed. She's taking slow breaths in and out. I don't know why she didn't think to call or text me when she got here, but at least my workers are looking out for me. They are the only reason I knew where to find her since I was busy checking other gardens.

"How could you do it?" I ask as soon as she's within earshot without me having to shout to her.

Her eyes rush open. "Do what?"

"How could you agree to remarry him? You and I have something really great, or at least I think so." My voice sounds strangled, but I feel like someone or something is squeezing the life out of me, so that makes sense. Getting all of this out won't be easy, but there's no freaking way I'm letting her leave me without a fight.

I make my way closer, each step heavy and quick.

"Not to mention the fact that he abandoned you. Which, by the way, has he even apologized for that? Where the hell was he? He left when Hayzel was only a couple months old. He missed her first teeth, first words, first steps. He wasn't at her school programs or birthday parties. He didn't see her eyes light up when she saw Santa at the mall for the first time. He wasn't there when she had a fever of a hundred and three and needed to go to the hospital. He didn't buy her five gallons of ice cream when she had her tonsils taken out. *I* did. I was there for all of it."

"I know." Her voice is small.

"I was there for you, too." My voice is still rough. Not harder, but there's obvious emotion attached to it that I don't even care to hide. "When you were suddenly alone. When you had no idea if you could raise Hayzel on your own. After every bad date when you finally felt brave enough to date again. When you lost it every time Cal came back and never bothered to contact you. When you began taking steps to find your joy, what excites you. I've been with you every step of the way."

"I know," she whispers again.

We're finally no more than a foot or so away from each other, within touching distance. Except neither of us tries to. Our arms are down at our sides.

"So what the hell are you doing? Why did I just hear that my best friend—my *girlfriend*—is remarrying that jackass?"

"Trev." She stops and shakes her head, hopefully to herself more than anything. What if she means it to me? "Cal and I aren't getting married. I made him leave an hour ago."

"What?"

Shit.

I screwed this up. Big time.

How could I have assumed such a thing and not just talked to her calmly about it? How could I have let that stupid rumor get to my head and not have trusted her? But honestly, I know why. It was an apparent confirmation of my worst nightmare.

"Cal and I are not now, nor will we ever be, back together. You would've known that if you'd just called me or talked to me when you heard. In fact, you never should have listened to town gossip in the first damn place."

Clearly, she's pissed, but there's something else. Something's bothering her. She looks like she wants to walk away but doesn't. Instead, she slowly strokes one of the flowers on the arbor.

I soften my voice. "I tried calling and texting you. I even went to your apartment looking for you, but that's beside the point. I've been terrified of your answer. Reuniting with Cal was always your dream."

"Except it wasn't a dream anymore." Each word is barely above a whisper and laced with a dullness.

I freeze, fully alarmed. My muscles tighten. "What do you mean? What happened?"

She shakes her head, like she doesn't want to answer.

"Why was he still here, Sweet Cake? Why didn't you make him leave sooner?"

"How was I supposed to explain all my feelings about him to you? It's my fault he treated you like shit in school. It's because of me." She chokes out that last word.

"No." I press her into me, holding her close. "Don't ever say that. It was never your fault."

"I—" She pauses, her body trembling. "I wanted him to hurt me."

I instantly tense yet again. "He hurt you?"

Chapter 46

Kenzie

"If he touched you, I swear I'll break his hands and his face and his—"

I quickly shake my head, stepping back and squeezing his arms to stop him. "Not physically. I just needed—I almost wanted him to intentionally do something brutal, something deliberately cruel, thinking maybe that could be the catalyst to making me let go."

"What? Abandoning you and your baby wasn't reason enough?"

"That wasn't about us or me. He had his own issues back then. I needed him to be an ass now. I needed a reason to hate him."

"You tried hating him before and it didn't work."

I nod. "I know."

His voice softens. "Did he hurt you?"

I nod again, tears filling my eyes. The strength to hold myself up is gone. I lower my body to the ground, but before I make it all the way, Trevor's suddenly below me, pulling me onto his lap, my legs straddling him as we situate ourselves in the grass.

"I wanted him to hurt me," I continue, trying to keep the sobs at bay, "but it was so much more than I expected. More painful. More heartbreaking."

"Heartbreaking?" he asks, alarmed. "Sweet Cake, I don't give a shit how Cal feels or what he thinks or says or wants or where he lives. If he's hurting you enough to break your heart, that asshole has to go. Not just out of your apartment."

I know what he means, but there's more I need him to understand. "He only broke the part of my heart that he has."

"Which was always about ninety percent of it."

"He had most of my heart. You have most of my heart, too. Simultaneously. I've only ever been in love with you and him. But it's like my heart split into two. Cal's had one heart all these years. You've had the other. Only one of them was strong enough to survive. Only one of them was meant to survive."

Now I cry harder, the sobs unsuccessfully abated. "I'm so, so sorry for not being there for you back then. I believed in him when everyone else told me he was a jerk to you. I didn't listen. I don't know why, but I didn't. I *chose* not to. It's my fault. I loved him and let him love me even when he was so vicious to you. I can't ever make up for that."

"You wanted to see the good in him."

"I did. The other night, he helped Hayzel with her homework, and he was patient and calm, even when she had a minor freak-out that she wasn't going to get it finished before bedtime. He's apologized to me. Gave me answers I never thought I'd get, even if they aren't things I want to hear. But he's just not the man I need. Or the man I want. Or even the one I miss. He wasn't ever really that one."

"What Cal did to me and to you is on him and him alone. You understand?"

I nod. "But I'm sorry I—"

"That's not your offense to atone for," Trevor interrupts me. "It's his." He pauses. "Cal apologized for it. To me. To you. I hate the man, always will, but I can see that he's trying. I kind of hate it, but I see it."

He pauses again, then asks, "You still love him?"

I take a few moments to breathe, to settle my body and calm my mind. Not that *calm* is really attainable, but at least *not as tense* is. As I do so, I see the fear in Trevor's eyes. I may not have flowery words right now, but I do have the truth. "I'll always love him. Always. But not in the way I love you. Not anymore."

He nods. "This is good. I can't expect you to pretend Cal never existed, but moving on from that is a good step."

"It wasn't only about me. He was also here for Hayzel. Said he wanted to be a real dad this time. He was MIA her whole life, and I thought it would be good for her to get to know him. I didn't want to take him away from her again. And all this time, I've been so stupid, because she already had a dad. She had you."

Now Trevor's eyes tear up. "I didn't care for her or help parent her just to earn brownie points with you."

"I know. You love her like she's your daughter. And I hope you still love me, too. I won't leave you, Trevor. Not for anyone." I'm crying harder again. There's no way we ever could've had this conversation without shedding some tears.

"I do love her like my own kid. Of course I do." He takes a strong breath in. My hands shake in trepidation of what he might say next. "I love you, too, Sweet Cake. Have since forever. I'll never leave you either."

"How can I ever apologize enough for not seeing what should have been obvious all these years?"

He smiles. "I'm sure you can think of a way."

I give a laugh. "I'm sure I can think of several."

"Starting with?"

I lean closer, only needing to move just a little, so I can reach his ear. Then I whisper a few naughty naked things we haven't tried yet from a book we saw in the bookstore. He moans just at the thought of this. I kiss his neck under his ear, and pull back to gaze into his eyes. "I'm in love with you, Trevor."

"I'm in love with you, too, Sweet Cake."

Trev cradles my face softly with his calloused hands and kisses me with the same heat as our first kiss. The same heat as most of our kisses. It zings through me. Somehow, we end up making out right here in the grass in front of the arbor. I don't know how none of the customers have made it over here, but I'm more than okay with it.

Eventually, we have to slow our kissing to a stop. I'm a little out of breath. Trevor is, too.

"Hayzel will be okay," he tells me once we've taken a few minutes to hold each other in silence.

"I hope so."

"She didn't want you to remarry him, either."

I don't think I should be surprised, but I am. "Guess my two best loves knew better than I did."

"Won't be the last time."

To this, I burst out with a laugh. He chuckles as I belatedly give him a small tap on his arm. "Hey," I say. "I'm offended by that."

"How are you besides offended?"

I smile, knowing he's well aware I understand it was a joke. "I'm happy with you, Trevor. It wasn't easy with Cal hanging around the Falls and in my apartment. So many memories and lost hopes. It hurts." I pause. "I know you don't want to hear that."

"I want to hear everything you want to tell me. Honesty, Sweet Cake. That's the only way to get through this."

"It really freaking hurts. But that pain doesn't diminish what I feel for you. I am so in love with you that I can't imagine my life without you. I don't want to. The idea of that hurts, too. There's just one thing that can make this better."

"Oh yeah? What's that?"

With a flirty grin, I lean to kiss him, my hands wrapped up in his shirt. Our kiss is soft at first, but that only lasts a few moments before Trevor's hands are on my ass, pressing my body into his, and we're full-on making out again. I kiss away his fears and he kisses away my pain.

I can feel that Trev aches for me the way I ache for him. It's been too long since we didn't have the dark cloud of Cal hanging over us, threatening to dampen all our happiness.

Eventually, we need a breather once again. I give him a little kiss on the side of his mouth, loving the tickle from his barely there beard. Then he pulls his hands from my bottom, gently placing them on my cheeks.

"You are sunlight and stars. Rainy days with a book and cold nights in front of the fire. You are daily visits to the diner and menu items that are for me and me only. You are cake so delicious, I've completely and willingly forgotten other desserts exist. You are my every freaking thing, Sweet Cake. You were the breath of fresh air this farm needed when I took over and was desperate for guidance. You are the inspiration for everything I do here. For everything I do, period. You and me? We are what other people dream of. We're best friends and lovers. We're made for each other. No blast from the past or crisis in the future can change that. It's us, always. Please, *please* tell me you think it's only ever going to be us from now on." His voice strains at the end of this beautiful, glorious speech.

"I promise," I whisper, tugging on his shirt at his chest, pulling him to me, not that he had much more room to move. But I want him to know how much it means to me to be close to him. "I will never do anything like this again. I will never give you a reason to doubt me or make you think I'm doubting us. Never again, Trev."

He nods. "I believe you. Also, I want to marry you."

I don't reply right away. I can't. My brain must have short-circuited or something. That, or I'm far too happy for it to function. "Seriously?" I ask lamely, letting go of his shirt and holding him to me with my arms. "Even after everything that just happened with Cal?"

"Yes."

"For real?"

Trev gives me a little kiss on the tip of my nose before resuming eye contact. "Yes, Sweet Cake. For real. Everything that's happened with Cal doesn't matter. This has absolutely nothing to do with him."

"But it's so soon. We haven't been together that long," I protest. I have to know for sure that Trevor is one hundred percent certain about this because I'm not about to jump into a marriage if one of us has doubts. I know for a fact that person is definitely not me. I've never been more sure about anything. I have made some gigantic mistakes lately, though, which could factor into Trevor's decision-making.

He returns his hands to my ass. My legs and arms are completely wrapped around him.

"Like I said, it feels like we've already been in a ten-year relationship. Even before the dating aspect, we saw each other every day. Went out to dinner and lunch and drinks and coffee and the movies and grocery shopping all the time. We cuddled on my sofa every week. Fell asleep in each other's arms. We still do those things in our relationship, with the added benefit of living together."

"And the amazing sex," I add with a grin.

He smiles, dipping down to kiss just above my exposed collarbone for a moment. "That too. We are *wildly* in love. Can you think of a reason for waiting?"

I can't. There is no reason to wait. No reason not to want to shout about our love from the rooftops. Only I'm crying too much—happy tears this time—to say this. I'm not sure Trev understands what's going on. His brows scrunch together.

"If you want to date more, we can. Official dates. Official engagement. Give ourselves loads of time. You want to wait ten or fifteen years? Let's do that. But . . ." He shifts to kiss my neck under my ear.

Then he continues in a soft tone. "If you love me as much as I think you do and if we've had the kind of friendship I think we've had, then this is what I want. This is what feels right for us."

"I wish you would have told me this years ago," I whisper.

"You weren't ready years ago. You weren't ready six months ago. You weren't even ready six weeks ago. You needed Cal to show up and remind you of the ass that he is."

"Trevor—" I warn, but he interrupts me.

"Okay, okay. To show up and remind you that he is not the guy you want him to be or remember him as in order to know for sure."

I nod. As much as I hate the fact that this is true, there's no denying it.

"You're ready now."

It's overwhelming how much Trevor loves me. It doesn't feel like I deserve it. I give up trying to contain my still-flowing tears. They spill out freely, with me madly wiping them away as quickly as possible.

"Aren't you?" Trevor asks, concern in his eyes and on his face.

"Without a doubt," I reply with a shaky voice, leaning up and sliding my hands on his cheeks, steadying him for a kiss.

When he immediately deepens the kiss, rolling me onto my back in the grass and sliding his hands under the waistband of my leggings, on my hips, I become acutely aware that we are most definitely in the wrong place. Sitting straddled on him was one thing. Him on top of me with my legs around him is another. While sex outside can be amazing, sex where anyone, including his staff, family, and/or customers can see us, is an awful idea. I tell him so.

Trevor rolls off me, stands, and reaches a hand out to pull me to my feet. Before we move further, he kisses me again, one hand still holding mine, the other slipping into my hair, holding my head steady while we explore each other once again. With quick movements, Trevor lifts me up, my legs around his waist, his hands on my ass. I give a laughing groan into his mouth.

Pulling back with a guilty smile, he takes a quick glance around. "Maybe this really isn't the best place."

"You think?" I grin.

He carries me in the direction he just looked. "If this pays off, it'll set the bar pretty high," he warns with a sexy tone.

I'm definitely intrigued. "Trevor, everything with you is better than the last thing. I will always want what's coming next."

Chapter 47

I carry Kenzie down the gravel drive to one of our barns. Honestly, the first reason I chose it is because it's the closest building I could think of. It's also the best chance we'll have of privacy. Mostly, this barn is just used for storage, one of two on the property for such a purpose. More importantly, it's the only building nearby that has a private office for me. Our land is so expansive, my grandpa needed places for his workers to get ahold of him, back before cell phones were a thing. This office has one of those phone lines that were put in. It also has a desk I hope is sturdy enough to hold our weight.

Kenzie's still wrapped around me, planting kisses along my jawline as we enter the barn. Two of my younger workers are in here. I forgot I sent them to rearrange the hand tools and see what we could put up in the local farm auction next month.

They glance at us with smirks, one barely holding in a laugh.

Yeah, yeah, yeah. The boss needs to get laid. Funny. And I guess, since I've never done this with a woman at the farm like this since high school, maybe it is hilarious, but now is not the time to share a laugh over it.

"Hey, guys. Get out."

Immediately, they set down the tools they were holding and walk out, but not before more chuckles and smirks escape. One of them closes the large door for us, which I actually really appreciate. I hadn't thought about that being left open. Kenzie's still kissing my jaw and now down my neck.

When it feels like enough time has passed for them to be far enough away, I carry Kenzie through to a tiny room off to the left. It's dusty in here, but not too bad. Polly asked one of the workers to clean it a few weeks ago during part of our regular building checks. There are windows without curtains, but now that Kenz has slipped her hands under my shirt and is caressing my bare back, I couldn't care less. If someone really feels the need to come down here and see a show, they'll definitely find one.

Carefully, I set Kenzie on the empty desk the long way, holding it tight with my hands and giving it a quick shake.

"Don't think it'll break anytime soon," she says, pausing a moment to bite her lip before giving me a sexy grin. Then she leans back on her hands, opening her legs a little more. "And I know I can handle anything you want to give me."

We are definitely wearing too many clothes.

I strip first, even though Kenzie tells me being fully nude isn't necessary. May not be necessary, but it sure as hell is more fun. Then I take my time stripping her, sending each article of clothing out of reach, each toss eliciting a beautiful laugh from my gorgeous girlfriend.

She scoots back, indicating she wants me up on the desk with her.

I oblige as she whispers, "I want to feel all of you on me. All of your skin. All of your weight. All of you up here with me. No separation."

When we're wrapped up in and around each other, about to share this experience together, I know without a doubt that I wish this could be a daily thing, and also that there will never come a time where Kenzie isn't the only woman in my thoughts, my heart, my bed, my life. I've known it since forever, and having it reaffirmed has now reaffirmed another desire of mine.

·❤·❤·❤·❤·❤·

We curl up on the faded and torn black leather chair a while later. I'm not sure how long it's been, but we're both completely satisfied and also spent. Our breathing has at least returned to normal now. Kenzie's straddled in my lap facing me, no clothes keeping us from feeling all of each other. I'm ready to go again, and she is, too. Her skin is warm, flush. We're heating each other, raising temperatures and desires. However, there's something I want to do first.

Kenz speaks first before I have a chance to.

"Did you mean it?" she asks. "When you said I'm your every-thing?"

I meant it so much, I don't have an answer so much as a request. "Marry me, Kensington."

She sighs that sweet sigh. "I love hearing you use my full name with love, and not annoyance or anger."

"Is that your answer?"

Now Kenzie giggles. "No."

I decide to play a little more. "Is *that* your answer?"

She laughs. "Ask me again."

"If you told me no as an answer?"

"No, the thing you asked that you think I'm replying to."

For a moment, I pretend like I don't know what she's talking about. Then I say, "I don't think I actually asked. I think it was more of a statement."

"A demand?"

I consider this. "Maybe."

With cheeks that are becoming even pinker, she asks, "A naked demand?"

"Well, we are naked."

"Hey, I told you that you could have left your pants on. Them being around your ankles never stopped you before. And my bra didn't have to be flung across the room. I could have kept my top on."

"First, yes, the bra absolutely did, and second, no way did I want a single scrap of fabric getting in the way." I slowly slide my hands on her sides, from hip up to rib cage and back.

Kenzie presses her hands on top of mine, forcing me to caress her with a little more pressure. "Your bare ass is on that chair," she smirks. "It might need bleached now."

"No one bleaches leather, Sweet Cake. Anyway, do I have to propose to you with clothes on? Because I thought what I just did to you on the desk was enough to show you how much I love you."

"Will you stop being a pain in the ass and ask me again?" She's laughing, though, telling me she loves this as much as I do.

I hold still, making her look into my eyes again. This moment is heady and flirty, but I want her very aware of how important it is to me. "Will you marry me?"

"Yes," she says softly. Then she smiles before grabbing my face and pulling me to her in a long kiss.

Once we decide we need to breathe again, I push forward with the rest of my plan. "How soon do you think you could put a wedding together?"

This elicits a chuckle from her. Then she tilts her head like she realizes I'm serious. "How soon do we need it to be finalized?"

I grin, so happy to finally be able to share this detail with her after waiting for months. "What if I told you I had the barn remodeled as a venue space in hopes we'd be the first to use it?"

Her beautiful, plumped mouth literally falls open. "The grand opening is in a few weeks."

"Like I said, how fast can you put a wedding together? Because I know you're the best, and I know what you're capable of. You said so yourself. You've helped women throw together amazing parties on short notice. I think we can do this."

"What exactly do you mean by *this*?"

"Two weeks."

She's quiet, like she's thinking. She hasn't shrieked in shock, so that's a good sign. Eventually, she says, "With help, I think two weeks is doable, but that's calling in a *lot* of favors from Edes, Lourdes, Knox, Dottie, Mom, your mom, your staff. Charisma. Ooh, Jade for the dress. Lucy could probably help. Anyone and everyone."

Taking her hands in mine, I say, "Sweet Cake, they'd all be more than happy to help, even Lucy. We have supplies stocked for rental, like linens, chairs, candles, and whatever else you want to make everything pretty. Lourdes would be more than happy to find what she can or give you people to contact. It's possible."

Kenzie smiles. "They might hate us two weeks from now, but let's do it."

<h1 style="text-align:center">Chapter 48</h1>

Kenzie

So I know Trev and I asked half the town, it seems, for help pulling this wedding together in two weeks, but very few of them actually know the event is today and not tomorrow. This was easily done, since we told everyone that it would be easier to store whatever we were borrowing, buying, or renting from them at BFO a few days ahead of time, just so we wouldn't have to scramble.

The fact that this wedding is happening so quickly in the first place is perhaps less of a surprise. I mean, Trevor and I have only been dating for less than three months, but we've loved each other as best friends for ten years. We've also been living together for two of those months. I'd say we know one another better than most couples do by this point.

Edes

> Things are ready for the ceremony. Polly's being picky about the lighting for the reception, but I told her as long as she doesn't touch the cake, I don't care.

> Awesome! And don't worry about Polly. Let her fuss if she wants. She'll calm down soon.

> Got it. Oh, and your parents are giving me really strange looks, wondering why I'm here for family portraits lol

That's the other reason we're having the wedding today instead of tomorrow. Since all our loved ones helped put this together, Trevor and I thought we should find a way to make it special for everyone. We told them we wanted photos taken at the barn as a pre-wedding event, along with a luncheon. Little do they know. This has me smiling while Lucy drives us to BFO.

"What's going on over there?" she asks, a laugh in her voice. "Trevor texting you again?"

"Not for a few minutes."

Edes

> Dom just made a joke that I'm adopting all of you Larkins now. No one else laughed

> Here soon, right?

> Edes, you are one of the toughest women I know. You can handle my family.

> Have you seen the intensely quizzical looks your mother can give?

Okay. Time for deep breaths.

I tell Lucy to hurry if she can and why.

"Oh no." She lets out a laugh. "Well, we're almost there. It's going to be all right."

"I know."

I reach my hand up to my flower-crown headpiece. I wore a veil the first time I was married. Traditional all the way. With Trevor, I want things to be different. I want this to feel like *us* and not just some cookie-cutter wedding, cute as it was. I'm in a flowy ivory lace dress, very boho in style and so me. My wavy hair blows around in my face when I open the window for a moment for a blast of fresh air.

Lucy's in yellow, of course, because I wanted her to be able to wear her favorite color as one of my maids of honor. Charisma and Edin are in red and orange, respectively. Trevor and I decided on fall colors—one, because it's a good season for us and for BFO, and two, because it's pretty easy to find décor in those colors right now.

As we pull up to the barn, I see my mother start to relax that we've arrived. Then I step out of the car. The confusion shifting to joy on her face is absolutely priceless. She rushes to me in a hug.

"Why didn't you say anything?"

Dad comes over for hugs, too. "This is a surprise, pumpkin, but the perfect kind."

"Don't make me cry," I warn, happy tears already pricking at my eyes. At least I remembered waterproof mascara this time.

Once Dominic, Dawson, Pete, Dottie, Knox, Jade, and Wyatt realize what's going on, we send everyone down to the garden—my favorite—for the ceremony. Only my girls, Hayzel, Cal, Polly, Deb, and Lennox knew ahead of time—Lennox only because he's still licensed to officiate weddings. Iris knows, too, since she did my hair, but she won't be able to make it to the ceremony, only the reception.

"Hey," Cal says in a soft voice when all the others have walked down toward the ceremony space.

I know Trevor's waiting in the garden to ask Dawson, Dom, and Pete to be in the wedding for him. They're luckily all in suits, but I wouldn't care if they weren't. Today is about love, not what someone is wearing.

Lucy, Edin, and Charisma watch Cal and me for a moment, share a silent look with each other, then step away.

"Hey." I smile at my ex.

Things have been really good between us since our fight. He moved out as promised. Trevor and I told him to move back in the next day. As it turned out, Hayzel and I didn't want to go back to our apartment anymore. Cal's moving into his new house soon, and since he's staying in town, Hayzel will get to see him whenever she wants.

She runs over now and nearly tackles him with a hug.

This is the first time she's ever hugged him.

I don't need to hear his thoughts. I can see it on his face, in his watery eyes. This is one of the best moments of his life. Then Hayzel makes it even better. "I'm glad you're here, Dad. Mom gets to marry Trevor, but she says she'll always love you, too, and we're all happy about that."

Cal looks like he might burst. I'll have to give him a moment to breathe when we're done talking, just so he doesn't lose his composure. He doesn't like doing that. But I guess with getting his first hug and his first "Dad" from his daughter, he just might make an exception.

He proves me right as I see a few tears stream down his cheeks. "I'm happy about that, too, kiddo."

"I'm going to be the flower girl, or else I'd sit with you." When she pulls away from the hug, she looks up into his face. "Are you okay?"

"Yep. I'm really happy right now," he replies with a nod.

"Okay. Maybe we can sit next to each other at dinner."

"I'd like that." He gives our sweet daughter a grin.

"Hayze, why don't you find Aunt Lucy and Grampa, okay? I think we're starting in a few minutes."

"All right, Mom. See you in a little bit, Dad."

When he sniffles, I move closer to him.

"I never thought I'd get any of that." His voice is raspy.

"She's not worried about you leaving anymore. She knows that she can love me and Trevor and you, and doesn't have to pick between any of us. This is good."

He gives a slight head shake. "This is amazing." After wiping his eyes and taking a few slow deep breaths in and out, Cal makes eye contact with me. "Thank you for this, Zee. Thank you for giving me this chance to get to know her and get to know you again."

"Thank you for coming back," I whisper.

"You know, I wouldn't miss your wedding for anything, because while we don't have that kind of a future anymore, I'll always love you. We'll always be connected by our past and a different future. One where our daughter gets to have two dads. That's pretty cool."

I lean up and gently kiss his cheek. "Yes, it is."

"Hey." Trevor's voice comes from somewhere behind Cal.

We both turn to see Trev all decked out, looking handsome in his new suit. Trevor gives a soft smile. Then he steps closer to Cal, reaching his right hand out. Cal accepts it.

"Thanks for coming," Trev tells him as they shake, then let go. "It really means a lot to our girls."

Our girls. Me and Hayzel.

Trev and I have discussed this many times since he proposed. We could only ever see the future one way: as a happily blended family, Cal included.

This isn't their first civil conversation. Cal has properly apologized to Trevor several times. They've actually been able to talk without one wanting to punch the other. They can smile and laugh with each other for real. Maybe they'll never be true friends, but friendly is perfect right now.

·♥·♥·♥·♥·♥·

After the ceremony, during which Trevor and I recited our own written vows and everyone cried, we gather all the guests and wedding party in the newly renovated barn. Polly and Deb outdid themselves with the decorations. It is truly exquisite in here. From the looks of it, autumn exploded in the most magical, romantic way and carefully blanketed itself all over the beautiful barn.

Edin cries next to me, but she always cries at weddings, though not necessarily for the reasons other people think. There were no cake disasters, so I hope they're at least semi-happy tears.

"You got married on Sweetest Day. The second most love-filled day after Valentine's Day. And so romantic, too," she explains as we watch Trevor laugh with his brothers.

He keeps twisting his gold wedding ring around his finger in the cutest way, smiling down at it every so often.

"I mean, that's such a cliché," Edes adds in a faux snobby tone, switching from her wistful tone.

"Sweetest Day isn't even a real holiday," I tell her with a grin, knowing she'll object. The romantic part of her might be shoved way deep in her core, but I know it's still there.

"Yes, it is. It's a national holiday."

I shake my head seriously. "No, it isn't."

"Well, it's on the calendar. It's on mine, anyway. That's official enough for me."

We share a giggle.

"It's good to see you happy. I know weddings aren't really your thing anymore."

"I used to be so hopeful, Kenz. Now I feel like I cry because I've become a bitter old hag."

"Edes, you are not old and certainly not a hag. And you can choose to work on the bitter."

She laughs. "Oh, hell no. No man will ever love me or be loved by me, I can promise you that. Been there, done that."

I would laugh with her, but I know she's not joking.

"Maybe I'm just sad you won't have any men to bitch about and commiserate with me over."

Now I smile. "Well, I'm sure there'll be things Trev will do to annoy me, I can promise you that. I love him dearly, but it's inevitable."

"Nope. I don't accept that. It's not the same. You love Trevor more than life. Nothing will change that. You are not destined to be bitter."

"And you are?" I scoff. "That's not what I want for you. That's not what you should want for yourself."

"Yes, I am destined to be bitter. Always." She smiles, but I know she's using this as a way to hide the fact that these feelings are very real for her. "This is my life now, Kenzie," Edes adds solemnly. "It's best we both accept it."

Bonus epilogue

Kenzie

"I JUST GOT HOME, Cinn. Do you really need to tackle me immediately?" I ask Cinnamon, my giant orange Maine Coon cat. Well, *our* giant Maine Coon. Hayzel's, Trevor's, and mine. Our sweet family of three. I plopped down onto the sofa in search of relaxation, but apparently, the cat has other ideas.

"He wants a snuggle," my husband Trevor says from somewhere behind me, stepping closer to gently plant a kiss on the top of my head.

Still seated, I swivel around, catching his shirt with my hands then his lips with my own. "Missed you," I whisper, my face near his. "Maybe you and I can snuggle without the furry feline?"

Trevor lightly kisses my lips again. "Clothing optional?"

"After my shower," I say with a laugh. Then I yawn. "Which might be after my nap."

Though I'm officially an event planner, I do still work at Button's Diner occasionally, both for the camaraderie with the other staff and because I don't like depending on Trevor for all our finances. He honestly wouldn't care if I quit my jobs tomorrow and never worked another day, if not for the fact that I'd miss the work and the independence. I pulled a full double shift today to cover for Trevor's aunt Dottie, my favorite coworker, who's on vacation at the moment. My eleven-year-old daughter is spending the weekend at her dad's here in the Falls, in the house my real estate broker friend Gwenn found for him at the beginning of this year.

Initially, Cal was not happy about my goal of becoming a full-time event planner. With time, he realized that it's my passion. It's the kind of work I enjoy the most. Now Cal happily recommends me to anyone and every one he can.

Trevor's ringtone sounds. His voice is alert, his face taut, while he's on the phone. Though he doesn't say much, something is obviously wrong.

Once he ends the call, I immediately ask, "What's wrong? Who was that?"

My husband is most likely not the first person my parents, sister, brother, or even Cal would call in an emergency, but you never know. "Did something happen?" I add.

"Take a drive with me?" he asks, but his expression remains serious. "Something I want to check on."

I nod. "Of course."

Nothing I wanted to do at the end of shift matters now. I need to know what's going on, especially since he turns the truck down the drive toward our garden—my favorite garden on our personal property. Oh no. I wonder if something got into it and dug it all up. We've been having rodent problems at Bernhardt Farms and Orchard lately.

But then we turn onto a paved road.

Why is this paved?

Where did this come from? I haven't been down here in about a week, and I know for sure this wasn't here then.

I ask Trevor, but he doesn't give an answer. He only points to something ahead of us. Turning away from him, I face forward to look through the windshield. We've already slowed to almost a stop. I can't believe my eyes, but I also don't know what I'm looking at.

Well, I mean, I do, obviously. It's the cutest shed or some kind of small building, maybe the size of my old apartment's tiny kitchen and living room put together, in terms of square footage, though it's a little hard to tell with a fading sun and Trevor's headlights. This might be a greenhouse, I think, eyeing the gorgeous planters out front and the numerous exterior windows—all with a white prairie grid. I know this only because when Trevor needed to replace the windows in our garage, these are the ones I liked the most. The glass doors also have those grids, with the rest of the door frame a soft marigold yellow color. Then I realize there's a regular roof, not a transparent one.

"What is this place?" I ask, hoping for an answer this time. This building was definitely not here a week ago, either. While the wood looks aged, it's also clean and crisp.

Yet again, my husband doesn't reply. He simply opens one of the french doors and guides me inside. Suddenly, I'm surrounded by all my office décor, albeit in a slightly different way. This room is larger than the spare bedroom I've used as a home office, so the furniture is spaced a little farther apart. The honey-tinted wooden desk is positioned in the middle of one wall, with a large window behind it, most likely gracing the space with gorgeous sunlight. My boho vibe is well-represented, even up to the beaded wood chandelier.

Happy tears begin to fill my eyes, yet I still feel the need for confirmation from my hubby. "What is this, Trev?"

He grins, his neatly trimmed beard surrounding his beautiful smile. "Let me show you the back."

We walk toward the wall with two closed doors. Once opened, one reveals a tiny half bathroom, the other, a small kitchenette with a sink, counter space, cupboards, and a portable cooktop. Every room has windows. I can just imagine the kind of glow that'll be in here during the day, all soft and warm.

"How did you do this? There's plumbing and electricity. How did I miss all of this happening?" I'm so surprised at the enormous amount of work that went into this project that I plop myself down on the super cushy office chair. Opposite me are the two chairs I had in my home office as well as a short, tufted bench that's new. There's a quilted loveseat against the wall over near the right corner.

"Sweet Cake, with the double shifts to cover for Aunt Dottie, you haven't had time to blink, let alone go into your office. You definitely haven't had time to come down here. Edin and Lucy helped in here, by the way, and Edin transported and arranged your files and things so well that nothing is lost. She even took countless photos of your office before anyone was allowed to touch anything just so nothing ended up misplaced. It's all labeled now, too. I think going through the drawers and cabinets might be slightly orgasmic for you."

I laugh. "I mean, I don't like organization *that* much."

Trevor smiles. My cheeks blush as I assume he's probably thinking about things that truly are orgasmic for me.

"This is secluded enough to give you privacy and peace, but still close enough to access the main drive of the farm and the road without much time spent. Our guests at BFO won't mistakenly wander down here, so you don't have to worry about that. This is officially our private land."

"What made you do this for me?" I ask in awe, still attempting to blink the tears away.

"Why wouldn't I?"

We're quiet a moment as I wait for him to explain more.

Trev steps over, sitting on the desktop, his body turned toward me. "Sweet Cake, this is the very minimum that you deserve. I wish I could give you the whole world. Right now, I have to settle for giving you a new opportunity—if you want it, and only if you want it."

"What do you mean?" Then I see something on my desk. An item I hadn't noticed before.

Small.

Rectangular.

Boho flower design with burnt orange and burgundy blossoms. Golden details on an ivory background. My logo from all my other business cards. And my name. Kenzie Hoffman-Bernhardt.

Except there's one thing that doesn't make sense about any of this.

My title. Or at least, the title in close proximity to my name.

Executive Event Planner/Coordinator, Bernhardt Farms and Orchard

"What is this?" I find myself asking again, placing my finger on the card. Its smooth texture invites me to pick it up and cradle it between my thumb and index finger. I can't help but oblige.

"I thought we'd make an official offer," he tells me. "If it's a no, that's okay. Don't feel pressured to work here just because it's me and it's family."

I don't reply, giving myself time to let this sink in.

"You've put together amazing weddings, corporate events, and family reunions here. You've been in charge of more than anyone else in that regard, even with the corn roast again this year. People actively seek you out to hire you for their events. With how amazingly you've managed every gathering at BFO, and with your expert knowledge of this place and all our event venues, I thought maybe you'd want to take on a little more."

While this is an emotionally-charged moment—one I know I should luxuriate in due to its importance—still, I try to hold back the tears. Try to not fall apart. Hot teardrops splash down onto my warm cheeks anyway.

"What about your mom? Doesn't she want this title? This job?" I ask, needing this question answered before saying anything else.

"Mom knows this job is perfect for you, if you want it. I intentionally had this built on our land, not BFO's. That way, it won't be seen as a conflict of interest if you decide to keep your own event planning business, using other venues."

"I'd have a steady planning job as well as a freelance one?"

"In a way. I don't want you to give up on your company. I just thought maybe you'd like to use some of that magic for BFO in an official capacity. You'd be given a staff to assign specific jobs to. I'm sure Mom will offer to help you in any way. Only take on as much as you can without exhausting yourself or feeling overwhelmed. I'm not pressuring you, I swear, and I'll never force you into anything exclusive."

There has to be some way I can express how much I appreciate my incredible husband and all the thought he's put into this surprise. For the time being, I only have these words. "I'm exclusively yours in every other way, I promise."

Trev brightens. "So that's a yes?"

I nod and jump up to be in his arms.

When he lowers his lips to mine, he lingers for only a moment before pulling back and asking, "So that exclusivity you mentioned. What things are only for me?"

Lifting up on my tiptoes to better reach him, I cradle Trevor's cheeks, his stubble beard soft and a bit ticklish on my palms. This time, we have no desire to end our kiss. Our more-consuming desires leave us naked on the russet-colored loveseat, wrapped in one of the blankets from the blanket ladder—which will be perfect for tablecloth samples.

We, of course, *tested* nearly every surface we could, just to make sure it was sturdy enough for event planning supplies. Obviously, it's much cleaner in here than the working barns, but that hasn't stopped us in the past. While thinking of cleaning, though, I make a mental note to clean all of the surfaces we just used before I meet with any staff or clients in here.

"Was that the official welcome from BFO?" I ask.

Behind me, Trevor shifts his arms, holding me a little tighter before kissing the spot between my neck and my shoulder. "That was all me, Sweet Cake."

"I'm guessing my official welcome shouldn't be so . . . *nude*."

My husband's laugh vibrates into me. I place my hands on his, wrapping him around me even more. "Clothing might be required, but in my heart, we're always celebrating this way," he says, his voice light but also slightly raspy.

"Naked?"

"Together. Body. Mind. In love. Whether you keep the job at BFO for a week or fifty years, I will always be by your side to support and encourage you. To celebrate you. Always."

"And if I only keep the job for a day?"

"This building is still yours. The office space is still yours. I'm still yours."

In quick, fluid motions, I pull Trevor's hands off me and roll my body in his arms, facing him now. He envelops me once again, one hand sliding to my lower back, the other tenderly cupping my cheek as he kisses me like life without this contact is unbearable.

I love these kisses. These moments with my husband.

I love that I'm starting a new journey in my career in my new office, built specifically for me. I love my life now, no longer darkened by lingering questions from the past. I love that I can be this amazing role model for my daughter.

But right now—most of all—I deeply love my husband.

Extra bonus epilogue

Kenzie

JUST OVER FIVE YEARS ago, my best friend Edin found out she was pregnant. She's on her way over now with her husband and little Sienna plus baby Piper, who just turned one. So many of our friends are on their way, joining Trevor, Hayzel, and me for a Thanksgiving dinner the Sunday before actual Thanksgiving.

Does this mean I'll host two Thanksgiving dinners this year, with my family coming over on Saturday? Yes, it does, but I'm more than prepared for this. After all, I'm not a professional event planner for nothing.

"It looks and smells great," Trevor says, kissing the side of my neck and wrapping an arm around my middle before I can step away to the spice cabinet. "Thank you for doing all of this," he adds, giving me a squeeze.

"Thank you for helping," I tell my sweet husband, turning in his arms so I can hold him, too. "I hope our friends like everything."

"Sweet Cake, they're happy to hang out with us. Fancy Friendsgiving dinner or fast food doesn't matter, but they will appreciate the love and effort you put into everything."

I nod, kissing his lips for a few moments. No alone time right now for more, but short and sweet kisses are just as good. "We have enough chairs for the tables?"

"Yep. I brought the chairs up from the basement already. The kids' table is up as well. I'll take everything for the place settings, so you don't have to."

"Thanks, honey," I tell him, kissing him once more before I hear the red wine gravy bubbling too rapidly. I step away to stir it and turn the heat down a little on that burner. He fills a sheet pan with plates, glasses, and utensils, giving me a wink before heading to the dining room.

"Trevor said you might need help," Hayzel says a few minutes later, joining me at the stove where I'm stirring the soup made from roasted pumpkins grown right here at Bernhardt Farms and Orchard. Thanksgiving Day may be all about the turkey, but this feast is all about two things: winter squash and roast beef. Case in point, my make-ahead pumpkin mac and cheese is coming to room temperature so I can finish it in the oven. The other oven is already slowly roasting the beef. It's going to be another year of nontraditional foods for our Friendsgiving, and I love it. I've already added some of the beef juices into the gravy, making it that much better.

I glance over and give my daughter a quick smile. "I do, honestly. We have the kids' table set up in the dining room already, but can you get the basket of toys ready for them in the living room? And make sure the crayons for Sienna and Everett are out of reach for Piper. Oh, and Lourdes said they're bringing the coloring books for the kids because she let Everett pick some out the other day, so we don't need to worry about those."

Hayzel acknowledges this then leaves the kitchen, presumably for the living room.

"Can't believe she's already a teenager," my sister Lucy's voice carries over to me.

I turn and find her carrying her purse in one hand while her husband Pete holds the other, and also a dish that I assume is their contribution for dessert.

"You say that all the time," I laugh as I step over to take the dish from Pete and greet them with hugs.

"But it's true all the time," Lucy replies, handing her bag to Pete, who offers to hang it on the coat rack in the mudroom, along with her jacket. Then Lucy's hands are on her very pregnant belly, as is often the case. She's due any day now but feeling little, if any, pain or discomfort. She's already rolled up the sleeves of her yellow wrap maternity dress.

"Warm again?"

"Again. Still. Always. I think it's impossible that I'll ever feel cold during this pregnancy. It isn't like I have a lot of time left. The chilly weather has no affect on me. I only wore a jacket because Pete told me to."

"Because Uncle Pete loves you," Hayzel reminds her, stepping over to give Lucy a hug.

"Of course I do," Pete says, giving Lucy a kiss when she's done hugging Hayzel. "Trevor around here?"

"Dining room," Hayzel answers for me. "He offered to set the table so Mom doesn't have to."

Then Hayzel turns to me. "Toys are all ready. Crayons are safely up and out of sight so baby Piper can't get into them. What else can I do?"

A timer goes off, letting me know it's time to put the mac and cheese in the oven. I tell Lucy to sit and relax at the island, then ask Hayzel to stir the soup while I get the mac and cheese in and check the temperature of the roast. If all goes to plan, as it should since I've timed everything right, we'll be eating dinner on schedule. "Gwenn and Rhett should be here on time. Lourdes and Spence are running a little late but will be here before we eat," I tell Lucy.

"Yeah. She texted me not long ago. Something about a new tooth coming in and Everett being a little cranky. But I think maybe he'll feel a little better when he sees Sienna. They always have fun playing together."

Is it weird that Lourdes and Edin get along well enough now that their children could be considered best friends? Maybe a little, but I'm so here for it and happy about it. It's equally odd that my sister and Edin get along now, too, but again, it's also the best. They understand each other more now, and past mistakes just don't matter anymore.

We've all grown closer over the years, my friends and my sisters' friends, and even their friends, with all the weddings and gatherings we've hosted that gave us time to get to know one another better. Of those we invited this year, only Charisma is missing today, since she's currently out of town. At least she's going to attend Saturday's dinner. So will Hayzel's dad, his wife, and their little boy. Another busy day with a full house, and I can't wait. Trevor's sister Polly is hosting their family this year on Thanksgiving Day, meaning we'll see our families later in the week, which is why it's mostly only friends this time around.

I move on to deciding how to arrange the desserts on the counter so everything will fit when the ones that need refrigeration are added later, plus all the ones Edin will bring. All the main course dishes will be on the island top, allowing everyone to load up their plates buffet style before sitting down to eat in our dining room, giving us more space on the table.

After I instruct Hayzel to chop a small handful of fresh parsley for the cranberry and roasted sweet potato salad, I tell Lucy, "Edin, Broderick, and the girls should be here any minute."

Lucy shifts positions, and does so with a grimace. "Is Edin bringing half the bakery with her this time? I know she wanted to make cupcakes, and cookies, and pie."

With a laugh, I reply, "Probably more. Maybe a little less than last year since neither Charisma nor Dominic will be here, but she like spoiling us with treats, and I like letting her. But are you okay?" I add when she grimaces again.

"Yeah. Just feeling a little weird. The doctor says it's normal to be uncomfortable this late in the pregnancy. I'm okay."

I need to make sure, though. We talk about what's normal and what's not, and since she doesn't have any alarming symptoms, she moves the conversation to Pete's recent promotion. "He's thinking of setting more aside in savings with this new raise because he's worried about how expensive everything will be, especially with me having to take time off work."

"Your students will miss you, for sure," I tell her.

She smiles. "I'll miss them, too. Two months is a long time." She shifts again.

"Maybe it's the chair," I suggest. "You can go sit in the living room. You can also lie down in the guest room for a while, if you'd like."

Lucy nods, and I help her onto her feet. "Maybe I'll go find Pete. Ask him to rub my back a little."

She adorably waddles off—though I'd *never* say she waddles to her face because I don't want to make her cry—and Hayzel and I continue with the food. She's been stirring the soup every so often.

"I think it's a good consistency now," she tells me, and I agree.

Most of the timers start going off, letting me know the dishes should be done, just as Edin, Broderick, their girls, Gwenn, and Rhett all arrive. Everyone's in and getting settled, with the girls running to play in the other room, when Lourdes, Spence, and Everett come into the kitchen, right on time, as everything's ready to eat. On schedule, the way I like it.

Hayzel helps the kids sit at their little table as the parents fill their children's plates, including choices from the fruit and veggie platters I recently set out for them.

We're about ready to eat when I realize Lucy and Pete aren't in here. "I'll go check on them," I tell everyone. "Please eat. Enjoy. We'll be back soon."

I make it to the doorway when Trevor meets me and joins me in the hall. "Everything okay? Is Luce all right?"

"I think so, but she's been uncomfortable today. I'd feel better checking on them."

Trevor walks with me hand-in-hand as we search the house for Pete and Lucy. We find them in the little sitting room on the opposite side of the house from the kitchen. "Hey," I say softly as we enter the room. "Everything okay?"

Lucy sits on the wide love seat we have in here, next to one of our short bookcases. "I couldn't make it up the stairs, but I wanted to lie down, except every position kind of hurts now."

"Maybe we should go home," Pete suggests, his worried eyes on his wife.

But she shakes her head. "You already mentioned that, and I already told you no. I don't want to ruin dinner."

"You won't ruin dinner," Pete and I gently say in unison.

I can already see my little sister is about to object again. "But it's Friendsgiving," she adds, in a bit of a whine. Her voice is thicker, telling us she's fighting off tears. "Our friends are here. I don't want to miss it."

"We can all have dinner again another time. You need to take care of yourself and that sweet little baby."

Finally Lucy relents. Pete helps her stand, and Trevor and I walk them to the door, after they say goodbye to everyone. Though we're sorry Lucy and Pete had to leave, we have a wonderful meal full of fun conversations and lots of laughs. Edin and I are halfway through slicing up the pies while Spence and Lourdes open the cookie containers when I get new texts from Lucy.

> Water broke. No contractions yet.

> On our way to the hospital.

> Mom and Dad headed there, too.

> We'll update you soon.

Then she adds a bunch of happy face and nervous face emoji. I announce this to the others in the kitchen with me, who burst out with happy responses as I immediately text my sister back.

> That's amazing! Keep us updated. Wishing you the very best! Trev and I will come up and see you tomorrow. Love you sis

Trevor joins us in the kitchen. "Got some good news? We heard you cheering in here."

I tell him about Lucy.

His face brightens. "Hey, that's great! Won't be long now. Well, shouldn't be anyway. Hopefully."

Trev's been as worried about Lucy as he is about his own sisters. He loves her just as much. He might call me Sweet Cake, but he's the sweetest person I know.

We share the news with the others, who are equally as happy. Lourdes, Gwenn, and Edin text Lucy their well wishes while we all have dessert, then the families start to head home. Soon, only Hayzel, Trevor, and I are here once again. Hayzel heads upstairs to her bedroom to check her homework once more before school tomorrow. Trevor guides me to the island after he and I put away all the remaining food and wash the dishes.

"Today was awesome," Trev tells me as we hold each other. I sit in his lap in the chair, my legs perpendicular over his. "It's no wonder you're the best event planner in the state."

I laugh. "Region maybe, but not state."

"Yet. If you're not, you will be. But honestly, I don't see how it's possible that anyone's better than you. You really are the best, Sweet Cake."

I fight back against a yawn, but it's no use.

"Off to bed we go," he says softly, but he hasn't moved yet. He's probably waiting to see if I'm too tired to get upstairs on my own feet.

"What about Lucy? I should stay awake in case they need me."

He gently kisses my temple then my cheek. "She'll be all right. They'll call us if they need anything. You, Hayzel, and I can visit them tomorrow. For now, my beautiful wife needs a break. She's so worried about taking care of everyone else that she rarely takes care of herself."

When I open my mouth to argue that I do actually take a little time for me—admittedly not as much as I should—all that comes out is another yawn. Trevor slips a hand under my thighs, his other arm cradling around my back. He stands, lifting me with ease.

"What if I don't want to sleep?" I ask in protest as my amazing, sexy husband carries me to the staircase off the living room, my arms around his neck, my body as flush with his as I can make it.

Pausing a moment, he kisses my lips, nipping at my bottom one while we continue our trek up to our bedroom. Then he grins wide, a certain growl in his throat. "I said you needed to go to bed. Never said we'd be sleeping."

And this is why I'll love this man forever. Knowing what I need, giving me what I want, and loving me so wholly and completely that we will never let each other go. "I'm so glad my best friend kissed me," I whisper, smiling in return.

"I'm glad I did, too. And guess what?"

"What's that?"

He pulls me into him in such a way that he can whisper in my ear. "I'm going to kiss you at least a million times more."

I lean mere fractions of an inch to caress his scruffy cheek with my lips. "Besties forever, hubby?"

"Damn right, wife."

Uncharted Avenues Playlist

"BE MY FOREVER (FEAT. ed sheeran)" | Christina Perri, Ed Sheeran

"Hang on Little Tomato" | Pink Martini

"Unbreakable" | Janelle Monáe, Kelly Clarkson

"Realize" | Colbie Caillat

"All We Ever Knew" | The Head And The Heart

"Deep In Love" | Bonny Light Horseman, Eric D. Johnson, Josh Kaufman, Anaïs Mitchell

"Memory Lane" Haley Joelle

"Accidentally In Love" | Counting Crows

"Ho Hey" | The Lumineers

"Leave the Pieces" | The Wreckers

"Lucky" | Jason Mraz, Colbie Caillat

"Opening Up" | Sara Bareilles

"From Me to You" | Raining Jane

"Breathless" | The Corrs

"Fall Into Me — Acoustic" | Forest Blakk

"All We Have" | Mills

"The Morning Song" | Drew Holcomb & The Neighbors

"Just a Friend to You" | Meghan Trainor

"Somebody Like You" | Keith Urban

"jar of hearts" | Christina Perri

"Stronger (What Doesn't Kill You)" | Kelly Clarkson

"When You Say Nothing At All" | Allison Krauss & Union Station

"Can I Be Him" | James Arthur

"Let It Happen" | Just Friends

"You're My Best Friend" | Straight No Chaser

"I Want You to Want Me — Live at Nippon Budokan, Tokyo, JPN 1978" | Cheap Trick

"Hopeless Romantic" | Sam Fischer

"love is just a word" | Jasmine Thompson, Calum Scott

"Willow" | Taylor Swift

"Falling In Love With My Best Friend" | Tyler Ward

"What If I Told You That I Love You" | Ali Gatie

"What If (I Told You I Like You)" | Johnny Orlando, kenzie

"You Are The Reason" | Olivia Penalva

"Brand New" | Ben Rector

"Count on Me" | Bruno Mars

"I Saw Love" | Forest Blakk

Want more Lost Hearts Found?

WILL EDIN FINALLY LET go of the shadow of her past and look for a new love? Find out in **Holiday Distractions**, book 5 in Lost Hearts Found

Subscribe to my newsletter, and receive all the best news first, as well as free stories, chapters, insights into my characters, and so much more! **Sign up at https://lisakeiferauthor.com/newslettersign up**

If you enjoyed this book, please consider leaving a review. If you peruse reviews to see what readers liked about a novel, you might understand how important this can be. And thank you! As an indie author, I sincerely appreciate it.

THE ONE MAN I never wanted to see again is eating a delicious crumb-topped blueberry muffin I made from scratch, talking about the place I wish ceased to exist while sitting in my bakery.

What the fresh hell is this?

Since when does Broderick Saxton give interviews?

I mean, that's clearly what this is, as he's surrounded by three older ladies from town, all gushing about that damn Quill Bridge. They're also obviously taken by Broderick's handsomeness, but that's neither here nor there. He's an ass. What he looks like doesn't matter to me, nor should it matter to them. I'll have to warn those sweet old ladies to stay away from him once he leaves. He shouldn't even be talking to them anyway. He sucked as a food critic. I bet he's even worse now.

As I step from table to table to pass out orders for muffins, chocolate croissants, cinnamon bread, and honey biscuits—all made by me—I hear Broderick say, "I already spoke to Sal Leggero, and also Pippa Leonard, since her ancestor helped build the bridge. It's reported to be a magical, romantic place." Even his stupid voice makes it sound like he believes this garbage.

I can't help but turn my eyes his way. The women of the group swoon even more at the dimples and bright eyes of that asshole, smiling at his companions, but I know better. He's a snake.

I scoff out loud, heaving an annoyed sigh.

He turns to face me. "Excuse me?" he asks, smile still plastered.

Damn those dimples.

I will *not* smile in return. I refuse. "That's crap, and you know it," I tell him before walking away, back behind the counter.

Broderick kindly excuses himself from the table then follows me. "You have a problem with the bridge?" he asks.

The one I wanted to get engaged on? The one my fiancé—who couldn't bother with a proper proposal—never took me to before dumping me over the phone? Oh, no. Not at all. But of course, these thoughts knock that little hammer deeper into my already shattered heart.

Nope.

Not saying that out loud.

"It's laughable," I say instead.

He shakes his head like he doesn't quite understand what's going on here. Then he sticks out his hand. "I'm sorry. I'm Broderick Saxton, from the *Syracuse Falls Sentinel*."

I let his hand just hang there in the air. "I know who you are, and you should know who I am." Though I keep my eyes him, looking for a reaction, he gives zero indications of one.

Not even worth filing me into the recesses of his memory. Thanks, jerk.

"I remember you," I continue, unable to control myself.

He pulls his hand back, now aware that this is not going to go the way he initially planned. My tone isn't exactly sweet. "You reviewed my bakery in Auburn when I first opened. Enchanted Auburn Bakery."

Realization dawns on his face. I can see the moment he gets it. "I did," he admits with a soft nod. "I'm surprised you remember."

"You or the review?"

I suspect he thinks I mean this in a flirty way. He gives me a mega-watt smile. "Take your pick."

I grin, too, but it's the fakest smile I have in my arsenal, and I have many. "For such a suave, self-centered prick, one would think you'd consider yourself unforgettable." Both our smiles drop. "You seriously think I wouldn't remember? Of course, I'm sure that critique meant nothing to you, but it was super important to me, at least until you published it. You told all of Auburn that my bakery was shit."

Broderick doesn't flinch, but I didn't expect him to. He still keeps his cool, calm demeanor, though he is shaking his head. "No. No, I said it was great but had a few kinks that I was certain would work themselves out if given a bit of time, and they did."

I scoff again. "Uh, no. Actually, you said it wasn't as high caliber as other places in the area. That my food wasn't nearly as good as what you'd hoped but it was 'good enough.' You called me inexperienced."

"You were. You were very young. Nineteen versus, what? Twenty-nine now?"

How the hell does he remember my age? Can't lie. I seriously hate that.

"There's a lot of wisdom and maturity gained in that time, both in life and for you, in baking and running your own business. You've done well for yourself." He glances around Sprinkle Scene.

"Yes, I did, without any help from you. You know the critic from the regional website came the same week you did. She loved my cupcakes."

Broderick changes the subject. "So, you're not a fan of the bridge. Should I quote you for my story?"

"You'd like that, wouldn't you? 'Bitch Baker Badmouths Beloved Bridge.'"

"Nice alliteration. You ever think of changing careers?"

"Not funny." Why am I letting this man get under my skin? Why am I losing my cool?

A timer in back goes off. It's exactly what I've been waiting for. "I have 'good enough' muffins to get out of the oven. Don't stay too long. You might be forced to eat something ordinary or second-rate."

Val and Phoebe, my baking assistants who came with me from Auburn, have continued to serve our customers while I've argued with Broderick. They eye me now silently, knowing I'll probably put in an extra hour or two once we've closed to work off my frustration by whipping up a dessert that requires actual whipping with a whisk. Great way to burn off any emotion.

I give them short smiles, making a mental note to apologize to them later. They don't deserve to have to pick up the slack because I temporarily lost my head with a jackass who was still a paying customer.

No matter what Broderick Saxton says or does now, he nearly destroyed me back then, finding me at my most vulnerable and feeding me to the local sharks. I will never forgive him, and I probably will never forget him, but at least I'll never have to serve him again.

But then something clicks in my head.

He said he's working at the newspaper in Syracuse Falls, not Auburn.

That can't be right.

I remove the muffins and set them aside to cool, turn off the timer, then return to the dining room, finding Broderick at his same table. "You work here now?" I demand, ignoring the older ladies who still sit with him and are clearly enjoying the spectacle I'm making a little too much.

Does he really have to smile again? "Yep. Live here, too. Just moved into my house yesterday."

We stare at each other for a few beats.

"You know, Button's Diner makes excellent pie. Maybe you should go there from now on."

He laughs. Honestly laughs. "Paradise, getting rid of me is going to take a lot more effort. Besides, everyone in this town raves about your baked goods. I'm not going anywhere else. Kick me out if you must."

The ladies eye me intently, waiting for my reaction. I give my best smile—my sweetest fake one that looks the most real—and return to the kitchen. If he thinks this is over, he must be delusional. No way am I going to allow him in here day after day. Dimples or not. Broderick can go screw himself.

Also By Lisa Keifer

<u>Lost Hearts Found:</u>
Accidental Pasts
June Days
Winter Blossoms
Throwaway Rules
Holiday Distractions

<u>Auburn Hills:</u>
For Your Sweet Love
For Your Convenient Love